RUN COLD
The Tenth Edna Ferber Mystery

MOOD INDIGO
The Ninth Edna Ferber Mystery

"Ifkovic sets the bar terrifically high for future Ferber mysteries, but it's probably a safe bet that he can meet his own challenge."

—David Pitt, *Booklist* (starred review)

"Ifkovic adroitly squeezes huge amounts of research into the story, with glimpses of people in the arty New York scene as well as the poor on the streets. The novel's main strength, though, is its vivid depiction of a country in crisis in the depths of the Depression."

—*Publishers Weekly* (starred review)

"Ifkovic has done his research and brings the world of the 1930s rich and famous to life, but readers don't have to be fans of the period to enjoy *Mood Indigo*; they only have to enjoy a well-written mystery."

—*Mystery Scene Magazine*

"Ifkovic's dialog is the star. The witty banter between Edna and Noel is engaging and fun to read."

—*Historical Novel Society*

OLD NEWS
The Eighth Edna Ferber Mystery

"This is Ifkovic's eighth outing with Edna Ferber as sleuth, and he brings the characters of post-Great War Chicago to life: the accents, the clothes, the food, the traditions. The story itself is fairly gritty, with few details spared of the emotional and physical trauma that happened behind closed doors and is now being relived. Readers will be front and center for the action, the pain, and Edna's plans to trap the real killer."

—*Historical Novel Society*

COLD MORNING
The Seventh Edna Ferber Mystery

"Like Max Allan Collins in *Stolen Away*, Ifkovic develops a realistic scenario for what might have really happened to the Lindbergh baby. Largely unknown today, Ferber has emerged in this series as perhaps the most compelling of all the many real-life authors turned fictional sleuths in the genre."

—Booklist

"The seventh entry in Ifkovic's historical series continues to entertain with Woollcott and Ferber trading barbs and bon mots with Walter Winchell and Adela Rogers St. John from the Hearst syndicate."

—Library Journal

"The little town of Flemington, N.J., provides the setting for Ifkovic's intriguing seventh mystery featuring novelist Edna Ferber....History buffs will enjoy this one."

—Publishers Weekly

"Now that he's seen her through six murder cases, Ifkovic turns sleuthing novelist/playwright Edna Ferber loose on the biggest game of all: the Lindbergh kidnapping....Perhaps the finest hour yet for a fictionalized heroine who defends herself against undue prejudice in favor of a supremely unpopular defendant by saying, 'I have taken no position—except doubt.'"

—Kirkus Reviews

CAFÉ EUROPA
The Sixth Edna Ferber Mystery

"It's as smartly written as its predecessors, but, as each book does, it shows us a slightly different Ferber—here, she's not quite a girl anymore, but neither is she the experienced woman we see in other series installments. Another totally successful entry in a consistently interesting series."

—David Pitt, *Booklist*

"...Ifkovic successfully blends homicide with a loving homage to Budapest on the eve of World War I."

—*Kirkus Reviews*

FINAL CURTAIN
The Fifth Edna Ferber Mystery

"The story unfolds Agatha Christie-style, with an assortment of likely suspects, but it's best if one thinks of the novel as a Christie story written by, say, someone of Ferber's, or indeed Kaufman's, witty sensibilities. This is the fifth Ferber mystery, and she continues to be one of the more interesting of the historical figures who have found new life as fictional sleuths."

—*Booklist*

"Ifkovic's fifth Edna Ferber mystery provides a splendid view of the highbrow theater culture of another era."

—*Publishers Weekly*

DOWNTOWN STRUT
The Fourth Edna Ferber Mystery

"Ifkovic is assembling a sort of literary collage, building a picture of Ferber (this fictionalized Ferber, anyway) one piece at a time. Fans of mysteries featuring literary figures as crime-solvers will thoroughly enjoy this series."

—*Booklist*

MAKE BELIEVE
The Third Edna Ferber Mystery

"A vivid, atmospheric mystery about 1951 Hollywood. I loved Edna Ferber as a detective investigating a murder behind a film of her classic *Show Boat*. Add fascinating portraits of Ava Gardner and Frank Sinatra, and this is a winner."

—David Morrell, *New York Times* bestselling author

"This series is a lot of fun. Ifkovic has made a clever decision not to take the stories in chronological order, and his Edna Ferber is a wonderful creation, smart and sassy and determined and immensely likable. Fans of Hollywood-themed mysteries featuring real people—Stuart Kaminsky's Toby Peters novels, for example—will have a great time here."

—*Booklist*

"Ifkovic's series jumps ahead to author Edna Ferber's Hollywood days, when her novel *Show Boat* is being filmed and a blacklisted friend is killed. Mix in Frank Sinatra and Ava Gardner for an unforgettable read."

—*Library Journal*

"A host of Hollywood and Broadway personalities from Hedda Hopper to George S. Kaufman provide period color as a sharp-witted Edna probes for the reason behind Max's murder."

—*Publishers Weekly*

"Come for the whodunit, stay for the stargazing."

—*Kirkus Reviews*

ESCAPE ARTIST
The Second Edna Ferber Mystery

"Only a nitpicker would even wonder how much Ifkovic's version resembles the real woman, for the reader is entranced by her plucky spirit and sharp-witted investigative skills. Houdini, too, is a very well designed character. This isn't his first fictional appearance, but it's definitely one of his best, and if Ifkovic can manage it without overstretching the bounds of credibility, it would be great to see the escape artist and the girl reporter team up again. Who would have thought that, of all the real-life characters to have a second life as detectives, Edna Ferber, now largely forgotten as a writer, would emerge as one of the best?"

—*Booklist* (starred review)

"The author does a fine job of writing a sequel to *Lone Star*, set at the opposite end of Edna's life. Stylistically, it's as if we're in Booth Tarkington country, with a leisurely pace and a society with clearly defined boundaries. A gentle read."

—*Library Journal*

"Set in Hollywood in 1955, Ifkovic's debut...depicted Edna Ferber as a matronly but shrewd established author. This excellent prequel, set in 1904, shows her at the start of her career, a recent high school graduate working as a reporter for her hometown newspaper in Appleton, Wis."

—*Publishers Weekly* (starred review)

LONE STAR
The First Edna Ferber Mystery

"A pure delight."

—Jeffery Deaver, award-winning author of
The Bodies Left Behind

"A promising debut in what could be a long-running and highly entertaining series."

—*Booklist*

"Ifkovic handles the mystery plot competently, but the main pleasure is looking beneath the surface of the movie business to see the stars as people, in particular the doomed Dean."

—*Publishers Weekly*

"Ferber makes an appealing if unlikely detective and Jimmy Dean a splendidly charismatic enigma."

—*Kirkus Reviews*

Run Cold

Books by Ed Ifkovic

Run Cold

An Edna Ferber Mystery

Ed Ifkovic

Poisoned Pen Press

Poisoned Pen
PRESS

First Edition 2019

10 9 8 7 6 5 4 3 2 1

Library of Congress Control Number: 2018949100

ISBN: 9781464211133   Hardcover
ISBN: 9781464211164   Ebook

Poisoned Pen Press
4014 N. Goldwater Blvd., #201
Scottsdale, AZ 85251
www.poisonedpenpress.com
info@poisonedpenpress.com

Printed in the United States of America

For my good friends,
Susan and Dave Bogush

"There are stranger things done, in the midnight sun,
By the men who moil for gold;
The Arctic trails have their secret tales
That would make your blood run cold."

—Robert W. Service,
"The Cremation of Sam McGee"

Chapter One

Jack Mabie claimed he was the meanest man in Alaska. Yet the old man said it with a smart-aleck grin on his whiskered face, his watery eyes dancing with mischief. But something else was in those eyes—cruelty. I shivered, turned away. Miffed by my silence, he cleared his throat and repeated it. "Takes a lot of gumption and spit to get folks to hate your guts, ma'am."

I smiled at him. "Strangely, I get my enemies to hate me simply by being myself."

The old sourdough irritated me. First impression, indeed, but my first impressions were reliable. Not that I didn't believe he'd been a notorious frontier bad man from the icebox of the Yukon—there seemed to be a baker's dozen of such crusty geezers in every tin-roofed log-cabin roadhouse across the desolate Alaskan landscape—but Jack Mabie savored a reputation constructed decades ago in his younger years, lawlessness now recollected in a new world he had trouble understanding. The simple, venal soul of the old-time pioneer had watched as his frontier morphed into the pastel 1950s world of martini cocktail bars up and down Fairbanks' Second Avenue, pink and turquoise colors blinding a man who'd once only dreamed in gold.

A man in his late seventies—skinny as taut barbed wire, untrimmed whiskers tinted dirty yellow and charcoal, rheumy eyes in bloodshot sockets, scraggly hair dropping over his frayed flannel collar—he wore a drunkard's perpetual hang-dog expression. A small man, slightly taller than my own five feet, but hunched over, a bony left shoulder prominent now, a jawline that sagged and trembled, the result of a stroke he'd suffered during the last dark winter. Discovered half-dead in a wilderness cabin near Chena, delirious, feverish, he'd been carted to Fairbanks and restored to his grumpy self. He'd been forced to live in the Frontier Home, a house of craggy prospectors, wizened trappers, doddering men who drifted from their cot-like beds to the makeshift squalid bars nearby, like Omar's, a log-cabin shanty with fireweed growing from its sod roof. In the hazy blue light of morning, ambling through the ice fog that lay across the town like dust on old furniture, they'd stumble back for a fitful sleep and dream of timber wolves baying at the Northern Lights.

Jack Mabie wasn't happy there. City lights—and Fairbanks had more blinding neon and sparkle than he remembered—made him antsy.

Newfound notoriety came to him when Sonia Petrievich, editor at *The Gold*, her father Hank's weekly paper, learned through the mukluk telegraph about the meanest man in Alaska. Her breezy profile on Jack, filled with the over-the-top bravado and swollen exaggeration he generously provided, garnered attention. His cavalier account of strings of murders and robberies and shell games was a whole basket of evil gleefully recalled.

Suddenly, after dragging his feet on the frozen pavement and staggering back to the Frontier Home as the midnight sun hurt his eyes, Jack was greeted with hearty cheer and back-slapping camaraderie, and offered shots of whiskey and beer. A septuagenarian outlaw, the guy in the black hat from the old Republic Westerns out of Hollywood, was now applauded.

Jack became a ragtag remnant of old Alaska, the gold rush

days. The Klondike of '98. Fairbanks in '02. He reveled in it. He ratcheted up his stories of meanness—he boasted of murders he'd happily committed, his arthritic fingers counting them off, and got away with. "Don't got law on the Chilkoot Trail." As Sonia quoted him, "Ain't no peace officer around when you hang a man you don't like."

I'd first met Sonia Petrievich last summer when I visited Fairbanks doing research for my book, *Ice Palace*. For a week she was my constant guide, a warm, spirited woman who became my friend. Arm in arm, we wandered through Fairbanks streets, talking. I'd met her father years back in New York, a savvy newsman I'd taken a liking to, so I was not surprised I found his daughter frank and engaging and ready for battle. When I left, I had no plans to return, but a year later, driven, I flew back. *Ice Palace* was scheduled for publication the next year, in the spring of 1958, but Alaska drew me back—loose ends, haunting stories, unanswered questions.

I'd arrived yesterday, a chilly March day, slept the long night in my room at the Nordale, only to have Sonia meet me in the lobby the next afternoon and insist I meet Jack—"the meanest man in Alaska. Today. You can't say no. An original."

"I've met a dozen old-timers, Sonia. They tell me the same story."

Her eyes got wide with amusement. "He claims he's killed—indifferently murdered—dozens of men up North. Decades back."

I sighed. "Every pioneer I've met makes up stories, trying to top the one just before. Bonanza Creek. The gold rush of '98 was their idea. They dreamed it. They found the biggest gold nugget in recorded history in the golden sands of Nome. They almost married Klondike Kate."

Laughing, she held up her hand. "The meanest man in Alaska." Her fingers drummed the article she'd written in *The Gold*—as part of a popular series called "White Silence," the title taken from a Jack London story of the bitter Arctic—and announced, "I've interviewed eight old men so far…he's the cream of the crop." She'd leaned in, confidential, "Edna, he's a gold mine."

"Yes," I told her, "the one he never found."

So, one day after touching down in Alaska, I found myself in the Model Café, sitting across from Sonia and Jack, Sonia grinning mischievously and Jack obviously a little tipsy at two in the afternoon. Sonia and I munched on mooseburgers while Jack kept looking toward the bar.

Jack had demanded we meet him at a sawdust dive near the Frontier Home. Sonia described it as a peeled log-cabin tavern with Western-style swinging doors and a giant chromolithograph of a spangled dance-hall girl hanging over the bar. I'd balked at that. Exhausted from my trip across the country—New York to Seattle to Fairbanks—I had little patience with the tinny jukebox ditties of tractor infidelity and hoedown romance. No, I'd said, the Model Café was a pleasant coffee shop I recalled from last summer, perfect for conversation.

Of course, there was little conversation. Jack eyed me closely, his look sassy. "So I'm gonna be in your book, lady?" Before I could answer, he mumbled, "You gonna pay me, yeah?"

I didn't answer at first, but finally said, flatly, "No."

That surprised him, but he barely suppressed a belch, looked at Sonia as though she'd betrayed him, shrugged his shoulders, and whined, "But I'm the meanest man in Alaska."

I counted a second. "You've already said that."

His eyes got wide. "And you ain't believing me?"

I tilted my head to the side. "Why should I?"

"Lady," he sucked in his breath, "I'm a dangerous man." He hesitated. "*Was,* maybe…before that goddamn stroke." Then, reconsidering, "Still am." A deep sigh, almost an afterthought. "Mean."

I caught Sonia's eye. She was enjoying this.

From a satchel she'd slipped over the back of her chair, Sonia pulled out a clipping of her profile of Jack and spread it on the table. Jack, squinting, grinned, showing a mouth of missing teeth, blackened teeth, an ugly blister on his lip. He pointed. "See?"

I already knew the piece but glanced down.

The Legend of Jack Mabie, the Meanest Man in Alaska

The opening lines:

Jack Mabie, the newest resident of the Frontier Home, is the last of a rough-and-tumble Alaska from the gold rush days. A cocky man, a fighter, he boasts of his battles with the law and with average citizens—and his easy answer to any dispute—murder. The number is beyond calculation, he maintains. "Folks run from me back then," he says now. "Ain't no man tougher in the North, and there be lots of tough fellows."

On and on, language out of an old Beadle yellow-backed dime novel.

Jack sat back, tried to reach out his arm belligerently in a fighter's punch, but his shoulder twisted, and he moaned.

He shifted in his chair, uncomfortable, and suddenly seemed nothing more than an old, damaged man felled by a piddling stroke, a man who prided himself on a life of roughing it in the unforgiving Bush, now the victim of age and pain. He didn't like it. Frankly, I didn't blame him—at seventy-four I understood the inevitable unfairness of life. You spend a lifetime forging an image of yourself—the one you see when you look in your nighttime mirror, the one only you see, the one you demand—and then, in a flash, fate slaps you into frailty. I understood Jack's confusion better than he'd ever realize.

"Tell Edna about your life as a prospector," Sonia prompted.

Jack began a carefully rehearsed story. "The winter of '03,

cold as hell. Alone in a cabin up in Fox. Ma'am, you ain't known loneliness until you watch the Arctic night. Loneliness—it eats at you like a nasty worm." He held my eye, though his eyes suddenly shifted away. "Gold so close you can taste it—but you don't. You ain't find it in the Klondike in '98, at Dawson, but this time...you know you gonna. But you don't. You pan for gold—your fingers blue from the cold. Then you trap for pelts. That's the gold, they tell you. Frostbite, a can of beans, a few silver dollars jangling in your pockets." A faraway look came into his eyes. He shrugged his broken shoulder. "Dreams of fortune. Pouf." A sly grin. "Makes a man bitter."

"We all have dreams when we're young."

He shot me a fierce look, one gnarled finger scratching a scab on his cheek. "You don't get your dreams, you gotta take what you want."

"And if you don't get it?"

He twisted his head toward Sonia. "I always got it."

I caught my breath. "Even murder?"

He waited a long time. "Frontier ain't no place for the weak, the sniveling, the...coward."

"And you weren't a coward?"

His voice rose, broke. "Nope."

"You talk a lot about murder, Jack." I glanced at Sonia and tapped the interview in *The Gold*.

"Lady, sometimes murder is the only game in town—in those eat-dirt bars. You live by your fists, don't take no crap from anyone. Some asshole pushing up into your chest, I knows it's them or me. Dog eat dog, and I ain't gonna be the dog eaten. I like that when I walked into a bar, folks left." He grinned widely. "*Left.* A knife and a swagger sends a message."

Sonia began, "You told me about a fight over a cache of beaver pelts."

"Yep. Almost don't remember that one. Maybe 1910 or so. So far back. A man raids your goods, you got a right to..."

"Kill him?" I shot out.

"Ma'am, you city folks don't get it." He wagged a finger at me. "Miner's justice, they call it. No marshals or sheriffs around villages. You settle your battles with the fellows around you. Two bastards in a bar—and only one leaves. Me!"

"They found you hiding out in a cabin near Chena," Sonia chided. "Running from the law in Bristol Bay. You're *still* a criminal."

He waved a dismissive hand at her. "Ain't nothing, that nonsense."

Sonia turned to me. "Jack worked at a cannery in Bristol Bay last summer. Salmon season, mid-summer. June and July, peak time." Her eyes twinkled. "You got into a kerfuffle."

He squinted at her. "I'm an old man. Nobody talks crap to me and gets away with it."

"What happened?" I ate my last bit of mooseburger and pushed away the plate.

Sonia was grinning as she reached into her satchel, extracted another copy of *The Gold*. "Local police blotter. Last week." She pointed. "Down on Cushman, late afternoon. Jack tried to wrestle Jeremy Nunne—his old boss—to the ground."

Jack set his mouth in a grim line. "You know, I didn't know the bastard was up in Fairbanks. I knew they canned his ass…"

Sonia talked to me. "The reason he's here is because of"— she pointed—"Jack."

The small paragraph in the newspaper mentioned pushing and shoving, an incident that resulted in the police stepping in. No charges pressed.

"Scared of me, that fool. Me, I'm old but strong." Awkwardly, he flexed a bicep.

Sonia explained. "Jeremy is a young guy, nephew of the owner of Alaska Enterprises, which, as you know, Edna, is a powerful conglomerate of industries. Planted there as the new manager, a plum job for a wandering nephew, a man without a clue how to deal with the cannery workers—the Filipinos, Chinese, old sourdoughs like Jack, even the adventurous college students up from Seattle for the summer. He comes up against a man like Jack who hates authority"—Jack was nodding vigorously—"and the result is…chaos."

"I closed down the damn place for two days." Jack's eyes twinkled. "Stopped production. I slugged the bastard and beat it out of town, while the crazy Filipinos ran for the hills and this Nunne fellow calls the cops. Winter in a cabin in Chena. And then…"

"A stroke," I finished.

He ignored that. "The bastard."

"Why were you at the cannery, Jack?" I asked.

"Hard cash. A month in the summer. Ten hours a day. Brutal. A village called Egegik, down from Nushagak in Bristol Bay. A slimer. The rottenest job."

"A slimer?" I echoed.

"Well, ma'am, the salmon come down the chute and I gut them. You got you a fillet knife and you slit the throat down to the belly. When them suckers are decapitated, you pull out the guts and egg sacs. Messy job, you wear yellow oilskin pants and aprons, and you smell to high heaven."

"Sounds horrible," I told him.

"Yeah, but it puts silver dollars in your pocket. Of course, the money ain't last long—pool halls, movies, saloons, beer halls, and the goddamn N.C. store taking the rest."

"Tough job." I nodded at him.

"Yeah, a tough job, but you gotta make a living, lady." He sat back. "Some worse. The Chinks. The Filipinos drowning theirselves with their stinky perfume. Short season there, then I head north again for the winter. Trapping."

"But this time, one step ahead of the law." Sonia tapped him on the elbow, and he flinched.

He pulled in his cheeks. "They put in this green kid, bumbling ass, weak-kneed, college-educated sucker, tries to order me around." He gloated as his eyes scanned the bar. "I caused such a ruckus, no one knew where to run to." A triumphant grin. "Spoiled a lot of salmon, I tell you. You got you one month to do the job—can't afford to lose a day." A harsh laugh. "Lost two days, ma'am."

Sonia was nodding. "Jeremy was transferred to Fairbanks, put in charge of Northern Lights Airways, also owned by Alaska Enterprises."

"I didn't know the sucker was here."

Sonia hunched her shoulders. "Hence, the incident in the police blotter." She tapped the newspaper on the table.

"I want to get back to the murders," I said.

Jack grinned. "My kind of lady. Blood and gore. Only murderers are heroes in stories. Not dumb cannery workers."

A skinny young man called over to us, interrupting. Dressed in an airman's uniform, he was most likely stationed at nearby Ladd Air Force Base. He pointed at Jack as he rocked back in his chair. "You the meanest man in Alaska?" Jack grinned but looked confused. "I read about you," the airman said. I shot him a withering look, lost on the man who now addressed the other diners in a loud, rumbling voice. "I read about this guy." Pointing to the waitress, he ordered a boilermaker for Jack. Jack downed the whiskey shot but his fingers trembled on the beer bottle.

Jack was fading now. His eyes fluttering, he made a wheezing sound, his body drifting down into his seat. His gnarled fingers kept opening and closing. Popping his eyes open, he gazed across the room, focused on the bottles of whiskey on the glass shelf above the counter, and quietly echoed his own words to me. "My kind of lady." But his heart wasn't in it, and I sensed this talk—feeble though it was—was ending. Sonia, aware, offered to walk him back to the Frontier Home. His hand went to grab the beer bottle but knocked it over. Beer ran over the table and onto the floor. "Christ Almighty, man."

At that moment a group of men walked out of a back dining room. Dressed in black business suits under Chesterfield overcoats, two of the men wore fashionable horn-rimmed eyeglasses, all four sporting severe Eisenhower military haircuts, their faces assuming the look of a business meeting happily concluded.

Idly, I watched them, this new Alaskan dynamic that could be transplanted into a Manhattan cocktail lounge, a look uniform, bland, a tad smug. So I was not aware of the rustling at my table.

I sat up. "What?"

Sonia whispered, "Preston Strange." She nodded toward one of the four men.

"And he is?"

"An asshole," Jack roared.

I frowned at him. "That doesn't narrow down my list of souls."

Sonia kept her eyes on Jack, though she threw a sidelong glance at the men, all of whom had stopped moving, a rigid frieze planted ten feet away from us. "He runs Alaska Enterprises for his mother, Tessa Strange, the most powerful woman in Alaska. The most powerful business conglomerate in Alaska, including that cannery at Bristol Bay." To my continued bafflement, she added, "The uncle of Jeremy Nunne." She drummed the newspaper article. "Nephew Nunne, the victim of the recent assault by this crusty gentleman sitting here with us."

"The whole family is losers." Jack's benediction as his fingers pointed at Preston Strange. He half-rose from his seat, but Sonia touched him on the shoulder. He sat back down.

One of the men nudged Preston, who seemed loath to move. Finally, a gruff rumble escaping his throat, he took a step toward us. Though he glowered at Jack, he spoke to Sonia.

A phony laugh. "Sonia, I've often questioned the quality of the people I see you with, but I always assumed it was part of your job to assail lowlife for news for that rag you publish, but…a new low, no?"

Sonia smiled up at him. "Good to see you too, Preston."

He squinted at me, his pale blue eyes steely. "Ah, Edna Ferber, returned to pillage the spoils of Alaska."

I stiffened my spine. "You know me, sir?"

"We all know you, courtesy of Sonia and her vicious father and the tabloid slant of *The Gold*. Last summer you neglected to introduce yourself to my mother."

"I didn't know a royal audience was proper—or necessary."

"My mother is the most powerful woman in Alaska."

"Of course, but my visit last year was short."

"And under the protective wing of Hank Petrievich. And yet you are here again."

"You're very observant."

A hasty glance at Jack, a whistling hiss escaping his throat, he almost whispered, "You're writing a polemic on Alaska becoming a state."

"No, sir, a novel."

He cut me off. "Not what I hear." Another sharp look at Jack.

Irritated, Sonia broke in. "Alaska Enterprises"—she flicked her head toward Preston—"believes statehood is a mistake."

"Be that as it may." Preston's voice rose. He looked directly into Sonia's face. "I find your lunch companions…questionable."

"Then perhaps you should leave." Sonia pointed to the door.

Furious, Preston leaned into Jack. "You—you'll never work for Alaska Enterprises again, Jack Mabie. You disrupted production at Bristol Bay—unforgivable—halted production, our shipments to Bellingham delayed—a rabble-rouser, a…a Communist maybe. And then to assault my nephew on the streets of Fairbanks…"

Jack fumbled with the empty beer bottle, then dropped his fingers into the sticky, spilled beer on the table. He spat out his words. "That namby-pamby ain't got no business ordering hard-working real men around."

"You'll never..." Preston paused, rattled, his face purple, a vein throbbing in his neck.

"What? Slime another goddamn salmon. Christ, you can keep your worthless job."

Preston stepped closer. "I've said my say, old man. You touch him again..."

"Next time I kill him," Jack thundered.

Preston blanched, raised a fist. "You...you heard me."

Jack hiccoughed. "Maybe I'll take you off the planet." A sickly grin aimed at me. "I bet the applause'll be heard in the Lower Forty-eight."

Preston stepped away, nervous, but turned back. "Sonia, again...you really should rethink your lunch mates."

As he moved away, he boldly flicked a finger against Jack's shoulder. Incensed, Jack attempted to shuffle to his feet, jarring the table, scraping his chair, and sending our plates onto the floor. His hand reached for the beer bottle, but it fell to the floor and broke. Preston stepped back, stumbled, and turned toward the doorway. The three men had lingered in the entrance, watching, but now disappeared. Preston moved away, glancing back at us, his face a mixture of hot anger and hollow fear.

"You heard me," he yelled to us.

Jack sputtered, "I kill men worth more'n your spit."

But Preston had moved out of earshot, the door slamming behind him.

I looked helplessly at Sonia. Her eyes were dark and cloudy. "What in the world?"

Chapter Two

The day before, when Sonia picked me up at the airport, her shiny DeSoto humming, I saw a question in her face. "Tomorrow night," she'd said, "dinner at my parents' home? Everyone can't wait to see you again, Edna." A pause. "We were so surprised to learn that you were coming back."

"Not as surprised as I was, I have to admit."

I had no business returning in March, the end of a cruel Fairbanks winter. My novel *Ice Palace* nearly finished, there was no reason to be sitting on a Pan Am DC Clipper, New York to Seattle, then Seattle to Fairbanks. There was simply no reason for me to travel again. Especially north to Alaska.

Except one. That conversation. Abrupt words that stayed with me, haunted and alarmed me. Reason enough, somehow.

I didn't want to think about *Ice Palace*. It had plagued me, that challenging subject, but…it was nearly over. Yet there I was, winging my ancient body back to Alaska. For what?—the fifth or sixth time in five years? Brutal, forty-below temperatures in Kotzebue, twenty-two hours of hazy endless sunshine in Fairbanks, slipping on Taku glacier ice, Mount McKinley with its late-afternoon rose-tipped summit, a lazy afternoon in the Russian Orthodox Church in Sitka, hearty meals with ebullient businessmen in Juneau. My picture ran in *Look*, photographed with a Matanuska cabbage the size of a subway car. I'd become fascinated with all of Alaska, so it was all in my novel, from Point Barrow to the Banana Belt. I counted the visits on my fingers. Yes, this was my sixth. All because in the last days of my visit last summer, I'd had a brief, unsettling conversation with a young Indian who'd utterly captivated me. Noah West, Sonia Petrievich's lover. I'd been taken by his striking looks, his unassuming charm, his diamond-sharp intelligence, his gentleness, and his crisp, honest conversation.

I'd paid the Athabascan Indians scant attention in my research, focusing on their traditional rivals, the Eskimos. I'd spent time in the Eskimo village of Kotzebue within the Arctic Circle, dining on reindeer steak and shee fish at Rotman's Hotel. So Eskimos it was, not Athabascans. Or even the Aleuts. My audience knew Eskimos—they lived in igloos, rubbed noses when they kissed, sent ancient parents adrift on ice floes till death did them part, popular stereotypes, all—and few knew the more mysterious, elusive Indians.

But then this young lawyer, just returned to Fairbanks from Seattle, led me from the bleak concrete buildings of new Fairbanks on Second Avenue into the hardscrabble alleys of a fringe town, the area around Fourth Avenue beyond The Line, the red-light district where neon signs announced grimy bars and sad eateries. We'd been talking about Alaska as we sat in the lounge of the Nordale, and Noah West had said, "Come with me."

Sonia, at his side, nodded her head. "Go with him, Edna."

It was the night before I was to fly back to the Lower Forty-eight, so much to do, but sitting there with him, staring into his eyes, I'd sensed something in him. So, meekly, I'd followed him, Sonia waving us off with an enigmatic smile on her pretty face. With a dramatic sweep of his arm, he'd stopped walking and pointed over the rows of crumpled pickups and tethered, squawking dogs, and I saw a whitewashed clapboard shack.

Its neon sign said "Mimis," no apostrophe and the second "m" blacked out. His voice was flat yet laced with passion. "There's the novel you should be writing, Miss Ferber. That's the real Alaska."

And I'd found myself gazing at a corner of Alaska I'd ignored. Six or seven Indians huddled against the weathered building, all drunk, but worse, deadened. They didn't move. They congregated there like hunting trophies on a den wall, staring back at the black street with eyes washed free of life. Cigarettes dangled from twitching lips, beer bottles gripped tightly, knees buckled, skinny bodies and heads tilted like broken dolls. "There."

Then Noah West walked away, leaving me alone on that sidewalk.

Stunned, I found my way back to the Nordale Hotel and mechanically packed my bags. That night I couldn't fall asleep.

The next day I looked for Noah but learned he'd flown his Piper Cub back to his home in the North.

Now, less than a year later, I was back in Fairbanks. That image of those lost souls frozen outside Mimi's in the hours of the midnight sun was etched in my brain like a Kodachrome postcard tacked to the heart.

I felt I'd lost sight of the real Alaska, the frontier, the heartless icebox in the North, the blank-eyed old-timers still haunted by gold. I'd spent my time in overheated parlors, listening to prosperous old white men with cigars and cocktails, intimate groups that raged about statehood and exports and exploitation and—and these were the characters who populated my novel. I'd forgotten that Alaska was *still* frontier, rough, untutored, a violent, mysterious world deep below the glossy skin I'd written about. Noah West's Alaska—no man's land, maybe—was the dark night of the Alaskan soul.

Now, equally spurred on by Sonia's clippings of "White Silence" mailed to me in Manhattan, I was back. I wanted *that* Alaska.

The vacant-eyed Indians on that cold street.

"Where's Noah?" My first question to Sonia when she met me at the airport.

She shook her head. "Settling some Indian dispute in Valdez. He'll fly in tomorrow morning. He'll be at dinner tomorrow night."

"I hope so."

"Charming, no?"

"Very."

"He can't wait to see you again." Her eyes twinkled. "You'll be seeing too much of him, Edna. The Nordale lounge is his home away from home."

I loved the venerable Nordale. Not the most up-to-date hotel, a little tired and drab, but homey, like a remembered bedroom from a happy childhood. The busy lounge attracted a cross-section of Alaska. Scraggly drifters out of the Bush, their eyes with the wide-awake look of someone who'd survived an Arctic white night. Up-and-coming young professionals with their smart briefcases and California suits. Tourists from the Lower Forty-eight with their well-thumbed guidebooks, their cars parked outside bearing "Alaska or Bust" bumper stickers, their hands clutching birchwood carvings. Whole novels could be written in that room.

Yet it was the scene at the Model Café that disturbed my late-afternoon nap—what was that all about? Jack Mabie and Preston Strange. Two unpleasant men. Unable to fall asleep, I sat by my window, staring out at the bleak, dead landscape.

At seven Hank Petrievich sent a car for me, and I headed to the two-story clapboard Petrievich home fronting the frozen Chena River outside of downtown Fairbanks. Bundled in a hooded parka, a woolen scarf, fur-lined mittens, even the mukluks I'd been given on previous visits north—had I had a chance I would have shamelessly commandeered the coverlet from my bed at the Nordale—I thanked Henry, my driver, and rushed inside, where a fireplace blazed.

Sonia was late. "Long, long hours at the news office," her mother Irina whispered. "Her obsession." She hugged me. "Good to see you again, Edna."

Hank came from behind me, shook my hand vigorously, and repeated what seemed to be the prevailing sentiment, "A surprise, your visit."

"A few loose strings."

Irina turned her head, her eyes cloudy.

"Atmosphere," I added.

Yes, drunken Indians outside a seedy bar, clutching bottles of stale beer. A landscape of dreaming and loneliness. Despair. Even—the celebration of murder. Jack Mabie, folk hero.

"Sonia was thrilled when she heard you were returning," Hank said. "The two of you became so close…"

I looked into his beaming face, this man who looked younger than his years, towering, sinewy, with an ashy face under a huge bushel of white-gray hair, a man so tall he seemed to lope when he moved, like a romping wilderness beast. His handsome face bore an old-fashioned moustache, still blackened, bushy, in sharp contrast to his hair. There was about him a hint of the old frontiersman. He'd been born in Sitka, the old Russian capital, in 1892, of a pioneering Slavic family, had drifted to Fairbanks as a young man, made a fortune in fur trading and timber, and lived a baronial life in the boom-and-bust frontier town, publisher of the weekly *Fairbanks Gold Dust Gazette*, which locals simply called *The Gold*. A pro-statehood zealot.

Despite his money, he always appeared to be in a rumpled suit with a feathered fedora on his head. A boastful man, sure of himself—yet I liked him. Most men filled with braggadocio annoyed me, yet I found Hank amusing. Last summer, flying back to Seattle, I'd realized why I liked him: Hank Petrievich, despite his millions and his power, seemed nothing more than an eager little boy running through a backyard with his first BB gun, taking aim at birds winging their way over Fairbanks rooftops.

I caught Irina's eye, and the woman squinted, nervous. A small, mousy woman dressed in ill-fitting smocks that must have cost hundreds, she reminded me of a Calvinist schoolmarm with her gray hair pulled back into a neat bun, yet with hard blue eyes stuck onto a soft face. A woman who catered to a demanding husband, she spoke in a feathery, whispered voice. Perpetually dressed in black and gray and mauve, she struck me as Whistler's Mother transplanted to a frontier and left without the rocker she craved. But there was something about Irina that I never could quite grasp. Those steely eyes suggested intelligence kept masked, deliberately hidden behind the obedience. Not quite Patient Griselda by the fireside. Something else there: a fierceness, the quiet mama bear ready to take action.

Last year I'd concluded that Irina would have preferred a life out of the limelight, away from the boldface newspaper world, the politics, the entrepreneurs. She didn't want to be looked at. A life italicized unnerved her.

Irina, smiling, told me she'd prepared a true Alaskan supper, and I quaked. I'd had my fill of moose head soup, whale blubber ice cream, bush rabbit stew with spruce root and wild celery. But Irina surprised me with a credible steak—caribou, I supposed, since I was convinced all Alaskan steak was caribou caught on the run, the misguided animal wandering down Second Avenue at midday, blinded by ice fog—a steak a little too chewy but still rich and satisfying. Robust winter potatoes doused with butter and cream, and a rare green salad, flown in from Seattle, I was told. The meal finished with wild blueberry pie, a sweet confection in a brown flaky crust, delicious with a scoop of ice cream that did not originate from some part of a beluga whale.

Hank and Irina, and their son, Paul, were at dinner. I recalled Paul as a genial shadow, so unlike his hale fare-thee-well father. Paul simply was *there*, tucked into a chair in the corner. He reminded me of his mother, though he was as tall as his father, but thin, almost frail, droopy-eyed, handsome in a *Sorrows of Young Werther* melancholic way. A Russian blondness, pale, freckly. What little I knew of him I'd gleaned from his parents last summer. He was, Irina had whispered, unambitious. He worked on *The Gold*, but halfheartedly, a company drone, unhappy, and he talked constantly of abandoning Alaska. This stance, I knew, was sacrilege in a family whose members defined themselves by century-old genealogy and distance from "Outside."

What was clear to me was Hank's unabashed favorite—Sonia was his darling. Yes, she mimicked his passion for news and Alaska, but she had an infectious spirit—you liked Sonia because she laughed easily, held your eye, listened to your stories. A contradiction in some ways: a fiery muckraking journalist who wanted to be your best friend. Her writing was incendiary, purposely provocative, but she came off as the girl next door—friendly, bubbly, filled with neighborhood gossip.

Paul seemed a footnote in that family. Their mother told me, "Sometimes I despair of my two children. Paul the dark side of the moon, Sonia the noontime sun."

Once, having lunch with Sonia last summer, Paul nodded at us from across the room. "He doesn't realize how much he hates my father," Sonia had remarked.

Her words surprised me. "Why?"

"My father forgives Paul and me—especially me—our lapses and mistakes. I'm his...indulgence. Sometimes that's hard to deal with. Paul, I think, wishes our father spanked him more. Dad never learned how to deal with his children."

Now, tonight, with Paul saying little, the conversation turned to Hank's monomaniacal theme: statehood.

"Within a year," Hank crowed, his voice swelling.

"You think so?" I asked.

Irina added, "Richard Russell of Georgia said that no reasonable soul would consider living in Alaska."

No one laughed.

"I hope you put that in your book." Irina leaned into me.

"No, my book is a novel, fiction, a story of a family—two families…" I paused. "A romantic tale, though with a little satirical venom. *Giant* with ice instead of oil."

Paul held up his hand. "I think Miss Ferber has heard all this before."

Restless, he stood and began moving around the room, my eyes following him, though his parents' didn't. He walked to the sideboard, poured himself a drink, lingered there, then circled the table. When he walked by his mother, she instinctively reached out and gripped his wrist, a peculiar, affectionate though possessive gesture. He smiled back at her.

His remark hung in the air.

Hank looked at me, his face tense. "Are we boring you, Edna?" Then he glanced at his son. Standing, Hank poured himself another shot of whiskey, downing it quickly. He shivered. He was starting to slur his words, his eyes a little watery.

"Not at all," I lied.

But Paul's snide remark to his father had shifted the tone of the conversation. Tension built in the room as both men, standing, feet apart, eyed each other. Irina, nervous, jumped up, called to Millie, and the bashful woman emerged from the kitchen with a tray. The two women began clearing dishes while I sipped coffee and waited. The phone rang and Hank excused himself.

Silence. When I glanced at Paul, he was smiling.

"It must have been something I said, Miss Ferber." A rascal's twinkle in his eye.

I smiled. "It's usually me who clears a room, Paul."

A rush of movement came from the hallway as Sonia flew into the room, apologizing for her lateness, giving me a hasty hug—she smelled like lilac perfume and sweet powder—and then toppling into a chair. She poured herself a cup of coffee, leaned over to the sideboard, tipping her chair slightly. Deftly, she laced the brew with a finger of whiskey. She caught my eye and smiled. "The long, long Fairbanks winter." She took a sip and stared at me over the rim. A lazy laugh, warm.

I didn't answer. Paul slumped in his seat, his tongue rolled into his cheek. Brother and sister, both blond and fair, but Paul was a pale reflection of his sunburst sister. It dawned on me—twins.

"Twins?"

"You didn't know?" asked Sonia.

Paul was frowning. He stood back up, began moving idly, his fingers straightening a painting on the wall. His back to us, his shoulders tight.

I could hear Hank on the phone in another room, his voice rushed, anxious to end the conversation.

"That's why I always know what Paul is thinking," Sonia said.

Paul mumbled, but with a slight laugh. "If you knew what I'm thinking now..."

Sonia ignored that, reaching out and gripping my hand. "So happy you're here."

The outspoken daughter of a powerful man, Sonia had established a name for herself as an editor at *The Gold*. Dressed in a snug black wool dress, a gold chain around her neck, a jangling gold bracelet on her wrist, she was eye-catching. In her late thirties, perhaps, she looked as if she'd wandered away from some magazine shoot for a springtime-in-the-Rockies soap commercial—with her long blond hair, her blue eyes, her alabaster skin, her athletic body. The modern girl next door who read *Cosmopolitan*, tennis racket at the ready. A wicked serve. The girl who gave me heart palpitations as she drove wildly in the wilderness outside of Fairbanks. A girl who got her own pilot's license, winging her way over the Alaskan landscape. But as her father told me one evening—and not happily—his daughter had a tough soul and a fur-trap editorial reach. She skewered souls in her editorials, circling her targets like a one-woman army, hanging her opponents out to dry in the frigid Fairbanks air.

Last summer she'd given me sheaves of her columns, fiery exposés on the absentee salmon-canning industry, the steamship companies, the mining conglomerates, the fur-trading syndicates—their mean-spirited efforts to delay statehood. I'd saved one: "A Looted Land," a strident polemic filled with innuendo, rich in anecdote. A prosaic paragraph would stop, midstream, and suddenly there would be a delightful Indian parable, a Tlingit folk saying, an Aleut aphorism, or even a sourdough's pithy recollection from the gold rush days and the winter of '03. A gold mine for me, certainly, the scrambling writer.

"I thought Noah'd be here by now." She glanced toward the doorway.

"The two of you are always late," said Paul.

She looked up as her father returned, another drink in hand. As he slid back into his chair and apologized for the long phone call, he slurred some words. "A problem with the presses. Cheap labor." He looked to the doorway. "I wanted to talk to Noah about it."

Irina poured me more coffee, even though I held up my hand. Paul was smiling at me. "Perhaps something stronger, Miss Ferber?"

I said nothing.

Hank began, "Sonia told me you had an interesting lunch today—with Jack Mabie."

Paul returned to his seat. "The meanest man in Alaska."

"Tell me what's going on?" I asked. "This Preston Strange seems like a hothead."

Irina chuckled. "To put it mildly. To his mother's consternation. The corporate bigwig is a street brawler. He was always a hairpin trigger boy. Fistfights in prep school."

With a laugh, Sonia said in a fake whisper, "Edna, some Fairbanks scandal for you. For a brief moment in time, a few years after the war ended, I permitted myself to fall into the sticky arms of that man."

"You? Preston?" My eyes widened.

She sat back and sipped her coffee, watching me over the rim. "A short time, the streets like a spring carnival, the sense of relief after Japan capitulated—keep in mind Japan actually invaded parts of Alaska—and Preston wooed me. Preston had a moment of giddiness. He even sported a peach-colored scarf and a shiny Norfolk suit. Everyone was trying to look… brand-new. Like others, I was drunk with victory."

I chose my words carefully. "He seems an unlikely mate for you, Sonia."

Hank broke in. "Tell me about it. An oily confection."

Sonia shot a look at her father. "Two hotheads, me and him—I admit I can be a fishwife when challenged. It didn't last long. A couple months. I woke up and said goodbye. He returned to his undertaker's black suit—and snippy personality. I hid at the newspaper while he fled into his bank vault, but Preston doesn't like to be left. Deserted, dumped. There were bitter words."

"But that was years ago," I insisted.

Irina sighed. "Not for Preston. He still moons over Sonia."

"Every man moons over my sister," Paul added, unhappily. "They don't realize she's a heartbreaker."

Hank was smiling at his daughter. A father pleased with his children's antics—or at least those of one of his children.

The look he tossed Paul's way told me there was little Paul could do to please his father.

Hank reached over to the sideboard, poured himself a tumbler of whiskey. Irina watched his movements carefully and clicked her tongue. Settled back in his chair, both hands gripping the glass, he rocked back and forth like a contented cat, purring.

"Thank God for Noah," he said into the dead air. "Cool and calm and…" His words trailed off.

"Cornered," Paul finished, and his father grunted.

Sonia turned to me. "Edna, my work is my life. Everyone knows that. No marriage for me, no children. I've been saying that since I was twelve years old. The old maid. My declaration of independence from the kitchen. Yes, my dance partners, my—my foolish game with Preston. But when Noah returned from the war—battered, shattered, bandaged—suddenly we were a couple. I couldn't help myself. I fell in love with a man I've known—the family has known—since he was a small boy. A shock to the system, really."

"So you'll marry Noah?" I asked.

No one said anything. Paul grumbled, "She loves me, she loves me not."

"She *does* love him," Sonia, piqued, insisted.

Hank sounded frustrated. "Edna, Sonia keeps refusing Noah's proposals of marriage."

Again Sonia reached over and grasped my wrist. "Edna, a dilemma." For a moment she closed her eyes. "I suppose I will. There is no one else like him." Her index finger drummed her chin. "Yes."

In a hollow voice, Paul said, "Maybe."

She looked at him. "Maybe." An amused sigh. "I do love him. What a pity. Me, the career girl. I wake up and think of the newspaper—not love."

Irina's voice was hesitant. "Edna, that's one of the reasons

Preston hates Noah. Even though Sonia and Preston broke up long before, Preston insists Noah—an outsider, an Indian—is to blame."

Hank added, "Also Noah, a lawyer for Indian rights, has challenged in court Tessa Strange's business dealings with the Native employees. And won. Over and over. Unfair labor practices. Tessa Strange doesn't like dissent—only money. And her toady son Preston does her bidding."

Sonia held up her hand, protesting. "Enough of this. Edna cannot be interested in tepid romances in the land of the tundra. Sonia's sordid sallies."

"This explains part of what I witnessed today at lunch," I began, "but the presence of Jack Mabie seemed to throw Preston into a tizzy."

"Because he's his mother's handmaiden. Or henchman. Or hyena." Sonia laughed. "Tessa Strange snaps her fat fingers and a good part of Fairbanks trembles."

I turned to Hank. "You're not friendly with her? I mean, you publish an influential newspaper…"

He shook his head slowly. "That's the problem. *The Gold* is pro-statehood. Tessa Strange is not. Not now. We once were friends." He qualified that. "Friendly, maybe. Guarded friendly. She's a woman never to be trusted."

Sonia was eager to say something, sitting at the edge of her chair. Still laughing, she said, "Edna, Tessa Strange was a hellion as a young woman. Right, Dad? The wild stories no one talks about. An Episcopalian missionary above the Arctic Circle, especially in Venetie and over to Fort Yukon where Noah's grandfather still lives and where Noah was born, she had a profane mouth as she thumped her Bible. I would have adored her—then. Tessa was married to a weak-kneed missionary named Lionel Strange. One son, little Preston, who played with little Noah in that icy village, and then Lionel drowned."

Hank picked up the story. "In Fairbanks Tessa met a bigwig named Herman Bonner, money-bags adventurer, and the two got married. When he died a few years later, Tessa inherited his world of canneries, gold mines, commercial blocks in Fairbanks, you name it. Tessa suddenly became the most powerful woman in Alaska."

Paul added, "Tessa is mainly a recluse these days. Preston does her quiet bidding. His reach touches everything in Alaska."

"Which explains today's lunch. Jack Mabie."

"Exactly," Hank said. "Tessa planted her dead husband's nephew as manager—green, weak, sort of a nincompoop like Preston, though bumbling—and you come up against a wild old-timer like Jack Mabie, a notorious troublemaker."

Sonia stood and poured herself a whiskey from the sideboard. She didn't sit back down. Instead, leaning against the sideboard, one arm cupping her elbow, she watched us, a mischievous gleam in her eye.

Her father grinned. "Tell us, Sonia. You got that news-hound look in your eyes."

"The reason I was late to dinner." A melodramatic pause. "Tessa is on the warpath."

"Whatever for?" asked Irina. "This time."

"News from the mukluk telegraph—by way of gossip from the servants, news drifting into the newsroom. Tessa is storming about—or as much as a fat woman can storm about—furious with both Preston and nephew Jeremy, although Jeremy is monumentally scared of Tessa, always bowing as he approaches her. Word got back to her of Preston's antics with Jack Mabie today at the Model Café—with me, with him, even with Edna here." Sonia held my eye, amused. "Preston flicking his finger at Jack's shoulder as seen by a number of diners. You know, Fairbanks is a small village. The bad behavior of the unpopular town squire. This, coupled with Jeremy's police blotter notice the other day, has sent her into a rage."

I was baffled. "Such a small moment, no?"

"No." Hank's voice was firm.

Paul announced, "People don't like Preston, Edna. People are waiting for him to...to..."

"Crash land." Sonia made a ta-da noise.

Irina went on. "And with Jack Mabie in town—and suddenly known to all because of Sonia's columns—folks are hoping for a ringside seat."

Paul added, "Who cares about Jack Mabie? His antics happened decades ago."

Hank watched him. "But Sonia resurrected his evil reputation. Dime novel killer. Notches on his belt. Sonia exaggerates..."

"No," she protested.

The phone rang, and Hank jumped up. In the hallway his voice was mumbled with an edge. He returned to the table, shaking his head.

"That was Noah. He apologized. He can't make it. Exhausted from his trip. Edna, he said he'll see you tomorrow. He's looking forward to it."

Sonia joked. "You see why I can't marry him, dear family. He'll never be on time for supper."

I was disappointed. "I'm looking forward to it. Last year he impressed me. He made me look at a different Alaska. Bright, charming..."

"Good-looking," Irina added.

I laughed. "That, too."

Sonia was enjoying herself. "I'd slave all day in the kitchen, a frostbitten Betty Crocker baking cake after cake, a pineapple upside-down cake, only to eat alone at midnight." She winked at me.

Paul muttered, "The noble savage." But I noticed it wasn't said nastily or sarcastically. Oddly, there was a hint of reverence in his tone.

"Really, Paul," his sister admonished, "what a thing to say about Noah. I thought you'd learned years ago that silence is your only talent."

Paul made a clicking sound with his tongue. "Sonia, I was talking about you."

Chapter Three

As I stepped into the Nordale lounge with its scratched cherry-red tables and chairs, its walls covered with sentimental paintings of Arctic scenery, I spotted Clint Bullock sitting by himself on a straight-backed chair, legs up on another chair, drowsing before a roaring fire. I waved at him, though he had his eyes closed. Last year the bewhiskered sourdough had trailed after me, in his own words, "like a sun-besotted muskrat looking for a shady nook." At first I was put off by the old man's bumbling friendliness. But he was a goldmine of anecdote, this old-timer from the Cleary Creek gold rush days, one of the last of the original '03 pioneers who made Fairbanks a boomtown. Relaxing with him, I found a decent companion to bum around with, though I was hardly the kind of soul who bummed around—anytime.

With him, I lumbered through Rocky River beds, learning about placer gold, shuffling tin pans of gravel for gold dust. In over a half century, beginning with his shack outside Fox, north of Fairbanks, Clint Bullock had found no fortune. The only treasure he'd ever unearthed was the acorn-sized nugget he wore proudly around his neck. Now in his seventies, a small stooped man with a wrinkled, dried-up face covered with ungainly whiskers, Clint lived alone in a small log cabin in town. In the summer he chopped wood and fished.

Occasionally he mined for "colors," as he called his quest for gold. Through the long icy cold winters he burned wood and dozed in the Nordale lounge. Most nights, huddled there, he talked and drifted off.

"Clint." I nudged his shoulder.

He opened his eyes and smiled. "Heard you was here," he mumbled dreamily. "Can't stay away from me, can you?"

Within minutes the reception clerk placed tea at my elbow, and I nodded my thanks. I looked up into his face. "Mr. Thompson, I'm afraid I've encumbered you with a nightly routine."

He chuckled. "But one that's my pleasure, Miss Ferber."

Last night, settled into the Nordale, I'd drifted down into the lounge and requested a cup of tea from the night clerk. For a moment he'd become flustered. Groups of men lingered in the lounge, glasses of whiskey clinking as they toasted one another.

"Tea?" the clerk had asked.

"Yes, without whiskey." I hesitated. "With cream."

None was available, I'd learned, but he kindly brewed me a cup on a hot plate in the back room behind the reception desk, delivered it to me with a small pitcher of cream from an icebox in a back kitchen. Now, unfortunately, it would be a nightly ritual for him, though he insisted it was no big deal.

"Mr. Thomson…"

"Teddy," he interrupted. "Please."

A fiftyish man with a pale, drawn face, a web of wrinkles around his small gray eyes, balding, a thick chest in a tight hotel uniform, he did not strike me as a Teddy. But then neither did Teddy Roosevelt, whom I knew years back. The roustabout rough rider with riding crop and safari hat. The original teddy bear.

"Teddy," I said as he backed away.

Clint was talking. "Lots happening since you departed us,

Edna." He tugged at his bulky overalls, fidgeting with a loose buckle. The elbows of his shirt were worn, quarter-sized holes revealing pale skin.

"You mean besides the pall of utter winter darkness?"

"That's right." He cleared his throat noisily and blew his nose into a faded handkerchief he extracted from a shirt pocket. "You was here in June, twenty-two hours of hazy sunlight. Baseball at midnight. Girls half naked in the sun."

Shaking my head, I made believe I was shivering. "I'd forgotten how cold it could get here."

"Ain't nothing in March. Zero at night is a time to get outside, live on the creeks. It still ain't like my days trapping up in Eagle one long winter when the temperature never rose above fifty below, seemed."

I stared into his face. "Clint, what do you mean things have changed?"

He leaned in, confidential. "People can taste statehood, you know. We're that close, really. Sonia Petrievich done a series of fire-and-brimstone articles in *The Gold* that riled a few folks, mainly the salmon-canning folks from down in Seattle and San Francisco.

He reached into his breast pocket, extracted a briarwood pipe. Within seconds the pungent aroma of cheap tobacco filled the corner of the room. Clint waved the pipe at me, making a point, a grin on his face. "Only subject in town—until Sonia done that article on Jack Mabie."

"Did you know him up north?"

He shook his head. "Couple sightings way back when. I drifted up to Fort Yukon now and then. I headed north as a trapper and guide, tried to settle down in a wilderness cabin outside of Venetie. I was married to an Indian gal for two or three years, maybe, after the First World War. She died in childbirth in a blizzard like you never seen before, that beautiful girl from Circle City, near Fort Yukon."

"I'm so sorry, Clint."

"Just a step you take in life. Good. Bad. All steps."

"But Jack made a name for himself, right?"

"Stories shared around a campfire, you know. Wild tales of bad men. Jack Mabie was one of many. Mean son of a bitch, tell you the truth. He *scared* folks. Wiry, looking for a fight. The meanest man…"

"So he says."

"No, it's the truth. These days he's an old geezer like the rest of us, but back in the Bush he was a man most folks stepped around like when you spot a grizzly mama on the trail."

I sipped the hot tea—refreshing, a hint of some wild herb, rich like old moss. I smiled at Teddy, leaning over the reception desk.

I drew my tongue into my cheek. "Jack is savoring his outlaw reputation these days. I expect he'll get mash notes from dance hall girls."

"Because of Sonia's article. She romanticized him."

"You don't like that?"

"He's a murderer."

"He always escaped the hangman's noose."

"No matter." Clint's voice got louder, harsh. "He ruined lives. Yeah, he killed some bad guys, lots of them—he boasted about it—but with his temper, Christ, he murdered a simple missionary who got in his way. A man of God. Such a man ain't fit to be the hero of no story."

"I'm curious. Did Sonia interview you for her 'White Silence' column?"

A wide grin that showed broken teeth, yellow-stained. "She tried, that foolish girl. But I says to her, 'I'm an old wanderer who got up in the morning, put my pants on, and hoped I got matches to make me coffee and beans. No story there. Look around Fairbanks—Second Avenue filled with old men in sagging cabins sinking into the ground, staggering, limbs twisted. No thanks."

"Any life story, told with selection, is fascinating."

He grumbled, "Yeah, Edna, keep telling yourself that."

I pointed across the lounge at a man who'd lingered in the doorway, stepped in, backed out, then, in a rush, plopped his body into a chair, his eyes riveted on us. Startled, I whispered, "He looks out of place."

Clint followed my gaze. "Ty Gilley." Then, a piercing, sidelong glance back at me. "I don't trust him."

"For heaven's sake, why?"

"Look at him."

I did. A short, roly-poly man in a forest green summer suit, a matching necktie, a fluffy white handkerchief sticking out of a lapel pocket, he seemed a Leprechaun dropped down into stark territory. Slicked-back black hair, so inky black I assumed it was dyed, parted in the middle as if by honed knife blade. Like some silent movie gigolo, but his small, pudgy face held large, luminous eyes, so that he seemed perpetually surprised.

"And the problem is…?" I wondered out loud.

Clint's voice was clipped. "Too nosy. Asks too many questions and don't provide his own answers. In the wilderness you don't trust no man who asks too many questions."

I chuckled. "Wilderness?"

Clint pointed toward the street. "In Fairbanks you step out of town and you're in wilderness."

"What do you know about him?"

"In town since early last fall. Supposed to be an engineer over to the Ladd Air Force Base, but he got rooms upstairs here."

"Why nosy?" As I watched, Ty Gilley dropped his eyes down, but his hooded eyes watched us.

"He followed Sonia around for a while, peppered her with questions about the North. Her columns on 'White Silence' got to him, I guess."

"What's his story?"

"What we got—and he ain't talking much—is that he took the job because he's looking for his father. Ty fought in Japan, drifted, got a few bucks, headed up here. He claims his father left the family in South Dakota decades back, headed to the North, then disappeared. Fell off the map."

"People disappear in Alaska."

Clint nodded. "I guess he wondered all his life."

"And he thought Sonia had the answer?"

"Like—her columns got him going. The interviews with old-timers. So many lost souls up in the Arctic, Edna. You head for the bonanza and the sun swallows you up. Maybe someone knew his dad. Maybe somebody got a dirty little secret. He's…hoping."

I took a sip of tea and sat back. "He has a right to wonder, Clint."

Clint wasn't happy. "Sonia told him she ain't got news of the man who disappeared so many decades ago."

At one point Teddy walked by Ty, dropping evening newspapers on the tables, and Ty touched his sleeve. The clerk flinched, confused, and waited as Ty tugged. Suddenly Ty cleared his throat and spoke so loudly he could have been addressing the room. "You spent any time up north? The Klondike, maybe?"

Puzzled, Teddy stepped away, but turned back, a thin smile on his face. "Isn't Fairbanks cold enough for you, Mr. Gilley? The world up there got no appeal for me. God don't pay attention to folks up there." He shivered. "Don't make many stops in Fairbanks either." He laughed at his own joke, then walked away.

"Do you know any old-timers from up there?" Ty called after him.

Teddy shrugged him off. "This is as far north as I'm ever going, sir." He disappeared into the small room behind the desk.

To his back, Ty yelled, "I'll never understand the pull of the Yukon."

Teddy stepped back out and said, "You're not the only one."

Ty went on, "They say that up in the North you feel really alive." He waited a second. "Until you disappear."

Teddy drew in his breath, glanced around the room, rolled his eyes in my direction, and walked away.

Ty caught me staring at him, and for a moment his eyes got cloudy. Standing suddenly, he spun around like a dervish, held my eye again, and fled past the reception desk and up the stairwell.

Clint leaned into me. "Mysterious."

"It could be nothing."

"It ain't never nothing, Edna."

"You act like he's a criminal."

Clint grinned. "Hey, in Alaska everyone is."

Sipping the last of my tea, I changed the subject. "Clint, I didn't see Noah West at Hank's tonight. He begged off—tired."

He chuckled. "In and out of Fairbanks all the time, that busy boy. The Indians done drive him crazy. And Sonia, too. Him and Sonia been on and off lately. I seen them at the Pastime Cocktail Lounge last week. Moody as all get out. Sonia fussing, Noah glaring. Nobody happy."

"But they're in love," I protested, a foolish line.

"Don't mean they can't have the low moments." He closed his eyes a second. "When I was married, me and the missus liked to not talk for days on end. Silence is the glue that keeps folks married."

"I like them both. I was hoping to see him tonight."

Clint watched me, curious. "He lives in a small cabin a few streets over in what everybody but the Chamber of Commerce calls Indian Village." Clint smiled. "I'll walk you over to his office tomorrow, noontime."

• ● ● ● •

Late the next morning I met Clint in the lobby, and we walked the few blocks to Noah West's office on Fourth Avenue. It was a cold, brutal day, the air dense with ice fog. As we walked, Clint carefully cradled my elbow, though he shuffled along, a little wobbly. I gazed at the storefronts with sagging or peeling signs, hand-painted notices in grimy windows, here and there a flickering naked light. Battered cars parked diagonally, some with dented fenders and cobweb-shattered windshields, junkyard relics, many kept running against the withering cold. Worse, sloe-eyed young men huddled in rag-tag bunches, lost in caribou parkas, gazing out into nothing, loitering on the slick sidewalks. Only a passing girl, shuffling by with Woolworth earrings and Co-Op Drug Store lipstick, roused them.

Noah's office was in the middle of a row of one-storied, tin-roofed hovels, matchbox constructions, many with weath-ered log-cabin fronts. The sign in his window announced in jagged black letters, "Noah West, Attorney at Law. Native Alyeska Fellowship."

Inside was a small low-ceilinged anteroom, with a Mission-style green desk. A few chairs looked as if they'd been pilfered from the Odd Fellows Hall. A poster thumbtacked onto a wall: "Go Native." A scene of blue-white snow, a wilderness cabin, an unattended dogsled. No people. Underneath a motto: "You can only talk to spirits if you listen to the quiet inside you."

No one was in sight. Clint started to say something, but then I heard voices in a back room, Noah's pronounced bari-tone and a woman's trembling voice, pleading. Voices coming closer. Noah's voice was confident, laughing, and soon an old woman walked out, Noah's arm on her shoulder. Noah seemed surprised to see Clint and me standing there, but he smiled, nodded. Turning to the old woman, he said something in Qwich'in—or at least I assumed that's what it was. The woman looked up into his face and smiled. She hurried out.

"Miss Ferber." He grasped my hands. "Everyone is talking about your visit."

"That's the danger of visiting a town of five thousand. Visitors become the story."

"Only famous visitors." He nodded at Clint. "Lovers of Alaska."

"Are we intruding?" I asked.

"No, no. Of course not. Come. Let me buy you lunch." He was already reaching for his parka, which, I was delighted to see, was a brilliant red, fringed with beads, and covered with embroidered emblems. The hood was lined with a ruff of gray fur.

"Me, too?" Clint asked.

"Of course." Noah tapped him on the shoulder affectionately.

On the sidewalk Noah tucked his arm under my elbow.

"Miss Ferber," he began, but I held up my hand.

"Please call me Edna."

He nodded, smiling.

I smiled back. Leaning in, I looked up at him. What caught my eye was the profile: that angular high-cheeked face and the slightly crooked aquiline nose under darting black eyes, deep set and a little weary, as though he lacked sleep. In the cold air his ruddy complexion seemed curiously tropical: a beachcomber's coveted tan. A crooked smile that gave him a sardonic look, a hint of perpetual bemusement. That, and the shock of hair, long and straight and shiny black, bunched over his back collar. In the cold he didn't put up the hood of his red parka. A tall man, over six feet. Each time he glanced at me—huddled as I was in the thick parka and a swarm of scarves—he leaned down into my neck and smiled. I smelled woodfire, a hint of burnt spruce perhaps, wonderful.

Even though Noah held my elbow, he moved quickly—though finally he slowed down, as Clint and I moved at a snail's pace, a raspy sound coming from Clint's lungs—despite the fact that he walked with a limp, a rhythmic dragging of his right leg.

Last summer, arriving late for dinner at Hank's and being seated next to Noah, I was immediately captivated, but when he stood to leave, he reached for a cane and limped out the door. I'd been stunned. It was as though I'd failed to notice a crack in an exquisite Baccarat vase, but which, contemplating it, made the object possess more worth, fascination. The defect simply galvanized the work of art.

Noah opened the door of a small shack, pulling on the stuck, buckling door, and I looked for a sign. Nothing. An inn with no name. A small cardboard sign was taped to a window: "No Whores Allowed!" Clint nudged me to look, tickled. Inside, standing in the murky darkness, I spotted clusters of men sitting at oil-cloth covered tables, clouds of blue-gray smoke hovering near the ceiling from which naked light bulbs were suspended on frayed cords.

"White folks don't come here," Noah said.

"Probably the fault of the advertising."

Noah laughed out loud.

Seated by a front window cloudy with caked dust, Noah told a chubby young woman in braids—"Marla," he called her and she melted—what he wished. Nervous, I begged off lunch. Already my stomach turned. I smelled burnt oil, grill grease gone stale and unattended, and something sickly sweet, like spun sugar. But Noah seemed to know what he was doing. He slipped a cup of Labrador leaf tea across the table, and I sipped it. It had a calming effect—a subtle hint of some wild weed, musky, like dried flower seeds, marigolds, maybe. And then a simple lunch of dark flat frybread that, following his example, I dipped into a huge bowl of Bush rabbit stew.

"With a bit of ptarmigan game bird. To spice it up. And fried cranberries."

I sat back, watching Clint and Noah ravage the meal, their faces close to the deep bowls, spooning up the meat with torn pieces of dark bread. Then I discovered that my own bowl was empty, totally, a chunk of the nut-flavored bread wiping up the last of the stew.

"You're a woman who loves food," Noah said. "Usually I'm the first one finished."

"I questioned what I was eating."

"You gotta trust me."

"Obviously, I do. I usually peruse a menu closely, terrorize the waiter, exasperate my dinner companions, and then demand something not on the menu."

"I'm surprised no one's poisoned you," Noah said.

"They wouldn't dare." I lifted my chin. "I'll not allow it."

Sitting back, joyously sated, Noah lit a cigarette and Clint stuffed his pipe.

"Tell me about your Native Alyeska Fellowship, Noah," I began.

Noah exhaled smoke and snubbed out the cigarette. "You know, Alaska isn't like the Deep South these days, Edna. I mean, those civil rights battles. All that agitation in the streets and Negroes fighting to sit at lunch counters amazes us. The fire hoses. The vicious dogs. In Alaska we Natives were here first. There's lots of intermarriage, the old sourdoughs on the tundra needing women, falling in love with them, having children. But we're still second-class citizens. We lack education, medical care, legal rights. White civilization has done a number on us—TB, liquor, welfare, poverty, suicide. Growing up, we were told not to speak Qwich'in. The white teachers in the BIA schools would spank us if we did. I remember one sign in school: 'Speak English, Talk to the World.' Well, what about our world? So now I'm a voice for my Qwich'en

people, for others, a lawyer who can sometimes do wonders."
He smiled. "Sometimes, in court, Natives actually win."

I sipped my tea. "Last year you said statehood would ben-
efit Natives."

"I think it will. Statehood will settle land claims, get us
education. You know, we've been waiting to redress Native
claims since America bought Alaska from the Russians. We're
still waiting." He watched Marla clear the dishes, said something to her in Qwich'in, and she returned with generous
slices of huckleberry cake.

I bit into the cake, warm, buttery, speckled with crunchy
berries.

"Hank and *The Gold*—especially Sonia—are desperate for
statehood."

"Frankly, I am happy you and Sonia have each other," I said.

His eyes wide, he laughed a long time. "How you put
things, Edna. We're two independent forces—two planets
from different galaxies—who bounce off each other." He
hesitated. "I love you but stay away. Come back. Yeah, love,
but…"

"Hank and Irina are pushing the marriage," Clint said.

"That's not always a good thing," I said. "I imagine Sonia
doesn't take to suggestion."

"Especially from her parents," Clint added.

Noah was frowning. "I'm the bright little Athabascan boy
from Fort Yukon, sent to boarding schools for rich white boys,
to the University of Washington law school after the war,
returning dressed in sweaters and sharp-creased Eddie Bauer
khakis and penny loafers. Look what we did—we Arctic-rich
Pygmalions—with the little red boy. Part of the deal was
that I marry Sonia. Irina wants grandchildren. But I don't
know—this is also my world *here*." He pointed at the tables
with Indians. "But suddenly I'm in flannel and buckskin and
wolf fur and"—he waved his hair wildly—"my hair goes on
forever."

"The man in the flaming red parka," I commented. "Bull's-eye."

"Marry the girl," Clint said quickly, punching Noah in the shoulder.

Noah's eyes shined. "I keep proposing."

"Sooner or later," Clint stressed, "she's gonna say yes."

• • ● ● •

Outside the restaurant Clint and Noah each took one of my arms—I felt like a rag doll flopping on the icy sidewalk—and we walked toward the Nordale. Turning the corner, I sensed Noah's hold slacken, then tighten. He stopped walking, and Clint, off-kilter, jerked away, with me nearly toppling to the ground. The three of us shuffled, then stopped, a frozen tableau, as Noah acknowledged a young woman walking toward us. She'd spotted us first, and, striding forward, her face set in an impish grin, seemed ready to collide.

"Maria." Noah's voice was scratchy.

"Well, Noah." Her grin got wider.

Noah got flustered, something I didn't expect. He looked toward the street, gazed into the air, at the ground. He mumbled, "My sister Maria. Maria, Miss Edna Ferber." A thin smile. "Of course, you know Clint."

Clint half-bowed to her.

Close up, Maria was very much Noah's sister. Tall, willowy, she had the same ebony hair, long like her brother's, and that beautiful face, those deep-set black eyes and the pronounced cheekbones. But there was something shabby about her, a cloth coat with a shoulder seam unraveling, cloying drugstore perfume, blotchy rose-colored rouge dabbed generously on her cheeks. Noah was staring at Maria, and none too happily. She struck me as a bar girl, one of the pretty women I'd spotted last summer lingering in the red-light district, a notorious stretch of one-room shacks and endless neon-ugly bars on Fourth

Avenue. She stood before us, waiting, tapping a high-heeled shoe, baiting him. Her brother didn't say anything.

"Noah, you don't call."

"I've been busy, Maria."

She raised her voice. "Sam Pilot is in town. A month now."

"Where's he staying?"

A harsh laugh. "My couch."

Noah turned to me. "Sam is from Fort Yukon, too. A distant relative, but then we all seem to be related." To Maria he said, "What's he doing in town?"

"Getting ready to die—from the sound of his midnight hacking." A pause. "He's a tired old man."

Noah leaned into me. "A trapper from Fort Yukon. Tough as nails. A grandson of a famous shaman." He lowered his voice. "A common thief, if not worse."

Maria watched him closely. "He read about Jack Mabie in *The Gold*."

Clint was itching to say something. "Edna, Sam Pilot was the only friend Jack Mabie had from the old days. Partner in crime, they say. Shared a frontier cabin over a winter or two. Fistfights, black eyes, marshals running them out of the villages, shared cans of beans and sourdough bread and cheap wine from dandelion greens."

Maria went on. "He hasn't seen Jack in years—was surprised the old coot is still alive."

I said to no one in particular, liking the sound of the words, "The meanest man in Alaska."

"I never met him." Maria said. "Sam got a lot to say about him. He says Jack tried to kill him once. He plans to visit him at the Frontier Home—surprise him." A light laugh. "He says Jack owes him twenty bucks."

Noah wasn't happy. "Sam Pilot used to be a dangerous man, Edna. A killer."

"Now he's just—feeble." From Maria.

"I'd like to meet this Sam Pilot," I said.

Noah's glare was not kind. "An old Athabascan man who once told me only sissies go to school."

"But you didn't listen to him," Maria said quietly.

"I haven't seen him in years."

Maria clicked her tongue. "I have, unfortunately. He's old and cranky and smelly and…and now and then he shows up at my apartment."

"You could turn him away."

Maria scoffed. "I don't treat family the way you do, Noah."

With that, her head thrown back, she walked away.

"Your sister is beautiful," I told him.

A gritty tone. "She's forgotten that she was born in Fort Yukon. She's an Indian like me."

My eyes trailed after his sister. "It's her life, Noah."

He pulled away but turned to face me, his eyes fiery. "I love my sister, Edna. There's only the two of us here, brother and sister…" A helpless shrug.

I didn't know what to say. Again I turned to look at the departing Maria and noticed she had stopped at the end of the sidewalk, facing us, staring, arms folded over her chest.

Noah groped for words. "We don't understand each other."

I blurted out, "Perhaps you should work on that, Noah." My words stung him, his face closing up. "It might be your failing."

Startled, Noah started to say something, but paused. Then, his eyes dancing, he laughed, "Edna, you're the only person I know who can slice bread with her tongue."

Chuckling, Clint rocked on his heels.

I bowed to both men.

Chapter Four

The jukebox at Cleary Creek Roadhouse was playing a staticky version of Hank Williams' "Cold, Cold Heart" when Sonia, Noah, and I walked in. A honky-tonk girl in a flared square-dance dress leaned over the jukebox, her body swaying. As we passed, she looked up. She was mouthing the words of the mournful song, tears streaming down her cheeks. She offered us a feeble smile and pointed to a table, and I realized she was the barmaid.

"This is not a good beginning," I whispered into Noah's shoulder.

Competing with the jukebox was an old man, perched on a stool, blowing into his harmonica. A plaintive "Home Sweet Home."

"Jack's already here." Sonia pointed to a table near the long pinewood bar. He was slumped down in his seat, legs stretched out, eyes closed, a tinny wheeze escaping his throat. As we approached him, the harmonica player stopped, to a smattering of applause, and someone nearby whooped it up. Jack, startled, sat up, letting out a ferocious belch that caused the weeping waitress to titter.

Not a good beginning.

Sonia had insisted on another meeting with Jack—"There're one or two more stories I can get out of him"—and Noah, who'd not met the old-timer, was all for it.

"The history of Alaska," he'd told me. "A dying breed."

"Yes," I'd replied, staring into his eager face, "all contained in a bottle."

"Stories to tell you, Edna," Sonia had emphasized.

"Yes," I'd said, "hyperbolic tales of craven murder and, I suppose, simple meanness."

"The meanest man in…"

Groaning, I'd held up my hand. "Noah, please. If I hear that phrase one more time you'll encounter the meanest woman in the world."

Which was why, the next night, around eight, we sat with a sloppy-tongued Jack Mabie at the roughhewn pine table covered with beer rings and jackknife inscriptions scratched in. Kilroy, I noted, hadn't been there—or at least at my stained and wobbly table.

"You've been drinking," I told Jack, which surprised him, causing him to blink wildly. It was as though I'd insulted him by observing the color of his eyes.

Noah stuck out his hand. "Jack, we haven't met."

"You sure about that?"

Noah nodded.

"I know a lot of Indians." He growled. "Most losers, fools, and downright thieves."

Noah bowed. "I answer to all three conditions."

Jack called the barmaid. "You know, I'm sitting here and I ain't got another bottle in front of me." He waved his empty bottle.

The roadhouse was on a dirt road leading out of Fairbanks, a mile or so from Jack's Frontier Home cot, a desolate stretch of the Richardson Highway, and I wondered how he'd found his way there. He'd suggested the place, peculiarly, because it was a touristy place with sawdust on the floor, spanking new glossy prints of the frontier days on the walls. A table of Outsiders nearby, a family that looked fresh off a Pan Am flight. But the tables were mostly locals, backslapping folks who yelled across to one another, raised bottles of beer in salute. Jack already knew a few of them by name.

"You like this place?" I asked him.

"I like any place that gives me free liquor."

"I like any place that doesn't give me the willies."

Jack eyed me closely. "Lady, you talk mumble jumble."

Sonia grinned as she reached over and squeezed my hand affectionately. Then, still laughing, she leaned into Noah's shoulder, and he whispered something in her ear. Shaking her head and widening her eyes, she smiled back at him. For a moment the two stared at each other, companionable, private, the secret communication of lovers in a public place. A lovely tableau, I thought, perfect and rare, though it excluded me and the irascible Jack.

Watching them, Jack narrowed his eyes. "You two a couple, right?"

Noah nodded, his hand grazing Sonia's cheek.

Jack's penetrating look suddenly morphed into hardness. He hissed at them, "You know, pretty people always end up real unhappy."

"Why would you say that?" I asked him, piqued.

Dramatically, he pointed at Sonia and Noah, his baleful stare moving slowly—the word *menacing* came to mind—from one to the other. "She's like this beautiful blond girl out of a damn storybook. Once upon a time..." He glowered. "He's like...like a John Wayne Indian. Apache warrior. Marauder—war paint and poisoned arrows. No good can come of this."

Noah bristled and looked ready to say something, but Sonia, smiling, tapped the back of his wrist as she flicked her head back, a look in her eyes that said—*leave it alone. He's baiting you.*

Noah caught his breath. In a thick, unfriendly voice he said, "Sam Pilot is in town, Jack."

Jack waited a moment, scrunching up his face as if trying to recollect a face. "That old bastard?" Then he laughed. "I thought the ass was long dead."

Jack fiddled with the empty beer bottle. He upended it, his lips sucking on the glass. A hint of white foam speckled his upper lip. His tongue rolled out, made it disappear. The barmaid placed a bottle of beer in front of him, but he didn't look at it. He chuckled. "The only buddy I ever had. But a real bastard."

Noah was staring at him closely. "You know, Jack, Sam's a distant relative of mine."

Jack pressed a finger into Noah's chest. "All Indians say they're related. Ain't never met one who said he didn't share blood with everyone. Athabascans, well, you know, rabbits." He made a scary face. "Hocus pocus voodoo man. Christ, that man's eyes could set paper on fire."

Noah watched him, unhappy. "He's staying with my sister, Maria."

"Ain't seen that fool in a dog's age." Jack tilted his head, lost in thought. "Winter back twenty maybe more years. Shared a cabin outside of Old Crow. One more day and I'd killed the bastard."

"Ah, good friends?" I asked, smiling.

His brow furled. "Yeah, only friend I ever had. Truth to tell, always had my back, as they say. He saved me from a hangman's noose. More'n once." He deliberated slowly. "In fact, I saved his sorry ass from a gang of miners set on stringing *him* up." A feckless grin. "Tit for tat, the law of the jungle."

"Do want to see him?" Noah asked.

"Yeah, for old time's sake, maybe."

"I'd like to meet this Sam Pilot," I repeated, though no one was listening to me. "He strikes me as…"

Jack interrupted. "The ass owes me twenty bucks, you know."

Noah offered a thin smile. "Funny thing—he says you owe him twenty bucks."

"Nobody'll believe that crap. Everybody knows Indians is cheap."

Noah squirmed in his seat, and Sonia, leaning in, tapped his forearm with her finger. Again the quiet suggestion—*calm, calm, he's an old man. Crazy.*

"You promised me stories," I said loudly, grabbing Jack's eye. He'd been glowering at Noah, irritated, and I feared a spitfire exchange between the two men.

Noah sat back, amused now. He whispered to Sonia, "You see how the man you love goes off the rails? I'm ready to go to battle for a distant relative who sneers at me the few times we've met."

"Blood lines," she whispered back. "They make a man do foolish things."

Waving a dismissive hand at the couple, Jack cleared his throat. "Yes, ma'am." He swiveled his body away from Noah's, facing me. Then, to make a point, he shuffled his chair, dragging it at angles to me. "You're a woman what likes murder and mayhem."

"Tell me."

Jack took a long swig of beer, rolled his head to the side, and grinned mischievously. "Well," he began, lazily drawing out the word, "I come close to hanging off a cottonwood tree so many times. What you gotta understand is that murder ain't like you know it, ma'am. I mean, some bat-shit crazy mugger loose with a gun in a city street—or a husband thinking he can be free of the missus."

"You're saying…"

"I'm saying life on the frontier is different. Like the Old West."

I thought of my novel *Cimarron*, the Oklahoma land rush. The shifting code of law and justice. "A different set of rules," I agreed.

"Rules, hell," he stormed. "Ain't no rules. Only rule, if there is one, is survival. Christ, lady, you got your grizzly moms coming at you in the Bush and you chatter at them and hope to God they're listening. You lose your way and you kill a caribou, empty out his guts, and sleep in his carcass while the snow piles up around you." He paused, out of breath. "You get the picture, lady?"

Another swig of beer, a satisfied belch. "You get so lonely you tell yourself that if there is a hell after you die—you sit in a room and hear people talking and laughing somewhere outside. But you can't get at them. For eternity. Bone-marrow deep loneliness. A hunger…" His voice trailed off. "Okay, murder. You trap all winter, stow your pelts, wait for the first thaw, and you find a sucker done stole your cache. You track him down and—confront him. Red-handed, he is, standing there with your damn pelts. He lunges at you, you lunge at him. I win. Is that murder? In '98 you stake a claim north of the Bonanza claim, upstream, and you return to find this cheekacho sitting pretty there. He points a gun but got the aim of a dizzy girl. A knife to his heart. Bingo."

I said nothing.

Noah's words were laced with anger. "But you robbed… killed…"

Jack sucked in his breath. "Sometimes folks had stuff I wanted." A deep rumble. "I took it."

"And they died?"

"What can I say? This fool mocks me in a saloon. You lay in wait and ambush the guy."

Sonia rustled in her purse and pulled out a crumpled sheet of paper, yellowed pulp, flaky. "I found this in our files. Some village printing press back in 1911. *Yukon Call.*" She pointed. "One paragraph here." She read: "'Horace Rowers, deputy marshal out of Circle City, shot to death by Jack May. May, a scoundrel on the run. Powers attempted to arrest May for thievery.'" She stopped. "Jack May? Is it you?"

Jack was grinning widely. "Couldn't never get my name right. Yeah, the buffoon run up against the wrong man."

"But were you ever arrested for murder?" I asked.

"Yeah. More'n once. Skin of my teeth. The law was afraid of me."

Awkwardly he pulled an old leather pouch from a pocket, fingered it, and grinned. "Souvenirs." Stained, a flap half gone, the pouch looked ready to disintegrate. He grappled with it, and a few silver dollars clanged onto the table. His hand grabbed them. But he took a folded piece of birch bark, opened it, and smoothed out an old yellowed piece of paper.

"Back in the winter of '29—maybe '30—Sam and me locked up in Nome for robbery. Dumb-ass sheriff took our pictures"—a wide grin, posing—"'cause I'm good-looking. Next spring they wanna hang me for murder." He tapped the crumbling poster. "There I am, plastered all over Kingdom Come."

"They caught you?"

"Yeah."

"But you didn't hang."

Again the sickly smile. "The one witness somehow disappeared."

A cheap poster, now faded, creased:

WANTED FOR MURDER

JACK MAYBE

REWARD

TO BE HANGED

What little could still be made out showed a grainy picture of Jack, mostly gone but, oddly, the coal-black eyes and the jutting chin.

We watched him carefully fold the sheet and shove it into the pouch.

Silence.

"So you…" My words stuck in my throat. I thought of Clint's remarks. "You even murdered a missionary?"

"Says he was. Who knows?"

"Why?"

"Says I flirted with his wife."

"Did you?"

An impish grin. "Yeah."

"So you killed him?"

"He came at me."

Jack's eyes closed, and then popped open, his look particularly lascivious. A sickly smile. "Yeah, she was one pretty girl. Maybe she flirts with me. I'm a good-looking guy, you know, flirting like right in front of her husband, she twirls, smiles, he gets hot under the collar, threatens, she gets scared, accuses me of nonsense, and right in front of her boy and girl, and…and…"

"You kill a good man," I concluded, my teeth on edge.

Noah was steamed. "You enjoyed being one of the bad guys."

"What can I say? Soapy Smith over to Skagway. His gang robbed caches of supplies—died in a shootout with some fellow. They wrote a song about him. Others—O'Brien's gang, him hanged in Dawson. Took all the gold dust and nuggets on the Chilkoot Trail. Bodies floating down the Yukon." He offered an exaggerated grin. "The Blueberry Kid up to Cleary Creek, he killed him three men. The miserable son of a bitch never burned daylight, I tell you that. But"—a dramatic pause—"I was the meanest man in Alaska. The one Judge Lynch's Court never got to hang. Me and my Winchester .30.30." He breathed in. "End of story."

"Where did you meet Sam Pilot?" Sonia asked.

"Up around Fort Yukon."

"Nathan West is my grandfather," Noah added.

Jack looked surprised. "Hey, I knew him. Trapper. Some high-muck-a-muck in Fort Yukon. Like he's king of nothing."

"My grandfather," Noah said softly.

"You can't help that." Jack's eyes got a faraway look. "I remember his own folks don't care for Sam Pilot. Athabascan Sam, they called him then. Drifted in and out of the village, and this Nathan tells him to get lost. Sam drunk mighty hard back then. Ain't nothing worse than a drunk Indian who's dumb as a river stone."

"Your buddy," Noah noted wryly.

Jack chuckled. "They say you can't choose your family, but, Christ Almighty man, sometimes you can't choose your friends. They're just there like a rash on your neck."

Jack downed the rest of his beer, loudly bellowed to the barmaid who was back hanging over the jukebox—Patsy Cline was walkin' after midnight and the barmaid seemed to think that was a good idea—and demanded another beer. The harmonica player was struggling through "She May Have Seen Better Days." Slurring his words, drifting into silence, sighing heavily, hiccoughing, Jack slipped down in his seat. I nodded at Noah—time to leave.

But Jack dreamily began a curious ramble now, some of his words lost or unintelligible, others choked with sloppy emotion, still others infused with a venom. A curious monologue: "Yukon, the fellow turns an ace and you know he's cheating... Come outside and I'll...you come up against Klu-tok, the crazy Indian on the Mulchatana River, he killed him a score of men...his body in the winter cabin thanks to me...you know the guy...flashy dressed, a gun to your back...Klondike Sally...you say that to me and...a pocket of gold nuggets, jangling...he says...a damned fool he is...Sam says..."

On and on, disjointed, intoxicated, a Homeric sweep of scattered memory that finally dissolved into silence as Jack slumped in his seat.

I gathered my gloves and hat, nudged Noah and Sonia, and waited, tapping my foot on the floor.

Sonia, glancing around the room, suddenly froze. "There," she pointed.

In a dark corner, back by the kitchen door, stood Ty Gilley, nearly hidden in shadows, his back against the wall, his body facing us. Leaning forward, he had a palm against his chin. A light from a hallway silhouetted his head. Watching, watching.

I started. "Good Lord. What?"

"The man who came to Alaska looking for a lost father."

Once he realized we were watching him, he hunched his shoulders and turned his face away. But then, boldly, he leaned forward, staring into our faces. No—at Jack's face.

Sonia wasn't happy. "He's hounded me about my interviews." She never took her eyes off the dark shadow. "He hoped I'd have information that could lead to his father."

"And do you?" I asked.

She shook her head vigorously. "Of course not. He told me he took a job over to the Air Force base because he spent a lifetime wondering about his father, a man named Clay Fowler, a restless man, shiftless, so said his mother. Around 1917 he headed off to fight in France, but they got a letter from Anvil Creek, Nome. Then no more letters."

"He wants answers," I said.

Noah said into the silence, "But the world of the Yukon, the Klondike, Circle City, the gold rush, the frozen land… ice and snow…everything is a secret. Dark stories. Lost lives. Violence. White silence. Your articles told him…maybe."

Jack had been staring at Ty. He turned in his seat, and made a clicking sound. "Christ Almighty, man."

Noah went on. "Alaska is a place where people disappear. Plane crashes, sudden falls into the ice crevasses, landslides, blinding sunlight, starvation. Never heard of again. Every family got someone who never came home. It's like—like a haunted land."

Jack snapped at Noah. "Christ, man, sometimes men just walked away. They start walking and never look back. The *nothing* they're walking to is worth more'n that *something* they left behind." He took a large grimy white handkerchief from his pocket and blew his nose noisily. "Maybe his father just wanted to get away from his ma and *him*. Some men don't wanna look back." He shivered.

He was looking into the shadows.

When I followed his gaze, Ty Gilley was gone.

Chapter Five

Sam Pilot sat stiffly in the Nordale lounge.

When I walked downstairs, headed into the lounge to meet Clint, Teddy leaned over the reception desk and grumbled, "When I come on duty an hour ago, he's sitting there like a cigar store Indian, arms folded over his chest, staring straight ahead, silent, eyes like glass marbles. Like the dead, Miss Ferber. Somebody told me his name is Sam Pilot." He *tsk*ed. "Another drunken Indian somebody gotta boot out of here."

Clint motioned me over to where he was sitting, across the room from the imperious Indian.

"That's Sam Pilot."

"I know." I glanced at the unmoving figure, rigid as a statue, barely a flicker of his eyelids. "You ever meet him before?"

Clint lowered his voice. "Many years back. Seen him with Jack Mabie. One time at a gambling joint in Valdez. The two shot up the place. A pretty gal shot in the hip."

I peered at the unmoving man, though I noticed a quick move as he scratched his chin. "What did you do?"

Clint chuckled. "Skedaddled out of town. Gunfire ain't hold no attraction for me."

"A sensible man."

There were a few stragglers in the lounge, mostly clustered on sofas near the reception area. No one was talking, and, indeed, no one was purposely looking at Sam Pilot—though everyone was conscious of his presence—and the dark sense of menace. I caught one Outsider, baffled and tittering, throwing a sidelong glance at the Indian.

A tall, willowy man, rail thin, perhaps over six feet tall, with bronzed, leathery skin, without wrinkles despite his being probably in his seventies, he had a prominent hawk nose, high chiseled cheekbones under large, luminous black eyes. A lightning scar under his left eye, pale pinkish white against the dark skin. A jutting chin under a thick mouth. His most dramatic feature, though, was his hair—brilliant white, almost platinum, parted in the middle and cascading down his shoulders, ending just above his waist. The ghost of your nightmares. A little frightening, I thought, that regal look—a shaman's ethereal look, awe-inspiring, distancing. That, coupled with his stillness—each time I sneaked a glance I detected no blinking or slight shift in his body—made him appear unreal, a phantom.

No one sat near him.

I had trouble imagining him with Jack Mabie, that small wiry man, all angle and bone, tiny. Irrationally, I imagined the two as the dark, failed negative of that noisome popular image—the Lone Ranger and servile Tonto. White hero and darker sidekick. Natty Bumppo and Chingachook. The dark night in the wilderness. But that unwanted imagery slid into something more bizarre. Mutt and Jeff from the comic strips. Crafty Mutt, a schemer, and bumbling Jeff. A devil's dream, though: the tall bumpkin with his stumbling short friend. No—Sam Pilot and Jack Mabie occupied their own universe, sinister, dark, threatening.

"What's he doing here?" I whispered to Clint.

"Dunno."

But Pilot suddenly raised an arm in the air as Noah rushed into the lounge.

"I'm late," Noah said to no one in particular.

Noah approached Sam, extended his hand, but Sam did not shake it. Rather, the old man stood up, his bones cracking, eyes narrowed, face to face with Noah, the two men the same height, but Sam looked past Noah, pointing around the lounge. "I ain't never been in a fancy place. Why you make me come here?"

Noah acted flummoxed. "Maria said she'd drop you off and…" He stopped.

"Jack ain't here?"

"No, we got to meet him at Mimi's. But I wanted to *talk* to you first."

"Maria ain't told me that."

Noah pointed to a chair. "Sit back down. Please." He waved me over. "A few minutes. Sam, I also wanted you to meet Edna Ferber, a writer. She's in Alaska doing research for…"

Sam locked eyes with mine. Not friendly. A thick grunt, garbled. He dismissed me.

Still flustered, Noah seemed at a loss. Finally, looking into Sam's face—putting his face close to Sam's—he said, "Sam, Edna is my friend."

"Mr. Pilot, your friend Jack is a local celebrity."

He grunted but for a second I detected the hint of a smile, though he sat back down. Clint, muttering something behind me, stood and left the room. When I called to him, he waved his hand at me. With a ripple of laughter he said, "Life is safer in the wild."

I sat down in a chair facing Sam, though he turned away from me. Finally he stared at me. My chair was close to his, but I felt dwarfed by Sam and Noah.

I waited.

Sam spoke through clenched teeth, a rusty voice. "Celebrity, my ass. Jack—he always saw hisself as a hero. Bullshit artist, that man. Ask him how Jack London stole his life and put it into a book."

"So Jack tells stories, exaggerated?"

He counted a second. "Three-fifths fudge and a lot of nonsense."

"He said you saved his life many times."

He sucked in his cheeks. "That's true."

Noah added, "And he saved yours?"

"That's true."

"What isn't true?" I asked.

He didn't answer.

"Murder?" I held his eye.

Sam spoke through clenched teeth. "Everybody is a murderer."

I looked at Noah, then back at Sam. "I'm trying to understand the real Alaska. The raw underbelly." I stopped. Sam was whistling softly.

"You talk too much, lady."

Noah sighed. I waited, my eyes demanding that Jack look at me. His head rocked up and down, his eyes were cold, unblinking, but as I watched him his lips curled up slightly, giving a hint of stained yellow teeth, and then a rheumy cough from deep in his throat. "Christ, Jack's been talking a blue streak."

I returned his steely gaze. "The meanest man in Alaska."

"Bullshit." He scoffed. He pointed at Noah's breast pocket— "Yeah, now, hurry up"—and Noah handed him a cigarette. Shoulders hunched, he waited as Noah struck a match and lit it. Slowly, coolly, he inhaled the smoke, his eyes suddenly dark as he sent out a cloud of gray smoke into the air, followed it as it drifted up to the ceiling. For a second his eyes shut dreamily, and then he contemplated the cigarette in his fingertips. "Man." He put the cigarette between his lips, sucked in the smoke. "Heaven." He held my eye. "Killing a man ain't necessarily murder."

"What?"

He scratched his chin. The overhead light caught a purplish scab, a trace of blood. The cigarette bobbed between his lips. His eyes focused on the red-hot end, the burning ash, waiting until the last moment to flick the ashes into an ashtray.

"Ancient history. We're old men now." He held the burning cigarette toward my face. "You ain't never killed a man, have you?"

I started. "No." I smiled at him. "The temptation..." Laughing, I looked at Noah.

Seething, his voice clipped, Sam broke in, "You play games with words, lady."

"That I do."

"Stop talking, lady."

Silence, the old man wheezing. I waited.

Noah's voice was hesitant. "You looking forward to seeing Jack again? It's been what—many decades?"

"He owes me twenty dollars."

Noah burst out laughing. "He says the same thing about you."

He spoke over Noah's words. "He's a goddamn liar." A lazy drawl, menacing. "We'll hash that out, the two of us. A goddamn crook."

"But you two were wilderness buddies—winters in snow-bound cabins," I protested.

He stared into my face but didn't answer at first. "Brings out the worst in people, those winters."

"But you claim he's your friend," I went on.

A half-hearted shrug. "You ain't never been north, ma'am. Jack—he's a darn fool most of the day, a lunatic most of the night, but when the law got a gun to your head, when some bad-ass cowboy or Yupik fool thinks he can cheat you out of a silver dollar, Jack—he got my back."

"Frontier justice." I sat back, watched him.

He rustled in his seat and pointed at Noah. "We leaving

or what? This lady talks too much." He pointed at Noah. "I remember him as a sniveling little brat, sassy mouth. Smarty ass boy, big britches. Old Nathan hovering over him like he's the last Indian in a parade."

Noah snapped, "My grandfather protected me and Maria after our parents died. So young."

"Yeah, old Nathan, holier than thou, he done a great job."

Noah bristled. "Now…"

Leaning forward, Sam snapped a gnarled finger at Noah's chest, so quick a gesture that I jumped. "Yeah, that was before you turned into a white man."

"Christ," Noah began. He half-rose from his chair, but I touched his elbow.

Sam counted a beat. "And Maria sold her body to bums in the Row."

Noah tensed up, unsure of himself, but finally sat back, shaking his head and bunching his lips.

"But you're sleeping on Maria's couch," I noted.

He watched me a long time. "You gotta sleep somewhere. Maria is…lovely, kind. She remembers that she's an Indian from Fort Yukon."

"And I don't?"

"You wear that red parka with the Qwich'in symbols… phony. Strutting around like a cock in a henhouse. You're playing cowboys and Indians but you wanna be a cowboy."

Without asking, he reached forward, pulled a cigarette from the pack in Noah's pocket, and nodded toward the matches.

"Are we bothering you, Mr. Pilot?" I asked.

"No more'n than nobody else I bump into."

Noah was itching to leave, signaling to me, but I ignored him—Sam Pilot intrigued me.

"Miss Ferber."

I looked up as Teddy leaned in, a cup of tea in his hand. "Thank you, Teddy."

He beamed. "It's that hour of the night." He placed the cup of tea on a side table, though his sidelong glance at Sam Pilot suggested he wasn't happy with the strange man inhabiting the lounge. Sam hissed at him, which made him back up. He half-bowed, whispered a curt "You're welcome" to my thanks, and disappeared into the small room behind the reception desk.

"None for me?" Noah laughed.

I took a sip of the hot brew. "The privilege of fame."

"I've been coming here nights for years, me and Clint and dozens of others. Loitering on these old chairs. No one has ever offered us a cup of tea."

"What can I say?" I shrugged, delighted.

"I can't even get a shot of booze."

"The tea is lovely. A mossy taste…"

Sam Pilot had ignored the frivolous banter. Stony faced, eyes riveted to the doorway, he rustled in his seat, twisting his body left and right. A foot drummed the floorboards. Old leather boots, the laces frayed. A drumbeat, like hail on a roof.

"Sam," Noah began, "we were saying…"

A rush of loud noise as a man and a woman, laughing nonsensically, swept into the room and then back out, disappearing up the staircase, their laughter drifting down. I stared after them but was surprised to see Preston Strange and Jeremy Nunne pause in the entrance. I caught Preston's eye, and he glared, but immediately a man in shirtsleeves stepped up to them, shook their hands, and the trio disappeared into a small meeting room behind the stairwell. The outside door slammed, someone arriving. Ty Gilley stood in the doorway, dressed like a polar bear in an oversized white parka, hood down, a massive white scarf circling his neck. Mukluks on his feet. Sealskin gloves. Shivering from the cold, he looked into the lounge and realized Noah and I were staring back at him. Eyes hooded, he offered a tentative wave, then seemed to regret it, backing up and fleeing up the stairs to his room, the white scarf unraveling and floating after him.

"Ty has rooms here," I told Noah.

"I know."

Sam Pilot let out a low moan, a plaintive keening so raw that Teddy peered over the reception desk, question in his eyes.

Startled, I faced Sam. "What in the world?"

Like a mechanical toy, he moved his limbs stiffly, robotic. He sat straight up, threw back his head, and he placed an old arthritic hand on his heart. He held it there, his fingers trembling. He said a word, unintelligible to me, even to Noah whose eyes flickered.

"What?" asked Noah.

Sam said nothing, but stood slowly like a rusty automaton, his right hand still gripping his chest. The moaning stopped. He repeated the word, louder now.

"We have to go," Noah was saying, flustered.

Sam ignored us, moving slowly between the chairs, almost baby steps, headed toward the doorway. Noah called after him, and Sam paused a second, deliberated, turned to face us. His hand still on his heart, his face frozen, he raised his left hand. A statue, a little frightening. That long white hair caught the overhead light and gleamed. The smooth glow of that old face. In the shrill light his face looked—skeletal.

He disappeared from sight.

"What in the world, Noah?" I asked.

Noah's face was pale. Not looking at me, his lips trembling, he whispered. "He spoke Gwich'in." His eyes drifted to the empty doorway. "*Gwinah'in.*" Then, "*Niindhat.*"

"Meaning?"

"He saw it." He swallowed. "Dead."

Chapter Six

On a lazy Sunday afternoon, wisps of ice fog settled on Fairbanks, Sonia picked me up at the Nordale. "I was afraid you'd back out," she said as I slid onto the passenger seat. "Not your cup of tea, I imagine."

"You read my mind well," I answered. "A dreary afternoon to lie in bed with a good book."

On Sunday afternoons, once a month during the long winters, Hank Petrievich hosted an open house. Conceived as a pro-statehood gathering of kindred spirits, it had evolved over the years into a popular social event, an afternoon salon of sorts—and much talked about. No invitations were proffered, but woe to the disfavored soul or idle tourist or territorial government factotum who wandered in. Fairbanks society tacitly understood the boundaries, curiously as rigid as a private men's club. This month the open house, according to Irina, was preamble to the annual Fairbanks Winter Carnival, with the North American Sled Dog Championships ushering in four days of parades, floats, and ice sculpture. Schools were closed, routine meetings canceled.

Irina had informed me that some celebrated champion dog-sledders from Anchorage were Hank's special guests, but she'd confided, "You are the real guest this Sunday." I'd already spotted the quartet in the lobby of my hotel, blustery, backslapping dog-sledders, men too loud and too furry for my taste. Hardly celestial charioteers of the gods, these were hard-drinking men, all four of them in identical red wool shirts with white suspenders. An itinerant barbershop quartet with sled dogs. Sweet Adeline, my foot.

Of course, Irene had hummed, folks insisted on meeting Edna Ferber herself, the best-selling novelist who was a fierce advocate for statehood.

"You'll survive," Sonia told me now.

She reached for a clipping from a pile of papers beside her on the seat. From a rival newspaper, *The News-Miner*.

"In their gossip column," she pointed.

I read: "Edna Ferber, currently visiting Fairbanks, is finishing her novel on Alaska. Supposedly it takes place in Fairbanks, and local citizens will recognize themselves in her robust pages."

"Hmm," I mused out loud. "So this explains some of the looks I've been getting."

"Noah bet me that you'd skip the open house." She laughed. "We had a lovely lunch at the Model Café today. All he did was talk about you…"

I interrupted. "You two. My Lord. A breezy, modern couple, easy with each other. I come from a Victorian age, a different world. The world wars have redefined the word young."

"Those horrid wars gave us a reason to drastically invent our own futures." A gentle tap on my sleeve, affectionate. "When I got my pilot's license, I announced, 'Now no one can catch me in the heavens.' I felt free flying above the rest of Alaska." She was grinning. "Only Noah thought it was a good idea."

"I love it. I grew up marveling at a passing automobile."

Sonia got serious. "But Noah told me about Jack's reunion with Sam Pilot." She glanced out the window. "How did he put it? 'Curses, grinning over some inside joke, anger, shoving, happy, mad, bitter, silence.'" She shook her head back and forth. "A drunken ballet and a yelling match over that twenty dollars borrowed decades back, resolved when Noah gave each five silver dollars apiece. A brief meeting, maybe a half-hour. Sam hobbled off to Maria's. Jack stumbled back into the bar."

"A love story."

"Of the worst kind. Noah said Jack kept saying, 'Nobody writes the story of *your* life in the goddamn paper.'"

"See what you started, Sonia?"

"That reminds me. Here." Again from the pile of papers on the seat she slid a handwritten note over to me. "The pitfalls of journalism," she said, smiling. "The voice of the public, maybe the great unwashed."

I had trouble reading in the dim afternoon light, so Sonia switched on the car's overhead light.

It was scribbled script on wide-lined school tablet paper, the left edge jagged. Folded excessively—maybe an eight-by-ten sheet folded perhaps ten times—it was addressed to Sonia at *The Gold*.

Editor Petrievich—

> *I got something to say. Your articles in White Silence on the old men from the North are all offensive. I'll tell you why. You glorify evil. You celebrate murder. Your shameful words tell us our lives here in Fairbanks are crap because we go to church, follow the laws, go to The Lacey Movies to see a movie. No, no, no—you take a man like Jack Mabie and make him, I don't know, Paul Bunyan or Mike Fink. You like your wild stories. What about all of the folks he murdered—MURDERED—confessed years later, a smile on his face? Murder!*

> *And let me tell you, lady, anyone who celebrates the murder of God's innocents they are murderers too—on the road to hell.*

Like you, lady.
Maybe someone should murder you. Then they can make a story about you.
Dangerous territory, lady. God is watching you.
His words—Sodom and Gomorrah.
Lot's wife looking back.
Look over your shoulder.

An angry citizen.

The letter trembled in my hand.

"Good God, Sonia, how horrible."

Sonia dismissed it. "Comes with the territory—journalism."

"But never to be taken lightly. A nut, surely, and a scattered, confused man, though he does make a point—you romanticize Jack and the others, and naturally that bothers some. But what you're not paying attention to are the threats—'Maybe someone should murder you.' 'Look over your shoulder.' Threats, Sonia, maybe maddened, maybe empty threats, but death threats nonetheless."

Sonia rolled her eyes. "Really, Edna, I didn't think you'd take it so seriously."

Indignant, I faced her. "I'm not amused. I'm scared. Have you shown this to your father?"

"No, of course not."

"Or to the police chief?"

"It's not signed."

My voice rose. "I don't care." I counted a beat. "What about Noah?"

Her face closed in. "Oh no, Lord no. Noah's a lawyer and he'd feel a need to protect me, demand I hand it over to the cops. He'd bang on doors across town."

I sat back. "I'm not happy."

She looked perplexed. "I didn't mean to worry you, Edna. Not my intent."

I got silent, stared out the window at the bleak, shadowy buildings.

Suddenly her car jolted to a dizzying stop, slid on some slick ice, and edged toward a curb. In front of us an old Army Jeep had slammed on its brakes, and the driver was leaning on his horn. Behind us another car careened to the left.

"What in the world?" I peered out.

Through the ice fog, I saw a battered trash barrel roll across the street, rest against a lightpost, but then my eyes shot to a man flailing his arms, taking a step but faltering. The horn wailed again, and the man banged on the hood, let out a volley of *damns* and *shits*, and the driver leaned on the horn again.

Sonia pointed. "Omar's, the pit of hell."

As we watched, the door of the bar swung open, a naked light bulb hanging over the entrance, and suddenly, arms folded over his chest, Sam Pilot stood, imperious, though I noticed he wobbled, one hand bracing himself against the doorjamb.

"Jack," Sonia said softly.

Because at that moment we both realized that the drunken man causing the street to be blocked was Jack, who now staggered onto the sidewalk, swayed and bobbed, as he approached a watching Sam Pilot.

The street clear now, the Jeep sailed past, though the driver, cranking down the passenger side window, leaned over and gave an oblivious Jack the finger.

Sam Pilot silently approached a teetering Jack.

"Pull over," I demanded, but Sonia already had steered the car to the curb, idling, the two of us sitting quietly, specimens in a glass exhibit, frozen, both of us focused on the Mexican standoff, the drunken tableau.

I rolled down my window, ignored the cold air seeping into the car, and watched.

Finally Sonia spoke. "The nightly floor show at Omar's.

Lord, Edna, living in Fairbanks you get used to street brawls, folks toppling drunk onto the sidewalk, wives slapping husbands, curses, threats. The nighttime bars spilling guys onto the streets as you walk back from dinner or the movies."

"Drunken fools."

"No." Sonia threw me a sidelong glance. "Something else is going on here." She pointed to the two men.

As we watched, the men neared each other, slow motion, unsure of foot, reeling, and Jack turned to look up the street. Instinctively, I shrank back, which made Sonia smile, though he was not looking at our car. But at that moment Jack's hand brushed his jaw, and from where I was I could see a smear of blood. He looked at his fingers and bellowed. He raised his fist in the air and sputtered, "You ripped my skin."

Sam Pilot, in a loud, echoey voice, "I should have ripped your heart out."

Then Sam shoved Jack, who tottered against a parked car, and he swung wildly at Sam. But his swings missed, punching the air. Sam jabbed back, his reach stiff and feeble, missing his mark, the men's arms dancing around each other, but the awkward, angry dance reminded me of a Buster Keaton routine, some slapstick vaudeville inanity, two clowns beating up the air. A foolish cartoon.

A couple tourists passing by stopped, amused, one snapping photos with a Kodak, pointing and laughing, but there was nothing funny about this. Finally Sam stepped away, his back to Omar's door, but Jack kept rushing up to him like a pesky rodent, prodding, poking, hissing at him.

Sam, stiffening his body, stood like a flagpole, chin up, arms folded over his chest. But the more Jack jabbed at him, the more Sam grunted, chest heaving, lips set in a tight grimace. "This is not going to end well," I said. I looked into Sonia's face as she looked into mine. She looked sad but also a little frightened—and a little bit excited.

Sonia said, "There's a story here. This is a dirty secret from the old days in the North come down to Fairbanks for the final act."

I shook my head. "Maybe it's just a drunken brawl outside a sleazy bar."

Her voice clipped. "No, it's a chapter of my 'White Silence.'"

"Which obviously can't keep its mouth shut."

Suddenly both men seemed to calm down, like the eye of a hurricane, it seemed, the two so close, Jack staring up into Sam's face, his voice oddly calm but...lethal.

Jack yelled out, "You're a crazy old Indian, Sam. Always was." Then, his voice high, "Maybe it ain't him."

I echoed, "'Maybe it ain't him.'" I looked at Sonia, puzzled, and repeated, "'Maybe it ain't him.' What?"

Sam put his hand over his heart and stepped to the side.

"What does *that* mean?" I said.

"It means, 'My word is golden.' I've seen Noah do it. Or—'This is important.'"

"But what in the world?"

Emboldened, Jack repeated that line more than once. "Maybe it ain't him.' Each time louder, a little more plaintive.

Jack began jabbing Sam again, almost like a crazed man. And Sam, towering down at him, thundered, "You may be the meanest man in Alaska, but you can still die with a knife in your gut.' He mimicked a knife rammed into a chest. Jack stumbled backwards. Sam pointed a finger and said, "Die."

That one word was chilling, horrible.

Then, quietly, Sam stepped back and walked away.

Drunk, Jack spun around, banged into a post, started cursing the onlookers. He slipped onto the sidewalk.

Sonia laughed nervously. "Thank God this long, long dark winter will soon be over." She squeezed my hand. "You're pale, Edna—and frozen. Roll up your window. We're late for the party."

As she pulled away from the curb, I watched Jack struggling to his feet. I closed my eyes, and shivered. I said out loud, "A knife to the gut."

• ● ● ● •

Two days later, early morning, I sat with coffee and blueberry pancakes in the Gold Nugget Café across the street from the Nordale. So early, Second Avenue was largely deserted, a few delivery trucks pulling up in front of the Nordale. Alone in the café, I scribbled some notes in the pad I always carried, but I was tired. Yesterday Sonia and I went shopping for souvenirs—"authentic as all get-out," she guaranteed—at a small shop near the airport. Trifles for friends back in New York. A sleepy afternoon, Sonia and I dissolving into inane laughter for no reason—the most precious kind of laughter when friends become helpless with glee.

I smiled at the thought.

Suddenly a barking sound from the street, a man's thick, panicky voice. The waitress shot out of the back room, stared at me. The two of us rushed to the front door. A milk delivery-man, his face hidden behind a knit scarf, was pounding on the window.

He pointed to the alleyway next to the café.

His head rocked back and forth.

What we learned, a half hour later as police swarmed the street, was that a body lay half concealed in a snowbank.

Jack Mabie had been clubbed to death the night before.

Chapter Seven

No one spoke of anything else that long day in the Nordale lounge. The gruesome murder of the sudden celebrity Jack Mabie galvanized the room, not only the regulars—those souls who lingered there for hours, the diehards, the old-timers— but even the tourists from the Lower Forty-eight who found themselves intoxicated with the news—yes, Alaska was still a raw, shoot-'em-up frontier, old sourdoughs beaten up in alleys in the dark, windy night. Worse, one frisky wag, emboldened by the carnival spectacle, announced loudly that, indeed, there was some dreadful lout in Alaska who was meaner than the meanest man, now dead.

The tasteless remark had some currency as ripples of laughter moved from one corner of the lounge to the next—then to newcomers who wandered in. May Tighe, the day clerk, kept shushing folks, but finally she gave up.

I didn't find it funny. Late in the afternoon I sat with Noah and Clint, the three of us huddled by the fireplace. We had no news—no one did. Rumor moved like a wave across the snow-fogged Fairbanks streets, everyone with a different and more salacious story. Folks brought up the confrontation a while back between Jack and Jeremy Nunne that made it into the police blotter in *The Gold*, even Jack's unfortunate encounter with Preston Strange in the Model Café. "Yeah, I seen that man push Jack around. I *seen* it." Others recounted tales of Jack's nightly belligerence at Omar's, his rowdiness at the Frontier Home. Some folks remembered how he'd assailed them—or, at least, they thought the staggering fool in the street was—maybe Jack.

Noah was noticeably quiet, and a couple times I caught Clint's eye. Worry there. Sam Pilot, I figured—his blood, though distant. Blood, though ornery and combative.

A newsboy dropping off copies of the afternoon edition of *The Gold* only made matters worse. Of course, the late-breaking headline: PIONEER BLUDGEONED TO DEATH. Capitalized, bold. And beneath: "Jack Mabie was a well-known figure." Well, hardly. No details, given the newness of the murder. The first paragraph: "The meanest man in Alaska was found murdered in an alley next to the Lacey Street Movie House." A number of blows to the back of the head and neck. A bloodied club nearby. Chief of Police Rawlins was quoted as saying: "Jack was obviously headed back to the Frontier Home from Omar's in the wee hours of the morning." A quaint way to phrase it, I thought—the wee hours. A nursery tale.

Looking up from the newspaper, I was surprised to see Noah's face set in a stern grimace. "What?"

He didn't answer, but Clint, shaking his head, pointed to an inside column. "Sonia done it again."

"What?"

Clint had been rifling through his own copy of the newspaper. "She goes on a bit about Jack's bad-guy reputation and she…she puts in print what everyone is talking about—Sam Pilot's street brawl, but worse, Sam's threat to kill Jack." He squinted at the newsprint. "She even mentions Preston Strange and Jeremy Nunne. Their tussles. Them guys and Jack. I mean—upright citizens. Powerful men who…"

Noah broke in, unhappy. "Sonia's trying to fan the fire. Yellow journalism. Always."

"A rabble-rouser, she is," said Clint.

"What can Preston and Jeremy do?" I looked at Noah. "Documented encounters, doubtless known to the police, but trivial really, the stuff of…"

His voice thick. "No." He stood up and walked away. I followed his stiff shoulders, his rigid head.

Clint was muttering softly. "Sam Pilot."

"I don't follow." I looked from one man to the other.

Clint explained, his eyes on Noah's retreating back. "Noah may have contempt for Sam Pilot but Sam's his blood."

"Still and all." Helpless, not understanding.

"Sonia's playing with fire."

An hour later, I was sitting alone, bothered. May Tighe walked from behind the reception desk and stood in front of me. An old woman in a faded gingham housedress and pin-curl chestnut haircut, she smiled at men—a jack o' lantern grin with missing front teeth— and glowered at women. Maybe my age, maybe a decade older, a face of wrinkles and blemishes, she'd rolled her eyes when I requested a cup of tea. She never answered me—nor did I see a cup of tea.

"Here." She dropped a note into my palm. "Someone put it in your box, but since you are here all afternoon doing nothing…" She walked away.

A summons from Tessa Strange. In a tight script of red-ink block letters, written on creamy linen stationery, Tessa invited me to dinner that night. "A visit from you is now overdue." Scribbled at the bottom in black ink in someone else's hand was this: "My car will pick you up at 7." No phone number, no way of contacting her—just the assumption that I had no other plans or, had I, that those plans would be immediately abandoned.

I couldn't wait to go. Such summons, I gathered, were rare, and given the recent events, propitious.

Tessa Strange was a local legend. Twice-wed and long widowed, a woman in her late sixties, she lived a reclusive life in the biggest house in Fairbanks, a turreted Victorian monstrosity with a wraparound porch that looked down onto a pier where sternwheeler riverboats docked to allow tourists to snap pictures of the incongruous building. Her second husband had erected the rambling house at one of the turns of the Chena River. Each summer she painted it flamingo pink, though she maintained the color was (appropriately) candy salmon, but by mid-winter the house faded to a grimy gray. She entertained few people, but would venture out, perversely, at odd times—like a sudden appearance in the mayor's chambers or at a funeral at St. Matthew's.

Someone told me Tessa Strange weighed over four hundred pounds, others said three hundred, and they insisted she had her hair permed into a corkscrew mess of blue-rinse ringlets.

Bundled in a bulky parka—or parky, to use the common localism—gloves, scarves, and obligatory mukluks on my feet, as though headed into the bleakest Arctic night, I slipped into the backseat of the long town car waiting for me in front of the Nordale.

An Indian girl opened the double doors of the grand house, and I found myself in an octagonal anteroom dominated by loud burgundy velour wallpaper. On one wall an oil painting: a young, plump woman in a debutante's dress, a dangerously precarious tiara on her bushy head, and a little too much exposed cleavage for such a northern climate. Immediately I was ushered into a vast living room where a fire crackled and popped. Like most of Fairbanks, the room was obscenely over-heated. Here was a room so large it contained three different sofa sets, which tickled me—it was as though there could be three separate functions happening at once, each one inde-pendent of the others. But at the far end of the room sat the redoubtable Tessa Strange in a blue wing chair, Buddha-like, staring at me as I walked toward her.

A huge woman, as I'd expected, perhaps three hundred

pounds, maybe more, but dressed in what struck me as mundane nightwear—a flannel nightgown stamped with garish hibiscus blooms, a utilitarian smock that strained at her upper body, her feet encased in outdoor mukluks, fur-lined. Cascading layers of fat, neck and chin and arms and belly, a continent of soft tissue. Any slight movement led to a seismic rippling of flesh. She said nothing as I approached, and I thought of royal audiences, of supplicants pleading their cases, humbled before raised platforms.

When she spoke, I was surprised. Her voice was not the volcanic eruption I expected, but a little girl's squeaky timbre. "Miss Ferber, you're so tiny. I expect I could lift you in the air with an index finger."

"A feat I could never obviously reciprocate."

A moment's pause, then Tessa Strange burst into a cackle that dissolved into a smoker's thick cough. She looked around for a cigarette but did not touch the pack at her elbow.

"I was surprised at the invitation," I began.

Tessa motioned for me to sit in the wing chair at her side. Within seconds the Eskimo girl wheeled in a cart with tea. "Would you prefer hard liquor?" Tessa asked.

I shook my head. "Tea will be fine."

The girl poured tea, handed a cup to me, nodding, and then reached into a leaded-glass cabinet and extracted a bottle of whiskey, pouring a jelly glass full and handing it to Tessa. "Thanks, Raina." She looked at me. "Medicine. I have a bad heart." She drank half a glass. "I figured it was time we met. Last summer you ignored me. Hank monopolizes the interesting folks who come Fairbanks way."

I sipped the awful tea. "I gather that the two of you are not close."

Again the woman laughed. "Hmmm. Understatement, my dear." She stifled a belch. "But he's more foolish these days than wise." She gulped the whiskey, licked her lips.

"You don't see eye to eye..."

She broke in, her voice harsh. "On anything. On state-hood, for one."

"So?"

"Statehood will bring people here."

"And you don't like people?"

She swigged the whiskey in the glass and reached for a cigarette. "Not at all. Do you? My dear, have you *met* people? Look around you. Most people are horrible." A heartbeat. "I still haven't decided about you." Again the phony laughter, the choking. "I used to like Hank. Even Sonia." She sighed. "You see, he's the last of the Alaskan puritans. Ironic in that I spent my younger days as an Episcopalian missionary up in the Bush, while he caroused and made lots of money. Lord, I had to marry to get money, a husband who conveniently died before I murdered him."

"You were married two times?"

"I guess you've been told."

"People talk."

"The mother of Preston. Have you met him?"

"Yes, briefly."

"A wonder of jackass vacuity." She stifled a giggle. "People are afraid of me—but not of him. That's unfortunate. They think I'm a fat witch conjuring up spells in this…this coffin of a castle." She manufactured a gap-toothed grin. "I'm just a tired old lady who has to plan getting out of a chair. It's hard to be a damn *provocateur*—or a malcontent—when you spend a lot of time trying to stand up." Her tongue ran across her upper lip. "Yes, dear Miss Ferber—I'm going to call you Edna, you're as old as I am, if not older, from the looks of you."

I paused. "I take it you didn't invite me here to discuss statehood."

She eyed me closely. "Very good, Edna. I already know your position. But yes—another matter. This…the troublesome murder of that drunk." Now the eyes were wide, glassy.

"Jack Mabie."

"No matter the name."

"Yes, it does matter."

She waved her hand at me. "If you say so." She scratched her chin. "My spies tell me you witnessed Preston's stupidity at the Model Café, putting his hand on that…derelict."

"Jack Mabie."

Her voice rose. "I know his name. I remember it from the old days up North. A shiver down everyone's spine."

"Then say it."

Irritated, she spat out her words. "And you've been spotted with Noah West. Another one of my least favorite souls on this planet."

That surprised me. "He's bright, clever…"

She yelled at me. "He destroyed Preston's romance with Sonia."

"That's not how I heard it."

She belched loudly, closed her eyes dreamily. "I'm allowed to write my own history."

I sat back, stared into her face. "Why am I here?"

Color rose in her cheeks. "You have a lot of questions, Edna."

"And so far none of them answered."

Her eyes got small, cloudy. "You are probably the most annoying person your crowd in Manhattan knows."

I counted a beat. "I hope so, Mrs. Strange."

"Call me Tessa." A sharp look. "A powerful family should have nothing to do with murder."

"Preston?"

"A fool. A head for business but a hothead. His name in Sonia's scurrilous column. My nephew Jeremy, as vacuous as an empty nutshell."

I laughed out loud. "Character references?"

She didn't laugh. "Do know my story, Edna?" She didn't wait for an answer as she took a huge gulp of whiskey, shivered, and her eyes got droopy. She looked for the cigarette she'd placed on the side table. "You wanna hear my life story?"

"Tessa…" I opened my mouth to answer, but she held up her hand.

"Every gossip in town could fill in the scandal." She didn't pause, and her singsong narrative had a rehearsed tone to it. "A restless young girl in Sitka, religious as all hell but liked to dance with the boys, shuffled off to an Episcopalian missionary college by confused parents, met my husband Lionel Strange who was born in Topeka of missionary parents. That's what brought him to my attention. His folks were missionaries in a small village in the Yukon, Minto, on the Tanana. So I married the pious fool, came to Venetie, bore colicky Preston, watched Lionel drown in a river, drifted to Fairbanks, married money, watched him die of cancer, leaving me a rich woman." She breathed in. "And now the final act of this tragicomedy."

"It's a novel."

An edge to her voice. "It's a tedious flashback, that's all. I've honed it over the years—keeps people away from bothering me."

"Sounds like you're hiding another story."

That stunned her. Her eyes flashed and she sucked in her breath. "Never you mind. My life in your hands would be a—farce." She watched me closely. "This is the *Reader's Digest* of a fat lady's life. And not a pretty one. Now I'm stranded in Fairbanks in this mausoleum. And I plan on living to be a hundred, just to annoy the tongue-waggers."

I took a sip of tea. "I'm not going to die until my older sister Fannie goes first. I won't give her the pleasure…"

Tessa roared. "Good for you, Edna. Nothing keeps a woman alive longer than bile." She patted her fat cheeks. "And good for the complexion." She narrowed her eyes and hissed, "Everything I've built—in danger because of the murder of that derelict."

"I don't understand."

"Preston is being questioned in that murder."

"But surely…"

"Of course he had nothing to do with it, but Sonia will indict him in her columns."

"That's unfair."

Anger in her voice. "I know what I'm talking about."

"And you think that I can help?"

"You have that woman's ear. My spies tell me she likes you."

I rustled in my chair. "I'm afraid yours was a wasted invitation."

She fumbled with a cigarette, but changed her mind. She pressed a bell on a side table, and in seconds Raina walked in. "But you'll stay for supper."

Raina set a tray in Tessa's ample lap and wheeled a noisy cart in front of me. Supper in the living room. I ate smoked salmon that tasted like pats of sweetened butter—"Squaw candy," Tessa called it, "the best"—served on slabs of brown crusty bread, whipped potatoes, heavily peppered, and canned string beans so limp and pale they seemed to have been harvested in another century. I savored the salmon and picked at the potatoes. The string beans remained untouched. Tessa apologized, "I swear I had a jar of canned wild rhubarb from last summer. Saving it, I was. Raina or her no-good husband Joe—he's an Eskimo, so's you know, only mildly dishonest—pilfered it, most likely."

I heard the front door open, followed by a flurry of raised voices in the anteroom. Preston and another man sailed into the room.

Tessa grinned, nearly toppling her tray from her lap. "Now it's time for the evening's entertainment. You get to meet Jeremy Nunne, pebble-brained nephew. Lucky you."

The two men rushed through the long room, weaving in and out of the various sofa sets, bumping into end tables, divesting themselves of parkas and scarves—which Raina grabbed from them, sometimes catching them in mid-air—until the disgruntled pair stood in front of Tessa and me.

Tessa's voice was laced with sarcasm. "Edna, you've met Preston Strange, the fruit of my generous and overworked womb, born in an Episcopalian meeting house on a dark December night." She paused. "And my second husband's sister's failure, Jeremy Nunne." She paused again, dropped her voice. "Mild-mannered Mr. Milquetoast."

"Mother," Preston snarled, "I told you this woman is the enemy."

That surprised me. "I beg your pardon?"

Preston stared down at me. I saw flecks of food stuck to the corner of his lips. "Don't try to pull the wool over my eyes, madam."

Again a garbled cough, painful clearing of Tessa's throat, and the frantic reach for a cigarette. In seconds smoke filled her corner of the room. She glowered at her son. "Tell me what happened at the police station."

Preston glanced at me, hesitated, but said slowly, "I was questioned. For an hour." His face scrunched up. "Me—a prominent businessman in Fairbanks. The Chamber of Commerce. The Rotary..."

Tessa squealed. "A vendetta, Preston—are you dimly aware of what's gong on?"

Preston hurled a sidelong glance at me. "A simple formality, the chief said. Bullshit. Pardon my language, Miss Ferber. Because of that idiotic scene in the Model Café. And"—again the fierce look at me—"Sonia's gleeful mention of my squabble in that tabloid rag she edits."

"A formality," Jeremy echoed. "Everyone knows the Indian Sam Pilot did it. That brawl. Something talked about in town by *everyone*."

"They're hauling his ass in for questioning," Preston said. "But since when does an Indian ever tell the truth?"

Tessa turned to me, a rumble in her voice. "Do you see,

Edna dear, what Sonia has done? A bitter woman—she would damage us. An empire built on privacy, discretion—yes, even bluster. But…"

"But now…" Preston whined.

"Shut up, Preston. You brought this on yourself. A hothead like your father. Acting like a street thug. All our enemies will gather like a pack of wolves."

Jeremy cleared his throat. "I want to say something."

Preston groaned. "Your tussle with Jack Mabie also made it into the police blotter, Jeremy."

"I was walking by myself, quiet—and he harassed me. I pushed him away."

Tessa screamed. "Enough." She tossed her head back and forth. Rolls of fat moved. "Jeremy, Jeremy. How many opportunities you miss! Will this be the story of your life?"

"I'm not used to dealing with trouble-makers."

"Jack Mabie," Preston muttered. "Better off dead."

Tessa roared. "Are you listening, Edna? Will you repeat this to the chief of police? To Hank? To Sonia? Tomorrow's headlines. Preston Strange announces Jack Mabie better off dead."

Preston was furious. "Jeremy, tell my mother about your trip to the Frontier Home."

Jeremy swallowed, nervous. "I visited Jack Mabie at the Frontier Home—just before he headed to the bar."

"What?" Tessa thundered. "For what reason?"

He crossed and uncrossed his arms. "I felt bad about the nonsense in the street and…"

"And so he chose to lose his mind." Preston made a fist and stomped his foot.

Jeremy had hammock hands and a round basketball face. Beard stubble made his ruddy complexion appear unwashed. He had messy black hair and small black eyes, pinpoints. He looked monstrously unhappy. A football jock gone to riotous and pitiful seed.

"The police want to question me," he said softly.

Tessa said nothing at first, though I caught her surreptitious glance in my direction, an attempt perhaps to size up my reading of the two buffoons.

Finally, purposely blowing smoke into Preston's face, she said, "Which of you two will be named murderer by *The Gold*? A crap shoot, really. Tweedledum—tweedle dumber." She began coughing, a smoker's thick, pasty rasp, then said to me, "Do you see why I asked you here?"

Flummoxed, I stammered, "No, I *still* don't."

Tessa held up her hand and cleared her throat. "All right, dammit. You two have made fools of yourselves." She lit another cigarette and roared, "Raina, more whiskey." The young Eskimo woman bustled in and replenished the tumbler, though Tessa never looked at her.

Preston was mouthing Sam Pilot's name. "The Indian did it—a drunken brawl."

Tessa was shaking her head. "You didn't consider, Preston, that decisions like this are—political. Consequential. No matter guilt or innocence. Politics. Hank and Sonia have an agenda—statehood. Worse, a desire to embarrass us—to attack us."

"I still don't understand," I broke in.

Her eyes were watery. "You have the power to squelch this travesty, Edna. I have to believe you value—truth."

I stood up. "I have no role to play here."

Suddenly Tessa reached to a side table, out of breath, and grabbed a crumpled edition of *The Gold*. "Sonia, in her desire to exploit everyone for her readers' titillation, mentioned *your* name—you as horrified witness to Preston's ill-advised shoving of the late, not-so-great Jack Mabie."

"Yes, I saw that."

"Intrusive, no?" A sly smile. "The exploitation of a budding friendship."

"It didn't bother me."

She wagged a finger at me. "You don't lie well, Edna."

"Don't trust her, Mother," Preston said. "I wouldn't be surprised…"

Tessa was amused. "Everything surprises you, Preston. You know that." A chuckle. "I used to think it was part of your charm. Now I know it's just…imbecility."

I took a step forward. "I have to get back."

Tessa called Raina, who summoned Joe—and helped me into my parka.

Getting into the backseat, I looked toward the doorway. I was surprised to see Tessa standing there, her massive arms folded over her chest, her body filling the lighted doorway.

She raised her arm in salutation.

Already cold, I simply stared out the window as the car pulled away from the curb.

Chapter Eight

Noah and I found Sam Pilot hidden in the afternoon shadows of Omar's. Bothered by the nasty rumors floating around the lounge, Sam's name whispered as a brutal man who murdered his old partner, Noah was making repeated phone calls to his sister's apartment. "Maria was surprised to hear my voice again," he told me, a boyish smile on his face. "She's used to a simple Christmas call."

I ran my tongue into the corner of my mouth. "Maybe the gods are telling you something, Noah."

He hesitated. "Edna, you don't understand."

"Of course I do. I don't think *you* do. Perhaps a little understanding of a life lived differently from your own."

I could see him fashioning a rebuttal, but he simply shook his head. "You don't let a person get away with anything, do you, Edna?"

"Why should I?"

We were sitting in the lounge, and he said quietly, "I want to talk to Sam."

"Maria didn't know where he is?"

"She suspects Omar's." He breathed in. "Or a hundred other gin mills in town. She said he was questioned by the police, taken in a second time, and he came back moody and cold. He smashed a plate on the floor but she said he apologized, which stunned her. He *never* apologizes for anything. He wouldn't tell her anything except that they pummeled him with ridiculous questions, especially about his threat to kill Jack. She gathered that he stayed quiet, refusing their questions, crossing his arms and waiting for them to tell him he could leave."

"That's not going to help his case."

He made a helpless gesture and sighed. "He doesn't care. If he's innocent, he expects the authorities to believe him."

I laughed a bit. "That's not how it works."

"For the Athabascan that's the way it works." He rustled in his seat. "Come with me to Omar's. That's where he'll be." A quirky smile. "I know you, Edna—tempted to walk on the wild side."

Which was why, at four in the afternoon, an awful chill in the air as ice crystals floated in our faces, we walked into the seedy saloon. At first, blinded by darkness, I saw nothing, though the rancid odor of spilled beer and body odor slapped me in the face. A tiny place, slapdash peeled log cabin walls and a corrugated tin roof fashioned out of Mobil oil drums, an interior space with a few ragged pinewood tables and a makeshift bar up front, dimly lit from exposed bulbs hanging from wobbly wires, Omar's was a firetrap. Or a forgotten rung of Dante's inferno. As my eyes adjusted to the scattered light, I spotted an obese man with a knit snow cap tending the bar, unmoving, his body facing us. I stepped toward the bar, immediately assailed by the cloying whiff of smoke from the cast-iron coal stove, chugging and belching, a red glow to the hot metal, a bent pipe serving as ventilation to the outdoors. A smoldering sensation of dust in the air, a film on your skin.

An empty bar at that hour of the afternoon, it seemed. But no—dim late-day sunshine pierced the one side window, illuminating a shaft of dust motes across the room and spotlighting, almost like a stage beam, Sam Pilot, his back against a wall, his legs stretched out in front of him. Arms folded over his chest, body slumped down in the chair, he looked asleep. But as we approached I noticed a left eye flicker, open for a second, then close.

Noah stood in front of him. "Sam."

A long time answering. "What you want?"

"Answers." Noah's voice was clipped, biting.

"None to give the likes of you."

Noah glowered. "Well, you better get some."

"I ain't done nothing."

"You were at the police station all morning."

A shoulder moved. "Yeah? So what? It ain't the first time I been dragged into such places." A bitter smile. "But I always end up in places like—this." His hand lazily swept the bar.

"Somebody murdered Jack." Noah leaned down into Sam, his face inches away from the old man.

Silence, a raspy cough, then, "It ain't me."

"You threatened to kill him. Sonia and Edna heard you. On the street. Other people heard you. The reason the cops brought you in."

Sam's hand moved up toward his face, so slow and calculated a gesture it seemed staged. "So what? I threaten a lot of people. It's sort of what I like to do."

Stunned, I cleared my throat. "Why?"

For the first time he moved his head in my direction. He watched me closely. "Why are you here?"

Noah jumped in. "I asked her to come with me."

"A real man would come alone."

Noah's face tightened. "A man wouldn't hit his best friend in the back of the head with a club."

Sam waited a long time, his head slowly nodding up and down. The tip of his tongue slipped out, rolled across his lips. He stared into Noah's face, then dramatically reached across a nearby table and grasped a bottle of beer. Dreamily, eyes still focused on Noah, he drained the bottle, let out a satisfied growl, and slammed the bottle down on the table.

"Christ Almighty," the bartender yelled over. "Sam, you gonna break the goddamn bottle."

Sam ignored him.

"So your threat on the street meant nothing?" I ventured, hesitant.

He stared at me closely, his eyes dark. "You don't understand the North, lady. It ain't"—he flicked a finger toward the center of the room—"*this*. Jack and me. Living for winters in snowbound cabins. If we don't slam each other, if we don't threaten to kill each other, if we don't wrestle the other into a corner, then we go—crazy." A short maniacal laugh. "It's sport."

"Do you ever mean it?"

A wry chuckle. "Every time I say it. Otherwise why bother?"

"I'm not following this."

"Maybe you ain't supposed to, lady." He focused on Noah, and I wondered about his eyesight. "Why bring the old lady?"

I ignored that. "Sam, can I ask you about something you said?" I didn't wait for his response, "In the Nordale lounge you said"—I glanced at Noah—"I'm translating, 'He saw it.' In your street brawl Jack said to you, 'Maybe it ain't him.' Tell me, who are we talking about?"

"Nobody."

"Do you know a guy named Ty Gilley?"

"Never heard of him."

I was frustrated. "Those remarks have to mean something."

"No, they don't." He breathed in. "You ain't heard me correct, lady."

I looked to Noah for help. "Noah, talk to him."

Noah had been shifting from one foot to the other. "Tell us, Sam. Okay?"

"Ain't nothing to tell. I say a lot of things."

His face closed up, yet I knew, to my core, that Sam harbored a secret. His eyes fluttered, and his head dipped into his lap, his breathing louder, faster. A secret—and a damning one. A murderous one. "You're not telling us something."

He bit his lip. "You ask too many questions."

"You say such things and then Jack is found murdered."

"I ain't done it." For the first time a trace of anger in his voice.

Noah and I watched him, quiet, quiet.

"Then who killed Jack?" Noah asked suddenly.

He shrugged his shoulders. "He comes in here at night, gets drunk, picks fights with strangers. That's what he does, you know. Spits in folks' faces—insults, jabs at you. Sooner or later he's gonna lit into the wrong guy."

"The police think it's you?"

His face scrunched up. "Ain't no proof."

"I believe you," Noah said suddenly. He stepped back.

Surprised, I turned to him. "What?"

Flat out, cocky. "I believe him." He shrugged. "He didn't do it."

Sam was nodding at him.

"I'm not following this," I said out loud.

"I already told you that," Sam muttered, a smile on his face. "You an Outsider. You old white lady."

"Yes, I am that, but…" I stared at Noah. "An Athabascan thing?"

He was smiling at me. "A gut thing."

"Noah," I protested, "you're a lawyer. Surely you know…"

He stood up, stretched out his arms. "Blood talks."

Sam was nodding slowly.

Noah was backing away, signaling to me that it was time to leave.

Sam yelled to the bartender, sputtering something about another beer, but the bartender, rocking on his heels as he polished a glass, was staring at Noah and me. Sam repeated his request—"You goddamn deaf, Harry?"—and the bartender, mumbling "Yeah, yeah, you old drunk Indian," popped the top of a beer and slid it across the bar. It sat there, Sam staring across the room at it.

Impulsively, walking to the bar, I picked up the bottle. Behind me, Sam grunted—muttering something about my hurrying up, what are you doing, lady? It ain't your goddamn beer—as I debated what to do. Noah, flummoxed, made a what-are-you-doing? gesture with his hands, though a wide smile covered his face. As I approached Sam, he shuffled in his seat, attempting to sit upright.

"I thought I'd save you the long walk," I told him.

He growled as he reached for the bottle.

I held it high over his head, my fingers gripping it tightly. I watched as he attempted to lift his arm in the air, but with difficulty. His shoulder twitched and he winced, his face contorted.

"Gimme the goddamn bottle," he hissed.

I gave him the bottle and he took a swig.

I looked at Noah, who was smiling. "Maybe you're right, Noah. The arthritis I have in my arms makes little tasks daunting. Sam here—I can't imagine him lifting a board and slamming it with such force to kill Jack."

"I *told* you," Noah said, a smug look on his face.

"I told you, too." Sam slumped down in the chair, content.

"I mean, it's possible," I went on. "Jack was small, Sam tall. I *still* have my doubts."

Noah stared moving toward the door, his hand under my elbow. "I don't."

Sam called after us, his voice hollow. "Noah." We turned to face him. Slowly, almost ritualistically, he placed his hand over his heart. The other hand gripped the beer bottle. A shift in that voice now. Not the callous indifference. Now, strangely, he sounded frightened. "Noah, I have seen the face of God."

Noah's mouth fell open. Then, his eyes bright, he said, "I know."

• • ● • •

We sat in Hank and Irina's living room having coffee. Irina fussed around us, pouring coffee and slicing chunks of blueberry cake. Hank's eyes followed her jittery movement, at one point shaking his head, though I detected affection there. Irina acted fluttery, and Sonia finally reached out, touched her forearm, and whispered, "Mom, sit down."

Noah and I had been recounting the encounter with Sam Pilot, with me concluding, "I didn't understand half of what was said to me. A condition I'm not used to. Nor do I like it."

"The call of the wild." Hank rolled his eyes.

Sonia was amused by it all. "Half of what Noah tells me—in fact, whispers affectionately in my ear—is mysticism from—Stonehenge. Runic romance. His mash notes are shaman hieroglyphics."

Noah was shaking his head. "I contain multitudes."

While we all laughed and Sonia winked melodramatically at Noah, Hank didn't. "Somebody killed Jack Mabie."

Paul was sitting in an armchair near the fireplace, turned slightly away from our group. Sarcasm laced his words. "Headline news. Breaking news."

His father shot him a curt look, but turned to Sonia. "Noah tells me he believes Sam *didn't* kill Jack Mabie."

Sonia glanced at Noah, but addressed me. "Edna has doubt. I see it in her face."

"True," I admitted, "but all of Alaska remains a mystery to me, especially the white North, so I'm hardly in a position to—"

"Of course you are," she interrupted.

Swiveling in his chair, Paul sneered at his sister. "And what's your take, Sonia?"

Sonia glared at her brother, but shrugged, dismissing him. Restless, she stood up, circled behind Noah and let her fingers rest on his neck. Surprised, he twisted his head up, looking into her face, a quizzical smile on his lips.

"White silence, the end of the long story." Sonia rustled Noah's hair.

"What now?" Hank asked, shaking his head. "Sonia, what?"

She stepped away from Noah and dropped into a chair. "I have a theory—*maybe* it's a theory. The sins of the North end up here. I've been making notes for a piece for 'Town Topics.'" Paul groaned and wagged a finger at her. "No, no, listen. The North is filled with horrible stories of violence, anger, cheating, brutality, dreaming, hoping. Think of all the stories I've collected. Think of Jack the other day." She looked at me. "Sam and Jack, maybe ambushing gold runs from Dawson to Skagway. Bodies floating in the Yukon. Lynchings, floggings, Indians killing whiskey peddlers. A wilderness saga. But now, years later, these old pioneers drift down here to Fairbanks, linger in the bars, and the old angers resurface. The settling of scores years later." She bowed. "The end of a horse opera."

Noah sat up straight. "You're saying Sam harbored anger against Jack and killed him to settle an age-old score."

"Why not?"

"C'mon, Sonia, no."

Her voice louder. "The vices of the past come back to haunt us."

Now Paul laughed out loud. "You say that so much you should wear a sign on your back."

Hank shot his son a look. "For God's sake, Paul, that's a little…"

"Realistic?" he finished.

Irina tittered, "I don't like when we…"

"Talk?" Paul said to her.

Irina sucked in her cheeks and fiddled with the coffeepot.

"Proof?" I said to Sonia in the unpleasant silence.

Sonia was pacing the floor now, excited. She fingered a stone carving on the fireplace mantel. An Indian relic. She tapped it. "The mysteries we can't imagine. No proof. Common sense. Well, maybe a *little* proof. That squabble of Jack and Sam on the street—I was there. Sam threatened Jack's life. " She frowned. "It was chilling."

Anger swept into Noah's voice. "Sonia, for all your writing about the North, you seem to miss something important—the way these sourdoughs dealt with each other. Their world."

"I know what I heard."

I counted a beat. "Sonia, in your columns you also mention Preston and Jeremy. Their squabbles, public battles, their ugly encounters with Jack."

"I mentioned them for…human interest. But I didn't *accuse* them, Edna. Can you really see Preston Strange and Jeremy Nunne waiting in an alley to clobber the old drunk in the back of his head with a club?"

"Yes," I said emphatically. "Why not?"

She rolled her eyes. "Edna, the president of Alaska Enterprises has a lot to lose. Preston is a slimy worm, admittedly, a general annoyance—"

"Whom you dated," Paul interjected, though Sonia ignored his remark.

"But he's not venal. And Jeremy Nunne, that overfed frat boy given too much power by an indulgent aunt. No, I can't believe it."

Noah glowered. "And yet you assume Sam Pilot, an old sickly Indian, lay in wait."

Sonia was getting irritated. "I know, I know, I heard Edna's tale of arthritic proof." She barely looked at me. "But in a fit of anger it's amazing what strength a man can have."

Paul added, "Even Preston and Jeremy."

"Or Ty Gilley," I added.

That name stopped everyone cold. Confusion, puzzled eyes, even a sigh from Irina. Only Paul laughed out loud.

"What in heaven's name?" asked Sonia.

"I'm sorry—when Sam Pilot sat in the lounge and muttered those strange Athabascan words, Ty Gilley was standing in the doorway. Facing him. A hard stare. I think Ty's presence caused Sam to speak. Something triggered…" My words trailed off.

Hank reached over and patted Sonia's forearm. "Be careful, Sonia. A good reporter—"

She flashed back, "I am a good reporter, Dad."

Noah's voice rose. "Sonia, the police are investigating. They interrogated Sam for hours. Let them do their job. If you start rumors in the paper—in that chatty gossip column you write, local news—if you accuse…"

She yelled back, "I'm not *accusing*. I'm recounting talk I heard."

Furious, Noah shot out, "It's feeble accusation. Unfounded."

She crossed her arms, glared into his face. "Noah, you're being unreasonable."

He scoffed at that. "No, Sonia, *you* are."

Noah stood up, nodded at Hank and Irina, smiled apologetically at me, and said, "I'm going home."

Hank pleaded, "Noah, stay for dinner. Irina wants you here."

"No," Noah said. "Not tonight." He looked at Sonia, who avoided his face. He waited, but she never looked up. Hunching his shoulders, he swore under his breath. He stormed out of the room as the rest of us stared at one another. In the grim, painful silence, Sonia suddenly looked unsure of herself, her eyes dropped into her lap, her fingers interlocked. When she looked back up, catching my eye, she blinked furiously. The determined little girl, I thought, Nelly Bly with scattershot news passion, but a young woman who didn't understand what had just happened. Her eyes sought the doorway, and I suspected she was hoping Noah would walk back in.

Hank's words were slurred. "Be careful, Sonia. Be careful."

• ● ● ● •

Sonia insisted on driving me back to the Nordale. Bundled up, shivering in the cold car, I watched Sonia's profile as she maneuvered the car out of the driveway. A rigid chin, tension in her jaw, her hands gripping the steering wheel tightly.

"What's the matter, Sonia?" I asked quietly.

"I offended Noah."

"Yes, you did."

She looked into my face. "I do that a lot, I'm afraid. And I don't want to. Edna, I want to talk to you about something. Something's bothering me. I can't talk to anyone else." One hand flew off the steering and waved helplessly in the air.

"About Noah?" I probed.

"Well, yes, but more so…Edna, I'm so glad you're visiting in Alaska."

I laughed out loud. "That's why you're bothered?"

She shook her head. "I'm not explaining myself well." She breathed in, looked into my face. "I'm a journalist, Edna. My passion. I sit at my typewriter and get so—so insanely happy. But then…" She stopped. "I'm like my father. I live for that newspaper. But…I'm drifting. What I'm saying is that I've always been an independent woman, fierce almost, dedicated, and my passion for a career clashes with…"

"With the world you find yourself in."

"Exactly. My mother can't understand me. She's content to be at home, dithering around my father's life, obedient, smiling, telling us to eat more, sleep more, behave ourselves in public. My father expects it." Her voice got loud. "That's what bothers me. The expectations. Okay for her, but not for me. I look in the pages of *Look* magazine and see all these housewives in the floral dresses hovering like hummingbirds over the supper table. Fathers in business suits read newspapers while Mom shuffles the children off to bed. My mother keeps saying to me—marry, marry. They want me to marry Noah. They love him."

"You love him," I stressed.

She laughed. "Yes, I do. More than anyone else in the world."

"But you don't want to marry him?"

"No. Maybe. Yes." A sigh. "I don't know. A career is more important." A quiver in her voice. "Is that heresy?"

"You *know* what I think, Sonia. It explains why we're having this conversation."

She clicked her tongue and smiled at me affectionately. "That's why I'm glad I met you, Edna. Last summer. This year. All winter I smiled at the fun we had, you and me, arm in arm, wandering the streets, laughing. Your life thrills me. The way you carved out your own identity, your own space, a woman alone, you dug your way into a man's world and said, 'Hey, look at me.'" Another sigh. "I want that."

"I'm an old maid."

"I *hate* that phrase. As a girl I refused to play that stupid card game with Paul." She pointed a finger at me. "A little girl in pigtails as early feminist."

"Good for you. Some see it as a badge of honor—survival."

A long silence as she focused on the road. Her fingers gripped the steering wheel.

"And then there's Noah?"

She sighed. "Bingo. The wrinkle in the fabric. I've known him all my life but now, these days, a genuine love. Companionable, delightful."

"And good-looking," I chuckled.

She grinned. "That, too. But I can only fail him."

"Maybe he knows that."

"I don't know. He gets intoxicated when we're alone, thrilled with me, the puppyish look in his eyes. It—scares me."

"You're afraid of hurting him."

"I *will* hurt him. When he asks me to marry him, I say yes, then no."

I counted a heartbeat. "And tonight? What makes you talk of this now?"

She took a long time answering. "Sam Pilot. His blood, of course. And that article I want to write. I could see in his face that he wants me to avoid the subject."

"Maybe you should."

A harsh look. "Would you, Edna? As a reporter back in the day?"

"I'd follow my instincts."

"Exactly." She breathed in and faced me. "Edna, have you ever been in love?"

The question took me by surprise, and for a moment I got uncomfortable. Then, slowly, "Yes, as a young girl. My first years in New York."

"Your career got in the way?"

"My mother. The iron Madonna." I looked out into the bleak darkness. "A different world then."

Her car pulled up in front of the Nordale, but neither of us moved to get out. The heater blasted hot, dry air in my face, but I still shivered from the cold. Finally, reaching over, I touched her sleeve. "What are you going to do, Sonia?"

Her voice trembled, "I have to make a decision. I can't keep him…waiting. But anything I do will hurt Noah. It can't be avoided. And he's the one person in the world I don't want to hurt."

I struggled to say something. "He's an intelligent man. He'll understand."

Fierce, sad. "No, he won't." She sighed. "Let me walk you inside, Edna."

Outside, she cupped her arm beneath my elbow as we walked into a snow squall. Frost bit my cheeks. She pulled me closer and whispered, "Maybe I should marry him."

I stopped walking. "Yes? No? Maybe?"

"I know, I know. I'm a teenaged girl babbling over matinee idols' pictures taped to my bedroom mirror."

"And your article?"

She didn't answer at first. Then, finally, her voice faraway, "I already have the words in my head."

"Be careful, Sonia."

She opened the door of the hotel and I stepped in. "What do you mean? Why does everyone keep telling me that?"

"I believe that Sam Pilot has a secret that has to do with Jack's murder. His cryptic remarks, yes, but something about the way he acted today led me to think he knows something. We're talking about murder."

"Okay, but I owe it to Noah to investigate."

"I don't know about that, Sonia, but—be careful. If Sam Pilot didn't kill Jack, then somebody else did—and that person is still around."

"I'm a reporter."

"Don't let those be your last words, Sonia."

She leaned in and hugged me. I could smell her perfume, some spring-like scent. Lilac? Jasmine? She held on to me a long time, as though hesitant to let go, but finally said, "Goodnight, Edna. You give me strength."

She waved mischievously as she walked back out into the street.

Chapter Nine

Late the next night, a bitter wind howling off the Chena, Sam Pilot staggered out of Omar's and headed back to Maria's apartment, a few blocks away. He never made it. His body was discovered when a bread van, headed to the morning markets, blew a tire and the driver, careening onto the sidewalk, came to a stop against some old oil drums outside a grocery store. He spotted a ragtag shoe, bent. Then he realized it was a leg. He stared down into the contorted body of an old man with long, white hair glistening with ice pellets.

"No foul play," Chief of Police Rawlins announced. Not uncommon, such pitiful deaths. Omar's regularly witnessed a string of them each winter. Sam Pilot—one more. An accident. Unfortunate. An old drunk, falling.

That afternoon Noah approached me as I lingered over coffee at the Gold Nugget. He slid into a seat across from me, his face purple, his hands waving a newspaper. I nodded—I'd already read Sonia's rushed column.

"Edna, did you see this?"

I nodded. "Yes, Noah. But…"

His lips in a tight line, then, slowly, a bitter smile. "I guess we were warned."

I sighed, "Noah, you know Sonia. You know her incendiary journalism. She likes muckraking."

"I don't."

"I know that, but she has her own way of doing things."

He spread the newspaper on the table, his fingertips tapping the article, and read out loud: "'Arctic Justice: The Final Chapter.'" Sarcasm in his voice, though I thought I detected a hint of sardonic humor. "Her obsession with emphatic endings."

Good to her word, Sonia had dwelt in her rambling column on Jack Mabie's murder but her stated belief that Sam Pilot, Jack's old—and possibly only?—frontier buddy had followed through with his street brawl threat to kill the hapless old man. Somehow, to Sonia, it validated her thesis that the ancient animosities and creaky alliances forged long ago in the brutal North would inevitably find resolution years later. Strings tied. Scores settled. Vengeance exacted. End of the chapter. In her words—"A curious if bizarre poetic justice. Frontier justice." Obviously, in the hours immediately following the discovery of Sam Pilot's frozen body, she'd tacked a coda to her column—even more of a fitting conclusion. Sam, she posited, haunted by his drunken killing of his one friend, himself an old man nearing the end of his life and filled with remorse, had drunk himself into a stupor. Wandering from Omar's in the early morning hours, reeling, in a fog, he'd somehow willed his own death. The end of a long periodic sentence that began a half-century earlier in the white silence of the Arctic Circle.

"Insane," Noah now thundered.

"But effective," I countered.

Noah was mumbling. "She condemns a man—she *convicts* a man. Sam Pilot cannot defend himself against these accusations."

I waited a moment. "Noah, are you bothered because Sam was your blood?"

He twisted his mouth into a grimace. "Yes, of course. Who wouldn't be?" Then, pointing a finger at me, he added,

"But, you know, I'm more offended because I'm a lawyer. This goes against everything I believe in. *We* believe in. We— Americans."

"You believe Jack's murderer is still walking these streets?"

"Without a doubt. Not Sam."

"You're convinced of that?"

"In my soul."

"Blood?"

He nodded. Grinning, he placed his hand over his heart. "*Shidril'*. That's it, Edna."

When I looked confused, he smiled. "My heart."

• • ● • •

Late that night I walked into the Nordale lounge to discover Sonia wrapped in conversation with Clint, who didn't look happy. Spotting me in the doorway, Clint waved me over, a look of relief on his face. Sonia, intent on reading notes on a pad she'd rested in her lap, gave me a puzzled look. I hesitated, stepping first to the reception desk to ask for my mail.

Teddy checked, joked that I was forgotten by the Outside. "Not even a Sears Roebuck flyer." Then he leaned in. "You missed the battle."

"This probably involves Sonia, right?"

He nodded, whispering. "A flash fire yelling match between Sonia and that Indian."

I frowned. "Teddy, he has a name. Noah."

He didn't look contrite. "I know his name."

"What was it about?"

He pointed to the newspaper on his desk, opened to Sonia's inflammatory column. "The sins of the past come down to fair Fairbanks." He glanced in Sonia's direction. "Well, I agree with her. Sometimes the past won't stay—past."

"You're a philosopher, Teddy."

"Miss Ferber, I'm a man who sorts the mail."

"Noah left angry?"

"Like a bat out of hell." Then, looking over my shoulder, he muttered, "Folks who don't live in this hotel riling up guests, causing paying guests to avoid the lounge."

I smiled at him. "The Nordale lounge is Fairbanks' agora, Teddy. Sooner or later everyone gathers here."

He rolled his eyes. "Agora? Whatever that is."

I left him shaking his head and joined Sonia and Clint. Sonia, looking up from jotting something in her pad, offered me a thin smile. "Edna."

"Sonia, working on a sequel?"

Her pencil pressed against the page, the lead tip snapped. "Noah just left."

"In a huff," Clint added. "Them two"—he flicked his head toward Sonia—"squabbling like two muskrats pecking at each other over a caribou bone."

"Poor Noah." She locked eyes with mine. "He'll never understand me."

"No one can," Clint quipped and she chuckled, reaching over to tap his arm with the pencil she still held.

"I'm doing a follow-up article, Edna. 'The Legend of Sam Pilot.' The mystery of that man. The Athabascan from Fort Yukon who died in a cold corner of Fairbanks."

Clint was frowning. "Sonia, the man is already dead."

"But it's an intriguing story." Then she paused, thought a second. "Maybe Noah is right. Maybe Sam didn't kill Jack."

"What?" I exclaimed, shaking my head. "After all your pronouncements. Your…your article."

She flashed her eyes. "I'm a journalist. The story goes on. Maybe Noah is right. Maybe there's someone in town who killed both men." Her eyes got wide. "Now that's the story I need to pursue. The sins of the North become the murders of the present."

"Be careful."

"I've learned that something else happened here yesterday. Teddy told me about it. May Tighe, too. Day and night staff. Sam walked in here and sat in back, up against the wall, legs stretched out, quiet, unmoving, eyes half closed. And he sat still for most of the afternoon and into the early evening. Teddy said it creeped out the guests. After the supper hour no one dared walk into the lounge, so threatening was Sam's posture."

"Why?" I wondered.

Clint answered. "It's true, Edna. I stopped in early evening. He was there. Scary as all get out. Like a sphinx or something. A statue. The hotel manager, Silas Taylor, was buzzing with Teddy, telling him to get him out. Teddy told me—'Ain't my job.' And he hid in the back room."

Sonia was anxious to talk. "But Teddy did tell me something interesting. When Ty Gilley came downstairs, headed out, he spotted Sam sitting like a mummified corpse. Hesitating, he walked up to him, and he actually talked to Sam."

"What about?"

She shrugged. "I cornered Ty a little while back. He was antsy but said he asked Sam that same question he asked me. 'Did you ever know Clay Fowler?' His father. His quest for answers about the missing father."

"And what did Sam tell him?"

"He never answered," Sonia said. "*Refused* to answer. Ty said he felt foolish, standing there, the old Indian barely looking at him."

I was thinking out loud. "You know, I always feel Ty isn't telling us something. Maybe not the *whole* story."

That piqued Sonia's curiosity. "Me, too, Edna. Half-truths. I kept pushing at him, but he wanted to get away from me."

Clint scoffed. "Maybe your next article, Sonia. 'The Legend of Ty Gilley.'"

She pursed her lips. "That isn't as crazy as it seems. His

father—another mystery of the Arctic. A whiter shade of silence." She gathered her coat and gloves. "I need to check in at the office."

"It's late, Sonia," I said.

"It's never too late to write a story."

When she was gone, Clint stood up, stretched. "Gonna amble home." But he flicked his head toward me. "Edna, walk with me."

Surprised, I agreed, putting on my parka, mukluks, and fur hat.

"Edna, we're not going caribou hunting. I live feet away."

Walking there, I said, "What is it you want to tell me, Clint?"

But he didn't answer.

Clint lived in a log cabin in the shadow of one of the new white-cement skyscrapers in Fairbanks, a drab monolith that boasted an elevator—a novelty in town, just ask the Indian boys who doggedly rode it up and down. Clint had built the two-room cabin decades before, living in it since then, its beams sagging, its Arctic porch tilting to one side, surrounded by a vast tract of open terrain. A line of such cabins peppered the street. Single men, sheltered inside. Sven the Swede's cabin. Hatless Manny's. One-Armed Joe's sinking cabin, half disappeared into the permafrost.

Clint begrudgingly watched the city grow up around him. Tall buildings haunted him, like the Polaris or even the eight-story Northward Building. His own curse was the seven-story bleached-white atrocity that looked down on his cabin. Tenants, should they desire, could watch the hunched-over prospector hobbling to his outhouse or dumping his honey bucket down in back.

Cars buzzed in and out of the parking lot that bordered his yard, and now and then some foolish soul parked a Chevy or Ford in his dirt-packed yard. Once only: a tongue-lashing from the spunky Clint could go on for an hour or so.

Locals were familiar with Clint chopping winter wood that he hauled from outside of town, or pumping water from his well, even moseying back to his makeshift clothesline, Clint scratching himself in his yellowed long johns. With his messy, grizzly beard, his floppy hat and his suspenders and denims, he found himself being asked by tourists to pose for snapshots, some believing he was an actor in the pay of the Chamber of Commerce. Another tongue-lashing, to be sure. And deserved, in fact.

I sat in his small, dark front room, the Yukon stove blazing, the room toasty. It was surprisingly neat, I noticed, with odd amenities: a vase of dried flowers on a table, a *Gone with the Wind* lamp, even a store-bought rocking chair. For the rest it was frontier land: a mounted caribou head, a brown bearskin rug, an Indian mask hooked to a rafter, a knotty-pine table that wobbled. In a back room, behind a heavy fur-pelt barrier, were his sleeping quarters. The stifling room smelled of burnt wood, turpentine, old yeast.

He brewed the spruce-root tea served in a chipped but spotless mug. I sipped it slowly—it was hot and biting, almost medicinal to the taste. "Got the recipe from an old Athabascan woman in Circle City. Cures what ails you."

I caught his eye. "What do you want to tell me, Clint?"

"For one, Sonia and Noah, Edna."

"You're bothered?"

"The cat-and-mouse game they play. Love me, love me not. I think it's a game with Sonia. A little thrilling, no? She likes the excitement of..."

"Skirmishes? Maybe. But Noah..."

"Noah is too serious a guy, Edna. You could see the love—and the hurt—in his eyes. The scene at the Nordale was... ugly. You know, Sonia is the only person able to rile Noah. He's calm, peaceful, slow to anger. Sonia makes him into a different person."

"What will happen to them, Clint?"

"Everybody hopes they gonna get married and have kids."

I sat back. "No, that's not going to happen."

"Then that's the biggest sadness Noah will ever have in his life."

"But that's not the only thing you want to tell me, is it, Clint? Something you couldn't say in the Nordale?"

"Smart lady." He poured me more tea.

I waited. "Sam?"

He nodded. "Noah whispered to me that Sam was murdered. Not just an old drunk freezing to death. Murdered."

I caught my breath. "But why?"

"Noah heard they found wood splinters matted in his scalp. The chief, he says Sam fell against some wood piling, old wood, splintered, and shavings got mixed in with the blood. Froze."

"But Noah doesn't believe it?"

"Nope." He shook his head emphatically. "Noah says somebody clobbered Sam with a club—just like they done to Jack Mabie."

• • ● • •

Lying in bed, unable to sleep, watching the hour hand strike eleven on my desk clock, I closed the novel I was reading. Herman Wouk's *Marjorie Morningstar*. It made no sense to me. The phone rang, its jangle loud in the late-night quiet room.

"Edna, I know it's late. I apologize." The wavering voice hesitated. "I really have no business…"

"Irina," I said into the phone, "it's all right. Tell me. What?"

Her voice sounded far away, as though she'd regretted dialing and now held the phone away from her mouth. "It's just that…"

"Irina, tell me."

"Sonia told me she had a bruising fight with Noah in the Nordale. In a public place. I don't like that."

"But I gather they like to do battle. Irina. They'll kiss and…" I stopped. A tiresome cliché at the tip of my tongue.

Horrified at myself, I said to her, "You have me talking like a character out of an Elinor Glyn purple romance."

She hesitated. "I don't know about that, but Edna, it's more than that." I could hear her swallow nervously. "She caused quite a row at the house tonight. Words with her father, who fought her. She snapped at Paul. She ignored my pleas that she calm down."

"What are you talking about, Irina?"

Again the long pause, the heavy sighing. "Those articles she published in *The Gold*. The one about Sam Pilot. It's caused all sorts of nasty comment. Fury, threats. She said she had a call from Preston Strange—"

I interrupted her. "Him? Why?"

"Well, you read it. She mentioned him by name *again*. Part of Jack's history. He wasn't happy, she said. He threatened a lawsuit. Against *her*. Against the paper. Against Hank. And his nephew, that Jeremy Nunne, even he called, but she laughed at that. She said he sputtered and hemmed and hawed, and ended up apologizing for something he had done—but she had no idea what he was talking about."

"He's sort of a nebbish, Irina."

"A what?"

"Never mind. Irina, Sonia loves to fan flames. That's how she sees her journalism."

"She said something about that dead Indian. Sam Pilot. Sitting in the lounge at the Nordale. Just sitting there. She said it told her something. It answered something. She said the pieces might be coming together. Maybe."

I sat up. "What?"

Irina ignored me. "Hank was furious, Edna. He stormed out of the room. They never do battle, the two of them. But he told her she was turning his paper into a cheap rag."

"But they've had that disagreement before. Two different editorial viewpoints. He should be used to it, no?"

Her mouth close to the receiver, her voice trembling. "I'm

not explaining myself well. Edna. Not *that*. Noah. What she said about Noah."

I sucked in my breath. "I'm not following you, Irina."

I looked at the clock: late. I should be sleeping. Tomorrow a long day. Obligations.

"In her fury Sonia said she'd talked to you about her—her career. Career. I hate that word. So…clinical, no? For a girl? Her life. Your life. Your success. Her admiration. Well, we all admire you, but…"

"But what?"

"She told us that she told Noah at the Nordale that they should not be together."

I counted a second. "I hadn't heard that."

"That's what she said. 'I love you to death, Noah,' she said she told him, 'but I can only hurt you. Talking with Edna made me see it. Maybe some distance.' What in the world did the two of you talk about? Did she misunderstand you? Hank went crazy. He'd been drinking and he raged. Paul tried to calm him down."

I spoke to myself. "I hadn't heard that, Irina," I repeated. "I'm surprised." But then, the words tripping out of my mouth, I realized I wasn't surprised: Sonia, fiercely independent, her hunger for a meaningful life. Her words on the page. Her love for Noah got in the way of it. Sadly. Horribly.

"She said Noah didn't take it well. He stormed out of the Nordale, bumping into folks. That—that quiet man. She drove him…" She stopped. "Edna, I don't know why I'm calling you." A pause. "Except that this house is echoey with bitterness and anger. Sonia's gone to her apartment. Paul went upstairs, glowering. Hank passed out in our bedroom." A slight chuckle. "And me on the phone bothering you at this late hour."

"It's all right, Irina."

"Is it? I don't know what's right anymore." An abruptness

to her voice. "Tomorrow will be better, Edna. Yes, it will. Good night."

I started to say good night but I heard a dial tone. Irina had already hung up the phone.

• • ● • •

Midnight. The hotel quiet. The street outside dead. Still awake, shuffling in my bed, a wisp of cold air seeping through the old windowsills, I abandoned hopes of sleep. Eight hours a night, I demanded of myself. A routine. Rigorous. Eight hours, unbroken sleep, a brisk morning walk, up and down Manhattan streets, though I'd forgo that cherished routine in frigid Alaska. Restless, I got dressed and wandered down into the lobby.

Deserted, the cleaning crew's pails and mops bunched together by the front door. As I moved past the reception desk, I could hear wispy snoring from the small room behind the desk, and smiled: doubtless Teddy taking advantage of the empty lounge to drift off into sleep.

I picked up a copy of a newspaper from the counter, the *Fairbanks Daily News-Miner*, a rival to Hank's *The Gold*, tucked it under my arm, and walked into the lounge. I was surprised to see Noah sitting in one of the chairs, half-asleep, his head dipped into his lap.

"Noah," I said, startling him. "What?"

"Too cold to wander the streets."

"So you come here?"

"I always come here. And tonight my home was too… close. The walls too forbidding."

"Your home away from home."

"My own private fiefdom." He grinned. "Until you stepped in." He pointed to the reception desk. "Teddy never knows I slip in here."

"I heard about your kerfuffle with Sonia."

He waved a hand at me. "A bad day."

"I'm sorry."

Dumbly I repeated Irina's line to me. "Tomorrow will be better."

A puzzled look on his face. "Did Shakespeare say that?" Still that infectious grin on his face. "Tomorrow and tomorrow and tomorrow, creeps in this petty pace from day to day."

"You okay?"

For a second his face closed up. "Of course."

"Sonia."

"Will be in my life tomorrow…and tomorrow." He waved a hand in the air. "Romeo and Juliet?" He paused. "A midsummer night's dream."

"But it isn't summer." I watched his face. "She left you?"

"She's always leaving me."

"But Irina and Hank fear this time it's serious."

That bothered him. "Sonia scares her parents. Especially Hank."

I raised my voice. "But she said goodbye."

A wistful smile as he shuffled to his feet. "Time for bed. For both of us, Edna."

"Wait, Noah. Earlier Clint told me you believe Sam was murdered, contrary to what Chief Rawlins believes. The splinters."

He counted a beat. "Of course he was murdered."

"And you know this how?"

"I know it." A sheepish smile. "And now you do, too."

As he walked by me, he leaned in, and surprising me, he gave me a quick hug. I hadn't expected it. His warm breath on my neck: a hint of cedar, strong, appealing. Then he stepped back. "Sonia keeps making bad decisions. I hope this isn't one of them."

"Tomorrow," I laughed.

"Maybe another bad day in all our lives."

Chapter Ten

Friday morning I lingered in my room. I'd planned on spending the morning sifting through a stack of pamphlets I'd borrowed from the Fairbanks Public Library—"Take your time, dear," the jittery old librarian told me, "but don't crease them"—a gold mine of anecdote-packed accounts of Alaskan settlement, lawsuits, family sagas. But the task palled—instead, my mind wandering, I sat by the window and stared blankly at the snow-tinted buildings and pavement. A land in which ice lay under the surface of everything.

At mid-morning, famished, I dressed and headed downstairs, only to be called to the reception desk by May Tighe. "Hey, Miss Ferber, here."

She handed me a letter, the envelope bearing the logo of the Nordale.

"My bill?" I quipped.

But May grumbled and turned away. Facing away from me, she muttered, "What the hell does that mean?"

Smiling, I slipped into the lounge, took off my parka, and tore open the envelope. It was a typed note from Sonia:

Thursday night

Dear Edna,

Important! I have to fly to Tanacross early tomorrow morning before dawn, so I wanted to get this to you. Edna, I can finally connect the dots. Jack and Sam. I know. Answers. But I'm missing some pieces. I'll be back early evening, supper hour, last-minute work at the office. Can I pick you up at nine at the hotel? We can talk at the road-house by the airport. Very private there. If not free then, leave message at my office. Otherwise, I'll see you! Important! I repeat—I can connect the murderous dots.

She signed her note in ink and then, an afterthought, wrote beneath it:

PLEASE! (bad manners!) Please!

Then, oddly, below that humorous addition, big block letters, smudged black ink:

DON'T TELL NOAH! SECRET! IMPORTANT! I'LL EXPLAIN.

Startled, I reread the note, baffled. Staring into the lounge, I noticed a few loiterers watching me. What did they see? Probably my confusion, my worried expression. I folded the note, slipped it back into the envelope, and got ready to walk out of the lounge.

I wandered into *The Gold* offices on Second Avenue, just up from the Nordale in the shadow of the Northward Building, that eight-storied ice castle. Spotting me in the doorway, Hank waved me in as he puffed on a cigar. Sitting behind a big oak desk cluttered with copy spilling over the edges, his sleeves rolled up and reading glasses loose on his nose, he gave me a big smile. "Edna, I was thinking about you." He stopped when he saw the serious look on my face. "Now what happened?"

"Nothing. Or—I don't know."

He rolled his tongue into the corner of his cheek, his eyes darkening. "What?"

"Sonia left me a mysterious note at the hotel."

"She flew out real early this morning for a visit to Tanacross,

a small Native village, some ceremonial potlatch, an obligation to an old friend of hers. She was in a rush, as usual, late
getting started."

"Her note suggested urgency."

He seemed unhappy. "Everything she does is urgent these
days."

"You have no idea what she wanted to tell me?"

"Not a clue."

After a lunch with Clint at Mimi's, I returned to my room
on the second floor—back by the staircase at the rear of the
building, a room I chose because it was away from the clamor
of the street—I found myself doing what I'd done all morning.
I gazed out the window at the barren landscape, a parking lot,
sagging log cabins, stunted spruce and alders bent under ice,
and in the distance a rise of white hills. If I stood on tiptoe at
the window and shifted my head to the left, I could see the
distant summit of Mount McKinley—Denali, to the Natives.
The Great One—with its snow-shrouded peaks. Late in the
day it wore a rosy hue. Too tired to linger at the window, I
just lay on my bed, staring up at the ceiling. The old chenille
spread, a little frayed and linty, cut into my flesh. I thought
I'd nap before leaving for an obligatory supper with the head
of the Fairbanks Chamber of Commerce and some schoolchildren who'd read one of my novels. *Cimarron*, I'd been told.
I'd have to say a few words to the bubbly youngsters. Three
hours at the high school, they'd promised me, imploring—just
three hours of my time. I smiled. *Cimarron*—another frontier
I wrote about. The Oklahoma land rush.

Well, I thought, some game was now afoot. I looked at my
wristwatch. Dinner and reception with the schoolchildren,
over by nine, as promised. And Sonia's show-and-tell to follow.
Not a bad day's bill of fare.

• • ● ● •

The evening's events were predictable, if pleasurable. The head of the Chamber of Commerce was appropriately fawning in his generous remarks, the cafeteria food at the high school gelatinous and fearsome, save a bread pudding that tickled my fancy, and the nervous high-schoolers said nice things about *Cimarron* and I said nice things back.

But my mind was elsewhere, back at the Nordale lounge where I arrived a few minutes before nine, warming my hands before the blazing fireplace. Sonia hadn't arrived yet. But everyone else was there—Clint, Ty Gilley hidden behind a newspaper. Even Jeremy Nunne was talking with someone, although when I turned around, he was gone.

Clint beckoned me to the corner where he was slumped in a chair, a pipe in his mouth.

He was sitting with a young man I didn't recognize. Introduced as Harry Hilmar, a machinery salesman from Walla Walla, the young man kept tugging at the bulky wool sweater he wore, doubtless given to him by a loved one who feared he'd freeze in the Alaskan icebox. "We was talking about statehood," Clint told me.

What else? Three verities in the land of the Chinook: death, taxes, and the debate over statehood. Death, of course, preferable to the last.

Harry struck me as a genial bumbler, given his propensity to pick at the fabric of his sweater, as well as his curious manner of suddenly thrusting out a moist tongue, frog-like, to gather the drool that seemed to collect at the corners of his mouth.

"What exactly do you do?" I asked him.

"I represent generator parts, mostly governmental contracts, over to Ladd Air Force Base."

I stopped listening.

"Harry here is a real jackeroo greenhorn."

"Yeah, a cheekacho." I used the name for an Outsider who'd yet to endure one full Alaskan winter.

"I sure am," Harry beamed.

For a while, Clint and Harry talked about prospecting. Harry had been to the gold dredge across town, which Clint portrayed as a waste of money: "Give me a tin pan and a stream anytime." But Clint had found a receptive audience, regaling the young man with tales of old Fairbanks—thirty-three saloons in a four-block stretch of First Avenue. His friendship with Chee-chaco Lil, whorehouse madam extraordinaire. Claim-jumping, armed miners. Hordes of killer mosquitoes and black horse flies driving men mad. Life in the hungry bush. Barroom fights and dollar-a-dance girls. Ten bucks for a dozen eggs. Life in Fort Yuk, as he called it. I smiled whenever Clint glanced at me. I assumed he was making it all up.

Quietly, I watched as Mary, the young Indian girl who was the housekeeper in the lounge, moved silently about the room, emptying ashtrays, picking up glasses and cups, stepping out of the way of the loungers. Her look was a combination of Lower Forty-eight civilization—a white frilly blouse, the clinging black wool skirt, and the sensible oxford shoes—with a hint of something Indian—a beaded whalebone comb tucked into her hair and a bone ivory bracelet trimmed with a tuff of some fur, trinkets that clashed with her prim New England schoolmarm uniform. When she bent over, a necklace slipped out of her blouse. At first I thought it was an amulet, a chiseled jade stone, but when she turned, I realized it was a stone crucifix. So she had been educated at one of the Episcopalian missionary schools. Chubby, fat-cheeked, with straggly black hair, she looked like one of the Navajo women I had talked to in the Southwest.

Clint was telling Harry that the sourdough yeast he used to fry up his breakfast flapjacks dated back to a "good old gal who give it to me winter of 1914." Harry had no idea what he was talking about.

I checked my watch. I'd been in the lounge for nearly an hour and a half. Ten-thirty now. Sonia was late. Harry excused himself—"Need my beauty rest"—and I watched him walk away, headed to the stairwell.

"You missed Noah," Clint said quietly. "He was here earlier tonight. Around seven. Looking for Sonia—maybe. Sonia's talking double murder now, and scaring the daylights out of everyone. Noah slipped in, said hello, then headed home. He sat right in that chair you're in. I told him you was off to the high school."

I looked at my watch again.

"You waiting for someone, Edna?"

"Sonia. I'm supposed to meet her at nine. Here." I fidgeted.

"Well, you missed her."

"What?"

He looked puzzled. "I mean, she was here—like at eight, I think. She looked around, seemed to be waiting for someone." He smiled. "You, I guess. But she didn't come over to where I was. She was talking to Teddy, then sitting by herself, going over some papers she had."

"I'm sure the note said…" I rushed my words. "When she came here earlier, did she stay long?"

He shrugged. "Nah. She went up to reception, but by then I was yammering with that guy Harry. She took off, I guess. When I looked over to reception, she was gone."

"Lord, I missed her." I shook my head. Had I misread the time in her note?

"There's always tomorrow."

"I don't like waiting."

He chuckled. "Try living in a wilderness cabin all winter long up in the Yukon Flats. You learn patience."

"Thank you, but I'll stay in New York in winter. Everyone there is impatient, let me tell you. A hint of ice on a sidewalk, and people weep out of control. I fit right in." I sighed. "Good night, Clint."

Upstairs I walked down the long hallway, weary, but I paused, extracted the note from my purse, reread it. Nine o'clock: clear as day. Why me? I'm the Outsider. Outsiders, folks from the Lower Forty-eight. I smiled. Cheechakos. Lord, I hurled that bizarre term at that hapless Harry Hilmar, military machinery man, he of the drooling mouth and frog-like tongue. A johnny-raw, that boy. Must make a note about him, a description. Maybe use him in a novel. A story. A character…but not tonight.

Sleep. I need sleep.

I opened the door and stepped into the dark room, reaching for the light switch on my left. But I stumbled, struggled to right myself, and when the light suddenly flooded the room, I realized that my foot had kicked a body sprawled in a heap on the floor. I stifled a scream and pivoted wildly, this time toppling onto the body, then crawling away. My hand touched the dead woman's head, and I found myself staring at a face with eyes wide-open, glassy, brilliant, staring back at me.

Chapter Eleven

I sat in the small room behind the reception desk on a plaid-covered lumpy sofa covered with coffee stains. I squirmed, uncomfortable. I could still hear echoes of my own ragged screaming as I fell upon the body of the hapless Sonia. For those few horrid minutes I went blank, a condition I don't approve of in myself, but I recalled, with not a little embarrassment, a strange man grasping my arm and somehow maneuvering me into the hallway, down the stairs, and into the reception area where, spotting my trembling face, Teddy rushed over, his face white.

That was an hour ago—maybe more, time having collapsed—and I sat with an untouched cup of cold tea by my elbow, next to it a snifter of brandy, barely touched. For a minute I sat sobbing, grieving for that young woman. Folks skirted around me, Teddy quietly placing a box of tissues at my elbow. I did notice that he had been reading my *Giant*, open to the middle and placed facedown on a table, my dreadful profile staring up at me, a ghostlike photograph that probably looked more lifelike than I did now. A helter-skelter assembly of souls rushed in, rushed out, officious, noisy, crazed, dizzy with questions I couldn't answer. An ambulance siren, echoing against a howling night wind, grew louder.

At one point Clint straggled in, his face ashen, and he took a seat next to me in the tight room, mumbled something incoherent—I felt as though people were talking at me through a large, clogged funnel—but then, at one point, he seemed to disappear. Now oddly, he was back, sitting across from me.

"What?" I asked, irritated.

"You all right?"

I nodded. "What's happening?"

"Chief of Police Joe Rawlins's coming to talk to you. After they take care of things upstairs."

Upstairs: that beautiful girl, lying there, twisted and blank-eyed, a clot of thick brownish blood caking that lovely blond hair and forming a pool on the gray carpet. Sonia, no more. The laughing girl with her poisoned pen.

Then, a lightning flash in my head, I remembered something. When I'd been led down the stairs by that stranger, I'd spotted Ty Gilley by the front door, watching, stone sober, his eyes hard as diamond coal. A fleeting image: Ty, uninterested in the chattering woman being escorted down a creaky stairwell, slipping out the door. My mind raced. He didn't have on his parka or gloves. Or did he? Was he leaving? Or returning?

"What?" Clint asked. "You look like you're gonna say something."

I shook my head. "No."

He whispered, "Joe Rawlins says they'll move your stuff to a room down here. You can't go back up there."

Suddenly I wanted to, not so much to retrieve my suitcases and books and notes, and really not to see the body of that young woman lying there—no, I just wanted to be in that doorway, to walk in as I had earlier, unsuspecting, switching on that light and then toppling over. Somehow, being there, I could reconstruct that moment, I could see something, perhaps understand. But understand what? Yes. Why my room? Why kill Sonia there? What did I have to do with it?

Which, of course, was the first question that Chief Rawlins asked me when he sat down across from me.

"I have no idea," I told him.

The chief was a fortyish man with a weathered look about him, a mountain-climber's sun-baked visage, all those deep and pitted crevices. A red bulbous nose—a drinker, perhaps. Rail thin, Lincolnesque, with salt-and-pepper hair and beard stubble. A thin moustache, untrimmed. But he had stone-agate eyes that were unblinking and accusing one minute, the next soft and watery. A good-looking man, if you liked someone who preferred hunting grizzly bears to a soul who kept the home fires burning.

My answer seemed to stymie him. He waited.

So I demanded, "How did she get into my room? How did the...the killer get in?"

Teddy, sitting nearby, cleared his throat and glanced at the Silas Taylor, the hotel manager, who just arrived, his face pale and his eyes flashing. "Our locks are old-fashioned, easily manipulated. Lots of folks know that most keys can, you know..." He stopped. "Well," he sputtered, "we're a trusting people, we Fairbanks folks."

Icily, I held his stare. "Well, not everyone obviously is a model citizen."

He turned away.

Clint told the chief that Sonia had, indeed, showed up before eight, talked to a few people in the lobby, the regular nighttime crowd. Teddy said she'd talked about the potlatch she'd attended, bubbly, in fact.

"But I was at a supper..."

"Maybe not everyone knew that."

"We were to meet at nine."

"Yes," Rawlins noted, "we found the note in your purse."

"You opened my purse?" I was furious.

"Ma'am, it was on the floor. You must have dropped it. Unclasped. Contents askew, including the note."

"So there. I knew I wasn't insane. Sonia forgot the time of our meeting..."

He bit his lip. "No, ma'am, in her pocket we found a scribbled card, a note from the secretary at *The Gold*, saying plans had changed, you were busy later, for her to come here at eight."

"I never…"

"Of course," he cut me off. "Seems like she picked up her messages at her office sometime after she got back from Tanacross, and assumed you'd called her." He was nodding. "A ruse, obviously." He nodded at Teddy. "What did you tell me?"

Teddy, uncomfortable, made a raspy sound. He began talking but, scattered, looking into my pale face, he began again. "Miss Ferber called." He hesitated. "Or someone. Her room. Said for Sonia, when she comes, to have her go up to her—Miss Ferber's, I mean—room."

My mouth flew open. "From my room? A woman?"

He squirmed. "I didn't pay much attention. I mean, the voice sounded real sleepy, whispering-like. Like you were waking up, hoarse and raspy. So quick—a few words. I first thought—a man in Miss Ferber's room, so low…I'm sorry, I…" He smiled without realizing it.

"What?"

"Well, ma'am, like a whiskey voice, like someone at the end of a night's ferocious drunk. I get calls like that all the time—folks drunk in their rooms."

I pursed my lips. "Well, I have every reason to start doing so now."

"So we can't get anywhere with that. Man or woman, who knows?"

"What did I supposedly say?"

"Brief, to the point. 'When Sonia arrives, send her to my room.' That was it. No thank you, very abrupt." He bit his lip. "I started to say, 'Anything else, Miss—'but the person hung up."

"Yes, my usual gracious phone manner."

"Sonia was here. I mean, just missed Noah, she said, laughing, Noah'd be the death of her." He stopped, panicked at the words that popped out of his mouth. "I mean…"

"For heaven's sake, Teddy."

Squeamish, he looked down. "I don't know what to say." A helpless shudder.

"How did she seem?" the chief asked Teddy.

He shrugged. "Nothing peculiar. Nice. Like always. Always sweet. I told her the message. She walked away, took some papers from her purse, read them. Then she was gone."

The chief noted. "No papers found on the body." Puzzled, he addressed Teddy. "What did you think when you saw Miss Ferber in the lounge at nine?"

Teddy looked into my face. His lips trembled. "I could see she come from the outdoors, face cold. I figured she'd stepped out with Sonia for a bit—like was returning now." He swallowed. "None of my business, you know. Then Miss Ferber was gone. Up to her room."

"And into a nightmare." My voice shook.

"When did you get the note?" the chief asked me.

"This morning. May Tighe…"

The hotel manager kept looking around the small space. But now he interrupted. "Last night Sonia rushed in around ten or so. I was at the desk"—he glanced at Teddy—"Teddy had to carry yet another set of towels to Mrs. Leyerson on the third floor, a royal pain, that woman."

The chief glared at him. "And?"

"Sonia was happy to see me. I mean, she didn't seem—nervous. She told me she didn't want to wake Miss Ferber. Could I put a letter in her cubbyhole? I did, but then she asked for it back, tore it open, and scribbled something on it. I didn't see what. But I gave her a new envelope, she sealed it, and left. Her last words, 'Tomorrow a potlatch in Tanacross. I can't wait.' She seemed—normal."

The chief was talking to himself. "Someone knew Miss Ferber was away for the night. Someone knew Sonia was coming for Miss Ferber at nine. Someone called *The Gold* to change the time. Eight o'clock. Someone…"

"Who knew what she was going to tell me," I said loudly. "And what was that?"

I sucked in my breath. "Who killed Jack Mabie. Who killed Sam Pilot. She was hell-bent on that story."

The chief held up his hand. "Don't jump to conclusions. Her death could be something different…"

"No." I shook my head vigorously as my hand reached for the cup of tea. "No. We're talking three horrible murders here."

"Who said Sam Pilot was murdered, ma'am?" the chief said.

Suddenly I felt the walls of the tiny space closing in on me. Squirming in my seat, facing these men, I gasped for air. Why were we huddled in the tight little room? Outside in the lounge a babble of voices—doubtless hotel guests, townspeople, scattered souls drifting in after hearing of the murder. Macabre, ghoulish voyeurs.

My eyes lingered on a narrow cot along the back wall. Teddy's refuge—snoring when on duty. Now, exhausted, I wanted to lie down on that cot, close my eyes, fall asleep. A box of opened Ritz crackers, crumbs on the desk. A faded black-and-white photo of a family dressed in their Sunday best. An adolescent Teddy in a slough-boy cap and kickers. A snapshot of Teddy in front of the Nordale, his long arm pointing up at the sign. Rumpled blankets on the cot—I wanted desperately to leave these men, to snuggle under those covers, wrap myself in the covers, disappear. On the table a knitting basket, its contents spilling out. A box of chocolate-covered cherries from Lavery's Groceries. May Tighe's ratty sweater. Her needlework—a bit of embroidery, the beginning of a motto: "Laugh, and the world laughs with…" My mind recoiled. You! I finished the line in my head. You you you. I felt like screaming.

The manager was talking to the chief. "Never in this hotel. What do we do? Our guests…"

The chief said nothing.

There was clamor in the hallway as Irina and Hank flew into the room. I jumped, startled. The brandy snifter crashed to the floor and shattered. I looked at the manager, but he was nodding at me: Pay it no mind. But Teddy, fastidious, hurried to pick up the pieces.

Irina rushed toward me. "Edna, are you all right?"

The remark surprised me. "Yes, of course." I breathed in. "Irina, Hank, I am so sorry." I reached for Irina's hand.

Hank looked wild-eyed, moving back and forth, approaching the chief of police, then looking at me and Clint, as though uncertain where to look. I was waiting for him to say something, but he wore a blank look on his face, someone slapped, stunned.

Chief Rawlins said softly, "I'm sorry, Hank, Irina." The tone suggested an intimacy used for old friends.

"But we don't understand." Irina sounded helpless.

Silence.

Then Hank mumbled, his voice trembling, "They called us to the hospital but Sonia was already dead." His voice sounded faraway, disbelieving.

Chief Rawlins still spoke in that soft voice. "You spoke to Orville, Hank?" Hank nodded. The medical examiner? The coroner?

Hank nodded numbly and said, "In Edna's room?" He looked at me, puzzled, as though I held answers. For a moment I closed my eyes—I saw brilliant lightning flashes, sparks of electricity.

"'Fraid so," Rawlins acknowledged. "Someone got there before Miss Ferber was to see her."

Irina spoke. "Edna, why was she seeing you?"

I cleared my throat. "She had something to tell me. She was a little mysterious in her note to me." Looking at Hank,

I had a sinking sensation. He had been drinking. His eyes, though teary now, were bloodshot, droopy.

Chief Rawlins asked if Hank or Irina had any idea who'd do this, but the question, said so matter-of-factly, seemed preposterous in the small, cramped office. He swallowed and looked at neither parent. "Does she have any enemies?"

Hank babbled a bit, his voice cracking, and blurted out, "Of course, she had enemies. Any journalist has enemies—it comes with the territory. She was a fiery editorial writer, Joe. You know that. She liked—sensation…" He stopped, seemed to be thinking. "But people don't kill over something she said."

Chief Rawlins jerked his head back. He lowered his voice. "Who knows?" He scratched his chin, thinking. "But we can pursue that later. I'll want to go through her papers at *The Gold*, okay? Her apartment. Maybe something she was writing…"

"I think she had an idea who killed Jack and Sam," I announced.

Everyone stared at me.

Hank looked concerned, squinting at me. "Then why wouldn't she tell me about it? I'm her father—I run the paper." A long pause, but Hank went on. "You'd think…" He stopped, swallowed his words. He was sweating. "That makes no sense." Again, his voice trembled, and Irina, standing at his side, reached over to touch his sleeve. But he shook free of her touch, angry now. "Who would do this to my baby?" His voice now broke. "Who? Dammit."

He shifted from one foot to the other, but seemed to waver. He made little gasping sounds, trying to catch his breath. His dull glassy eyes looked to Chief Rawlins for answers.

Suddenly Irina was weeping, folding up, and Hank grabbed hold of her, pulled her into his chest. The two of them rocked back and forth, and I felt intrusive, witnessing such raw grief, both of them sliding into sloppy sobbing. Irina said something to me, but her words were incoherent. Hank reached out and gently rubbed her tear-flooded cheeks. It was as touching and simple a gesture as I'd ever seen, but it reminded me of a father dutifully placating a distraught child.

I heard footsteps running in the hallway, and Paul fell into the room. I watched him, the twin brother, the quiet moody one who disliked his sister. I watched as he ran past his father, maneuvering himself around the big man, until he virtually wrestled his mother from his father's hold, embraced her, and she found herself sobbing into her son's chest.

"Mother, they just told me." His voice was squeaky, dry. "I can't believe this."

"Our Sonia is gone," Irina bawled.

"They told me she was…" He seemed ready to say *murdered* but stopped, the word sticking in his throat.

Irina obviously finished his sentence because she dissolved into new spasms of sobbing, her head buried against his chest. There it was, then: a tableau of mother and son, both tight in grief, and looking up, I found myself watching the sweating, tipsy Hank, a man suddenly removed from this family portrait.

He looked ready to slug his son.

A deputy rapped on the doorframe and Chief of Police Rawlins nodded at him. The young man, red-cheeked and cherubic, motioned with an index finger, and the chief excused himself. I could hear them in the hallway, the two men mumbling at each other. In the room, Paul kept saying, "Tell me what happened," over and over. No one answered him. At one point, looking over his mother's head, he caught my eye, and again he mouthed the words: *What happened?* His eyes looked dull, curtained. I turned away.

What happened, indeed: I had entered my own hotel room, an old woman ready for slumber, and toppled over a body.

Chief Rawlins walked back into the room, and I noticed his gait—a loping, shuffling walk I imagined Charlie Chaplin executing. I realized that the man was nervous. He cleared his throat, and everyone waited.

A slow drawl. "It turns out we have a witness who…"

A flurry of excited voices, Hank yelping, Paul audibly breathing in, a gasp.

"What?" From Paul.

His mother grabbed at her throat.

"One of the guests on Miss Ferber's floor"—his eyes locked with mine and I realized I was looking guilty—"just told Deputy Jamison that he was coming out of his room sometime after eight, down the hall from Miss Ferber's room, and he saw a man leaving her room, shutting the door. He stopped, he said, because he'd dropped his keys, bent over to pick them up. That's when he heard Miss Ferber's door opening. He paid it little mind, he said, but he knew it was Miss Ferber's room because his wife had pointed it out earlier that day and she told him Miss Ferber was the author of *Show Boat*, was a real famous writer, and she got angry with him because he'd never heard of it or her and…"

"Chief Rawlins—" I interrupted but stopped.

Sheepishly, he continued, "Anyway, the man coming out of your room was facing the door, hunched over, turned away, hidden like. A man bent over. But he had on a parka with the hood up, which struck the witness as real funny, and then the man moved away as fast as he was able, rushing down the back stairwell that no one uses, which also struck the guest as odd. It's like a fire exit and it leads to a parking lot, deserted. Everyone else walks…"

I held up my hand. "What do you mean 'as fast as he was able'? A curious thing to say, no?"

The chief gulped. "Well, seems the man had trouble walking. He had a limp and…and was leaning on a cane…"

I got dizzy, my hand flew out, and I realized Clint had taken hold of my other hand. I looked at him. I saw fright in his eyes.

"I mean…" I stuttered.

"We got a description of his parka. A burnished red one, with some wolf fur trim around the hood, and some Native beading and embroidery on the edges." He paused, bit his lip, and refused to look at anyone. He didn't look happy.

Of course, he was describing Noah West's famous parka. The limp, the cane, but especially the distinctive parka with the Qwich'in markings. Noah's personal statement—his flagrant assertion of his Native background, in Technicolor. Everyone in the room understood that. He wore it everywhere.

My hand reached for the cup of tea. It rattled on the saucer as I picked it up. The brew was ice cold now.

No one said anything. Then, quietly, Hank said the word everyone was thinking. "Noah."

"Impossible," Paul thundered as his father looked at him. "Not the only red parka in…"

"Paul…" his mother said.

"I mean," Paul went on, "you're describing our friend." He was challenging Chief Rawlins. "Noah West."

The chief nodded. "I'm afraid I thought of him, too."

"Impossible," Paul emphasized again. "There's something wrong with all of this. There has to be."

Struggling, I offered, "Surely, there are others in Fairbanks who limp, who…"

Hank seemed in a trance. "Noah." A shaky, sad voice, blurred by whiskey.

Irina looked at her husband. "Hank, really."

Hank, loudly, "Noah." Sharper.

Paul fired at his father, "Surely you can't believe it's Noah. Dad, we've known him all our lives. It's Noah we're talking about. Our Noah. Our friend. A member of our family."

Hank looked up, his faced covered with tears. "What was he doing coming out of Edna's room?"

"Hank, you're assuming it was Noah," I said in a rush. "There is no proof."

A garbled, furious voice. "Didn't you hear the description? For God's sake."

"What reason would he have?" Paul stared at his father.

Hank, tight-lipped. "*She* told him—a separation. They fought—here. In the hotel. Yesterday she told *me*—told him. He loves—loved her— obsessed, he lost…"

Irina touched Hank on the arm. "Listen to yourself, Hank. You know Noah. We all do."

"Dad, you're not thinking straight." Paul was stammering.

Hank looked at his son, his cheeks crimson. "Maybe I am."

I spoke up. "Hank, you're jumping to conclusions." I glanced at Clint. "You're a rational man."

Hank stood with difficulty, swung around, frantic now. "But there's a chance he killed my daughter, and all of you are blind to it."

"But it's Noah, Dad."

He bit his lip. "Christ, Paul, you read the papers. Family members kill other family members all the time in moments of madness, of passion. Lovers snap. Minor spats erupt, things said, tempers flare, a hand strikes out…Noah…"

"Hank," Chief Rawlins cautioned, "take it easy. We'll question Noah West, of course."

Hank exploded. "Question him? What about arrest? What? Are you afraid of him? For Christ's sake, Joe, he's out there and my daughter is dead—dead." He stopped, looked disoriented. "I don't know. I just don't know. What's going on here?" He grabbed at his head, closed his eyes. "Somebody has to pay for this. Somebody has to. My baby girl. Maybe they fought. Maybe." He looked at the chief. "They told me at the hospital someone clubbed her on the head with something."

"Dad." Paul walked toward him, but the look on his father's face stopped him cold. "You can't just accuse Noah."

He yelled. "He wears a parka like that."

Paul raised his voice. "Look, I saw Noah tonight outside

and we talked for a few minutes." He looked at the chief. "We talked about some Native politics, and he was in a cheerful mood. He mentioned how Sonia was excited about her trip today—knew he'd want to hear all about it. He has friends in Tanacross. He laughed about that."

"Did you see him walk away?"

"Well, we shook hands, and I walked away. He said he was going home. He acted like he always acts...easy-going. Not like he planned to slip upstairs and...you know."

"What time was that?" the chief asked.

"Must have been around seven or so. I wasn't paying attention."

I was quiet. I looked at Clint, who spoke in a voice that seemed far away. "Noah don't hurt nobody. Noah left around then." He cleared his throat. "That boy ain't no killer."

Hank looked at Clint. "Everybody can be a killer." Said bitterly, coldly.

"Hank," Irina spoke quietly, "think what you're saying. You're a little...irrational."

Hank looked at her, his eyes narrowing. "Our daughter is dead and you defend the man who struck her down."

"We don't know if No—"

Suddenly he sank back onto the cot, pushed the palms of his hands up against his temples. He closed his eyes. "Christ, what's going on here? Will somebody tell me what's going on here? Noah said he loved her." He looked up, his expression that of a stupefied child. "But love can make people kill, right?" He waited. "People can lose it, right? Good boys fall apart. Look at Sonia. She's beautiful. Everyone talks of how beautiful she is. Noah used to tell me that he couldn't live without her. He made her happy. Wouldn't live without her." He looked at me now. "She said no. Lovers get off balance. Angry words—irrational action. Striking out." He stared into my face and I wanted to turn away, so raw his look. "Tell me,

Edna. You liked that boy, too. Tell me, why would he kill my little girl?"

I said nothing.

Hank covered his face and started to sob.

I heard Chief Rawlins tell Deputy Jamison that they needed to bring in Noah West for questioning. At my side Clint rustled, struggled to stand. I saw him tug at his side, wince, his body jerking from a sharp pain. "Where are you going?" I whispered.

"I gotta get to Noah before the cops do. I gotta be there. Just in case something happens."

I was frightened. "What can happen?"

"I just wanna be there with that boy."

Chapter Twelve

"He warn't home," Clint told me late the next morning when we met for coffee at the Gold Nugget Café across the street from the Nordale. "I banged on his door. I mean, the lights was on, but he ain't there."

I was worried. "That was after midnight. Where could he have gone?"

Clint's eyes twinkled. "A young man, good-looking, maybe a girl."

I shook my head. "I don't think so. Not with the way he's in love with Sonia. He..." My voice trailed off.

"What?" Clint swallowed a forkful of pancake.

"I was going to say he would somehow feel it was a betrayal, but how would I know that? I scarcely know him." I sighed as I smiled at Clint. "Perhaps I'm a romantic."

Clint scoffed. "I was thinking maybe he got one of them whores on The Row, you know by the..." Now he stopped, his eyes flashing. "What in Jesus' name, Edna?"

My face tightened, my lips a thin line, disapproving. "Clint, really."

"Don't mean to offend you, Edna, but this is Fairbanks, you know. Whores is part of the local economy. Used to be legal, fact is." He chuckled.

My tone icy. "Could we talk of something sensible?"

Clint tried to look contrite but gave up. "As I was walking away, the cops pulled up. I didn't linger."

The front door opened, a sudden burst of chilly air, and Chief of Police Rawlins stood in the doorway, looked around, spotted us, and walked over. "May I?" I nodded, and the officer slid into a seat. When the waitress bustled over, he waved her away.

"Officer Rawlins—" I began.

"Miss Ferber, pardon me, but I thought I'd fill you in on what we learned."

"Really?" I didn't expect such sharing. "But why?"

He shot a look at Clint, who was watching my face. The officer reached for a cigarette, lit it, and watched the gray smoke drift away from the table. "Truth is, it was your room where it all happened. I mean, you a guest and all. Just wanted to give you some reassurance." I waited as his eyes followed the cigarette smoke. "I don't want you worrying about your safety."

"I'm fine, sir."

He rapped the table and checked his watch. "The killer was hiding in your room, waiting. He came up the back staircase that no one uses. He got in, simple enough. Sonia knocked, the door opened, and she expected to see you. She started to back out, maybe, 'cause we found a tear in the shoulder of her blouse, like she was grabbed, then pulled in. A little bit of a struggle, some nasty bruises on her arms. But the killer knocked her down, then clubbed her on the head, a couple of heavy blows that probably stunned her, then killed her. Blood smeared on the carpet." He looked away. "Even on the doorframe."

I took a sip of coffee, breathed in. My hand on the cup trembled. "What kind of instrument?"

A heartbeat. "A cane."

I shuddered. "You know, I knew you'd say that. How can you be so sure?"

He nodded, impatient, glancing at Clint whose face was frozen. "You make me run ahead of my story, Miss Ferber." He lowered his voice. "Well, we figured the killer had to have her blood on the—instrument. We found a towel in your bathroom smeared with her blood. Killer wiped off the instrument."

"Interesting. So the killer was in no rush to leave."

"Probably *was*, truth to tell, but you can't walk out of the Nordale, even by the back door, with a bloody cane."

"You keep saying cane."

His eyes held mine, then shot to a frowning Clint. "This is what I gotta tell you, ma'am. Deputy Jamison located a cane this morning, tossed into the alley next to the Lacey Street Movie House, laying in some rubbish, some beer cans, just tossed there. Steel-tipped head, heavy-duty oak, solid, thick. No fingerprints, of course, wiped clean, but traces of blood on it."

My voice rose. "That can be anybody's cane."

"True." He eyed me, his look penetrating and hard. "You seem hell-bent on distancing Noah West from the murder, ma'am."

"Yes, I am. That young man could never do such a thing. Something I know to my core." My voice shook.

The man deliberated for a moment, but then decided to say nothing. He snubbed out the cigarette and thumbed the pack in his breast pocket.

A heartbeat.

Finally Clint said, "Chief, I guess you took in the lad?"

Chief Rawlins looked ready to leave, fidgeting with a shirt-sleeve cuff. He ignored Clint. "I just wanted to give you information about your room, Miss Ferber, so you won't think there's a murderer afoot, randomly…"

I interrupted him. "Sir, I assure you I don't think anyone was aiming for me. There are a half-dozen people who'd love to slaughter me, but all of them live in Manhattan, and at least one of them shares my blood. But not one of them, I assure you, has the courage to do the deed."

"I only meant…" He faltered. "I mean, someone was in your room."

"Yes. Waiting for Sonia. Someone who planned to kill her. Premeditated. Orchestrated. Someone who knew I was out for the evening. Someone who knew Sonia planned to meet me that night at nine. Someone who changed the time. A well-oiled scheme, carefully executed. Someone who chose Noah. The only question I have—actually I have more than one, but one pressing me at the moment—is why choose that time, why choose my room? There is a message being sent to me, I'm afraid." I paused. "Someone was afraid that she was going to tell me something."

"What?" asked Clint.

"The name of Jack and Sam's murderer. She had to be stopped from telling me."

Officer Rawlins looked uncomfortable. He tapped the pack of cigarettes, then looked to the doorway. He didn't want this conversation.

I looked at Chief Rawlins, my tone demanding. "But tell me, did you talk to Noah West?"

He clicked his tongue. "He wasn't home last night, as you know." A thin sliver of a smile as he turned to Clint. "We saw you slinking away, sir." Clint saluted him. "But this morning we found him at his home, rousing him from his bed, and took him in for questioning. Of course, he denies it all, and that's where it stands. Told him to stay put, we'd be getting back to him."

"You didn't arrest him?"

He deliberated. "No." He clicked his tongue. "Don't want to be—hasty. These are well-known folks."

"Sensible of you, sir. It would be a miscarriage of justice."

"That remains to be seen." He stood up. "This investigation is just beginning."

I reached out and touched his sleeve. "But your heart is set on arresting Noah West. Based on that witness's description." I rushed to add, "That very convenient description. Too pat, it seems to me. In your heart…"

"Not my heart, ma'am," he broke in. "But my instincts say he's dirty."

• ● ● ● •

Clint and I walked to Noah West's office in Indian Village where we found him sitting alone in his anteroom, his swivel chair pulled up to a side window. He was simply sitting there, idle, staring out the window into an alleyway. He didn't face us when we entered, though I detected a slight turn of his head, the flicker of a response.

"Noah."

He didn't move.

Clint walked up to him and put his hand on Noah's shoulder, letting his fingers linger there, a fatherly gesture. Noah turned slightly, looked up. "I'm all right." A hint of a smile, but he didn't look happy.

"I don't think you are," I told him.

He started to say something, but his voice cracked as he attempted to get control of his emotions. An actual smile, all those brilliant white teeth. "We're supposed to be stoic people, we Dené."

He swiveled the chair around, facing us, his eyes moist, and he motioned for us to sit.

"You don't look all right to me," Clint said.

"What did the police say?" I asked. "Chief Rawlins."

Noah closed his eyes for a moment. "They wake me at six this morning, pounding on my door, so loud that even Maxine Caln, next door, ninety if a day, comes running out in her nightgown and mismatched mukluks on her feet. And the first thing I learn is that Sonia is dead." He gulped, dipped his head. "I still cannot believe that. I never will."

"You hadn't heard about it?"

"How could I? I'd been playing cards with Tommy Hatch and his buddies, outside of town, a bunch of old school buddies from Fort Yukon and Arctic Village. We all got to talking, the way we always do. It got late, past three or so, so Tommy dropped me off in his pickup, sputtering all the way in the cold, and I topple into bed. I'm woken up a couple hours later with the awful news. I tell you—I couldn't breathe for a second. I stood there in the open doorway, half-dressed, groggy, the icy air flowing in, and I'm thinking that Sonia is dead. Is that what they're telling me? What are you saying to me? It just didn't come together for me." His lips trembled.

"I'm so sorry, Noah," I said.

His voice was scratchy. "Stupidly, I thought, God, how kind the police are. Everybody in Fairbanks knows Sonia and I are lovers, but how sweet, really." His eyes got moist. "Like notifying the next of kin. I felt touched. They didn't want me to hear it in the street. That's what I thought. But then, in seconds, I felt betrayed—stunned. 'You have to come with us,' Chief Rawlins said. And I'm thinking: What? To identify the body? What about Hank and Irina? All the odd, wrong things kept flying through my brain. I'm shaking from the cold. I'm groggy. I'm reeling from the news. And then I realize that I'm a suspect—this right after I realize Sonia has been murdered. Murdered, for God's sake. Jack—and Sam. Sonia fought me about Sam but…Sam. Murdered." He stopped, turned away, choked up. "They think I murdered Sonia." Said, the line seemed preposterous. "Murdered," he whispered. "That just seems… impossible."

"They took you to the station?"

"Yes." He smiled thinly. "Thankfully not in handcuffs. I kept thinking of Jack Webb and *Dragnet* on TV. But everyone was out in the street, Indians going off to their jobs in the restaurants, the garages, the warehouses, watching me get into the backseat of the squad car. The street just stopped, like a picture snapped, frozen in time. It was humiliating."

"But they didn't keep you."

His eyes locked with mine. "They kept after me. For the longest time. The grilling. Over and over the same questions, and I gave the same answers. The only answers I have, but not the ones they want. They gave me coffee so cold I had to spit it out. Bitter. And I'm thinking—they did this on purpose. Maybe. But Chief Rawlins…I know him. A decent guy in the past. Always. And I kept thinking that I had to get to Hank and Irina. I needed to be there with them. To grieve with them. With family. With Paul." A note of utter bitterness entered his voice now. "That's a laugh, really. That's when Chief Rawlins told me about the witness. The evidence—my famous flaming red parka with the colorful Athabascan trim, my cane, my limp. The whole picture. And I'm thinking—I'm not the only man in Fairbanks who limps, who uses a cane. Even such solid oak ones. There are a dozen souls around town like me—victims of frostbite, mining accidents, wilderness ordeals, plane crashes, even war injuries like mine. Lots of them. But you know what he said? 'You're the only Indian we know like that.'" He laughed. "Poster boy, again. War hero from Fort Yukon. Gwich'in lad now transformed into post-office mug shot."

"It's just questioning," Clint said.

His voice rose, hot. "It's accusation."

"But they let you go," I stressed.

"For now. What evidence do they have? An eyewitness, I suppose, who never saw the face. Rawlins acknowledged that—skimpy proof, no? He's not stupid."

"You been set up." From Clint.

Noah stood up. "I need coffee, some food. Something. I haven't eaten."

We walked a block over to Mimi's. At midday, inside the

dim room, the few tables were filled with Indians chattering away or eating bowls of beaver stew or plates of caribou and onions—I just assumed that because the chalkboard listed those as specials of the day.

Unhappy with the specials of the day—beaver?—I had vegetable soup while Noah and Clint chose the caribou. But I noted something else as we ordered. Noah, sitting back, seemed to relax, settling in, some of the bitterness dissipating, the tight, angry lines around his eyes vanishing, and in the shadowy light he looked boyish again. We didn't speak for a while, and I decided I would follow his lead. His silences, I sensed, were important to him. Clint, too, seemed to understand this, watching the young man with a gritty, fatherly possessiveness, seemingly anxious to talk but holding back. Noah gulped mugs of steaming black coffee, one after the other. He chain-smoked his Camels. He picked at his food. He relaxed.

He pointed his cigarette at both of us. "It was good to see the two of you walking into my office."

I said loudly, "I know you, Noah. I know what you are capable of...and, obviously, what you would never do."

"But you scarcely know me," he insisted.

I shook my head. "No matter. I know you."

Noah surprised me, putting his cigarette in an ashtray and reaching over and touching my wrist. His touch was so electric that I jumped. His smooth, warm palm held my hand, and my heart beat. Not good, I told myself. Not good, this. A fluttering of the heart. Nature's madness, exaggerated. An old woman, trembling.

For a second he closed his eyes. "You know what really got to me at the station, what really stunned me, was when they told me about Hank. What he said."

I looked at Clint. "Just what did Chief Rawlins say?"

Noah sighed. "You know, I understand his grief, his anger.

But I guess, at least from the chief's summary, that Hank immediately believed the worst of me, wanted me arrested then and there." Noah breathed in, the deep hurt back in his voice. "I've known him since I was a small boy in Fort Yukon. He's known me. He's been like a father to me. My own father died when I was seven. This is my family—Irina, Paul, Sonia. They welcomed me into their lives, their world. I could have been blood kin—the way I was treated. I was never made to feel like a poor Indian boy, some charity case shuffled off to school by do-gooders. Every step of the way—each achievement in school—they applauded me, swelled with pride. God, they sent me to prep school. When I dated Sonia, they were supportive, though that surprised them." He smiled. "And me, too, frankly. But Hank said I was the best thing for her. They worried about her...such a free spirit, a little wild." He spoke loudly. "She needed me...I...I gave her balance, I..."

Clint spoke up, his words rushed. "Hank is just feeling his hurt, Noah."

"No," Noah spoke harshly. "I can never look at him the same ever again."

Clint grunted, "That's a little harsh, Noah." He sighed. "The damn red parka."

"Tell me about your red parka, Noah."

A wistful smile. "Old Maxine next door made me that embroidery and beading that she herself sewed onto my red parka—a bunch of good-luck symbols, bits of wolf fur. How ironic that it identifies me as Sonia's murderer. Sitting in the back of that squad car made me feel...real Indian. I'm not a Petrievich, of course—never was. Now I'm the smart young Indian allowed to sit at the table who slaughtered the beautiful daughter."

"No," I said, my voice too loud.

Clint, angry. "Hank's a good man."

"Who isn't so good all of a sudden. Maybe he never realized

that he saw me as *other*." He tapped the table nervously. His eyes scanned the crowded room. "I can't get over the bitterness growing in me, and don't like it." He banged his fist on the table. "You know, I loved Sonia—I still do. It came out of nowhere, that love, and so it still sits inside me, like a part of me I was born with. And I wouldn't touch her. The Dené believe our spirits are one, you know. People, animals, trees. Interconnected. Like the caribou we hunt. There's a respect there. We shoot them but we thank the beast for serving us, for sustaining us. It's part of a grand scheme of life, you know. So I value that idea—it makes me think of my grandfather back at home, a man who taught me to respect life. Not just Qwich'in life, but all life. And," he sucked in his breath, "we certainly don't waste a loved one's life by taking that life away." He sipped coffee. "End of lecture."

Clint, quietly, "You ain't no murderer, Noah."

He smiled. "No, I'm not."

I tried to be logical. "You have to answer the chief, point by point. Like the business with the cane. I notice you don't use one today. And I noticed you didn't use one the other day. Last summer when I was here, yes."

He nodded. "I decided to stop using the cane months ago. I can walk, haltingly, it's true, but I wanted to rely on my own body. Yes, there are days when the pain is back, so I drag out the cane. But I try not to. I'm not toppling over."

"Someone purposely planted it in the movie house alley. It was easy to find."

"It's not mine. You know, I have two or three in my cabin. Ironically, all given me at Walter Reed where the doctors patched me up."

"There's no way of identifying it..." Clint began.

"And," Noah continued, "Chief Rawlins talked about me being at the Nordale around seven, which of course I was. Most nights I stop in to say hello to folks." He nodded at

Clint. "Like you, Clint. I check in. Lots of people know that. Everyone saw me talking—'animatedly,' according to Chief Rawlins—with folks there."

"You talked with Paul the night she died," I said.

"I was leaving, and we bumped into each other outside. Quick chat, friendly. That was it."

I sat back, nodding. "Noah, you know someone framed you—for a reason."

He nodded. "I know."

"This is hard to believe. Someone carefully orchestrated that murder and planned it so that you'd be suspected. You, in particular. That killer probably waited until there was someone else in the hallway, heard a door opening, heard movement, someone wanting to be spotted—otherwise why leave then? In any other scenario the killer would hope no one would spot him." I raised my voice. "You— they wanted it to be you."

"But why?" Clint asked.

"Because Noah is an easy target," I insisted. "Maybe your public spat with Sonia in the lounge the other day. Talked about. Gossiped. You know how Fairbanks is. A small world."

"The red parka," Noah added.

"Which you're not wearing, I notice."

"They took it from my home this morning."

"Of course," I said. "Evidence."

"Well, they are wrong about me," Noah said. He stood up. "I need to get back. Harlin Spence got drunk again last night and clobbered his wife. I gotta get him out of jail and back to work."

Noah dropped a few silver dollars on the table, held out his arm for me to grasp, and we moved away from the table.

But we stopped, stunned. The rhythm of the room shifted. The dark space, with a half-dozen tables occupied, had seemed quiet, subdued, as we ate our lunch. A tinny song on the juke-box, a country-western ditty, a scratchy record, low volume.

Nobody paid attention to the three of us. But now as Noah stood, the room suddenly came alive, like a movie frame unfrozen. As we moved slowly between the scattered tables, something was set in motion. A few men stood, young and old; a married couple, huddled together; even an old woman, toothless and shaking; some garage-mechanic boys, late teens, in dungarees; a cook in a filthy apron stepping out of the kitchen. They stood, these Indians, and as Noah walked by they tapped him on the shoulder, they patted his back, they mumbled in his ear. They nodded from the kitchen doorway, inclining their bodies toward him, acknowledging. I heard the strange Qwich'in dialect, a Babel of soft-spoken and over-lapped words, and I realized that they were showing, quietly and gracefully and certainly, a genuine regard and heartfelt support for the beleaguered young Athabascan.

Outside, in the cold, a red-faced Noah said to us, "Fairbanks is a small town. Everyone knows what has happened. The Dené"—he pointed back to the restaurant but also to the street where teenage boys leaned on pickups, cigarettes bobbing from sullen mouths—"they are telling me something."

I glanced at faces passing by. Everyone obviously knew what had happened to Noah—word of mouth about the murder of Sonia, his early-morning detainment, his questioning at the station. Everyone knew. And everyone wanted to nod at him, to mumble swallowed words, to communicate something. These were folks who understood that he was in danger, that he was one of their own, and a good, good man—not a rowdy troublemaking drunk, perhaps, or a wife beater, or a petty thief. This was Noah West, and he had been wrongly accused.

Watching, I was overwhelmingly touched. Tears came to my eyes.

But as we started back to his office, we also passed white folks, Fairbanks' other citizens, and everyone watched him closely, or made believe they were not watching him at all. No one touched his shoulders, tapped his arm, hummed in his ear.

Until, that is, we encountered Preston Strange and Jeremy Nunne leaving Stoffer's Bakery, Jeremy swinging a bag of pastries and munching on an enormous sugar doughnut. We almost collided, all of us, and Jeremy seemed particularly startled. We stood there, no one speaking in the awful moment.

Noah stopped walking. "Preston. Jeremy."

Jeremy seemed at a loss for words. But not so Preston. He sucked in his breath, looked around, narrowed his eyes, his nostrils flaring. He strode up to Noah and got close to his face. "I warned Sonia about you."

Jeremy reached out, touched his sleeve. "Preston, for God's sake. Do we need this? In public?"

"I don't care," Preston bellowed. "He should be hauled off to jail."

Noah's face reddened. He puffed out his cheeks. In a fierce, steely voice, he said, "Always the little brat, Preston."

His words startled Preston, who took a step forward. "Killer."

Noah arched his neck, glared into his face. "Maybe you're the killer."

Stunned, Preston rocked on his heels. Then, in a flash, his hand flew out, and he shoved Noah in the shoulder. Surprised, Noah flinched, but stood his ground. Jeremy looked horrified, blinking wildly, and pulled at Preston.

Preston's voice seethed. "Lawlessness. Celebrated in this horse town. And Paul. God, his own sister is murdered and he's defending the murderer. Everyone is talking about Paul taking his side."

Jeremy, his face beet red, grabbed Preston's arm and maneuvered him up the sidewalk. He hissed, "Another street brawl, Preston? Your mother is…"

"I don't give a damn about my mother."

Back in Noah's office, I noticed a change in him. Iciness covered him, and he even tucked in his head, turning away. He muttered something about work to do, Harlin Spence waiting to be sprung from jail. Feeling unwanted, I looked at Clint who nodded at me. Let's go. Let's leave the man alone. Frantic, I wanted to say something, though I was at a loss for words. So I simply walked away, mumbled my goodbye, but just as I left I glanced back to see Noah, still dressed in his parka—a dull gray one today and not that dreadful incendiary scarlet parka, that bullfighter's cape—slumped in his chair, facing out same window he'd stared out when I'd arrived earlier. He was a statue, his eyes riveted on the deserted parking lot outside, that squat space of packed snow and ice, with a couple broken-down jalopies, some rusted oil drums, shattered fence posts. A wasteland, that view, a place where people left their trash and hoped the snow would hide it.

Outside, Clint spoke into the silence. "You gotta save him, Edna."

"What?" I looked into his face. "What, Clint?"

He wagged a finger at me. "I know the Dené. I know how they're built, Edna. His pride's been hurt real bad, he feels suckered by folks who should love him, always said they loved him, and he'll let it crush him. He won't believe he's gotta defend himself because he's innocent. He don't understand that white folks don't play by such honorable rules."

"But he's a lawyer, Clint. Washington Law School, for God's sake. He understands American law."

"In his head, maybe. One part of him. But not in his heart. That's where the real Noah lives. In his heart he's an Athabascan."

"But what can I do?"

"Show him that he has to fight."

"How?"

"You got a big heart, Edna. Show it to him."

Chapter Thirteen

Irina Petrievich left a message at reception asking me to join them late that night. "We want to see you." A glass of sherry and some wild-raspberry strudel, Irina said in her note. "Please. We don't like leaving you alone at this sad time."

Paul picked me up at the Nordale and said little on the short ride to the Petrievich home. He sneezed, apologized. He sneezed again. Apologized. He reached into his pocket for a handkerchief. Sonia once mentioned Paul's history of long, nagging illnesses, in bed for weeks, shivering under blankets, plodding through the horrible winters.

"You have a cold?"

He grumbled. "You noticed?"

"Alaska doesn't agree with you."

"Truer words were never spoken, but they have nothing to do with my health. But, yes, our family doctor says I was born to live in the tropics. And the Fates plunked me down in a town where winter never ends and everyone is joyous when the temperature rises to zero." He shrugged. "I don't have the robust constitution of my warrior father."

I looked at his profile. "Do you go hunting in the Arctic with your father?"

He sneezed, apologized. "As a boy, yes. I did. The males in the family have no choice. Bonding, initiation, puberty reached when you shotgun a grizzly to death. I haven't gone in years. I see no need to freeze in a sagging wilderness cabin or tuck myself into a snow crevasse or skin the hide off a monstrous caribou. Outhouses have little appeal for me. So I stay here and ingest cough medicines."

"I was surprised at the invitation from your mother."

He glanced at me. "Why?"

"A time like this. Grieving. A family often wants to be alone at night."

He stared out the windshield. "My parents are committed to being...civil. The perfect hosts. And you're famous—here to visit them."

"No, Paul, I came to visit Fairbanks. Yes, them, too, because I consider them friends, but not..." I stopped.

He sucked in his breath. "I'm sorry. My words make me sound too...unforgiving. It's a sad house now. I think they don't want to be alone. They don't know how to deal with Sonia's death."

"And you?"

He looked away. "I keep to myself, Miss Ferber."

"I must tell you again how sorry I am, Paul."

He waited a bit. "I know." A heartbeat. "Me, too."

"You weren't close?"

He drew in his breath. "Nobody is close in my family."

He shot a quick glance at me.

"What?" I asked.

"I'm wondering what you think of me."

"Is that important?"

"Oddly, yes. I've watched you from across a room over the dinner table. You don't miss a thing. Sharp lady, you are."

"And what do you think I see?"

He deliberated a second. "Someone who isn't too happy with the family he was born into."

"But they're good people. Hank and Irina."

"They certainly are. But goodness has nothing to do with happiness. And now that Sonia's…gone, well, there's too big a hole in that house."

"It must be horrible for you to lose your sister like that."

But Paul stopped talking, hunched over the steering wheel as though unsure where he was going, and, arrived at the home, he rushed me inside, took my parka and scarves and gloves. As Hank and Irina greeted me, he slipped away, headed upstairs. I wondered why Paul still lived at home, a strange residence, given his professed disaffection for his family. He paused on the stairwell, turned, and caught my eye. In that moment I winced because his hasty look was cloudy and troubled.

We sat in the living room, the three of us. Hank was dressed in a suit but with his bolo necktie loosened. He looked tired, beat up, his wrinkles deep, rutted. Irina was in a black evening dress, a little too formal for an evening at home, and she wore a garish rhinestone brooch on the lapel. Her hair was pulled up into a French knot. Not very flattering, because Irina's small oval face now looked flat. She sat demurely on the sofa, both hands holding a goblet of water so tightly I feared the glass would shatter.

"We just feel so lost, Edna. We sit here and…"

"But," Hank interrupted, "we thought we'd spend some time with you. Your visit is so short. And this morning I was speaking to Ernest Gruening, who called with his condolences."

I nodded. "Yes, I got a telegram from him this morning. At the Nordale. Washington is cold, he says, but not from the temperature."

Irina sighed.

Hank bit his lip. "It's those damned Southern senators who hate us so fiercely. Strom Thurmond. Filibustering any debate. It has nothing to do with Alaska—they're just afraid of another vote against segregation. I…" A sheepish smile. "I can't seem to stop, can I?"

I didn't want to discuss statehood. Not now…not in this house of unbearable grief. Then why, I asked myself, was I sitting in Fairbanks in March, the end of a brutal winter? I could be in hot Arizona at a spa. Or—or in my toasty Manhattan apartment, sitting by a sputtering radiator as I gazed down into the cold New York streets. Or—a passable Sunday dinner with my lovely nieces at Passy, where the waiters bowed before me.

When I said nothing, Hank looked at Irina, then back at me. "We feel like we owe you an apology."

Hank's forefinger kept circling the rim of his whiskey glass. Every so often he took a sip, tentative and unsure, gazed into the glass, as though afraid it was empty. His eyes sought the bottle of whiskey sitting on a sideboard. He seemed to nod at it, an acknowledgment that the bottle hadn't moved. Slumped in the side chair, he sank into the cushions, his neck tilted to one side.

"I spent a few hours with Noah West." My words purposely bold, loud.

Irina spoke. "Yes, we heard." She glanced at Hank, who was frowning. "Dear Noah. You know, we'd hoped that he would be the one for her—to settle her down, you know. A good solid young man, a lawyer. Who cared deeply for her."

"Not now, Irina," Hank said.

She faltered. "A part of the…"

"Family," I finished for her.

"Yes."

I chose my words carefully. "He's grieving tonight."

She watched her husband. "Of course."

Hank looked away, uncomfortable.

Irina's eyes got wet. "I saw them married, you know…in my head…lovely…"

I waited a second. "Noah being an Indian didn't matter?"

Hank looked annoyed and spat out his words. "Of course not." He stammered, "I—we, that is—wanted him as a son-in-law."

Irina was nodding furiously.

For a moment he closed his eyes and seemed to relax. When he opened them, he wore a dreamy expression. "Edna, we've known Noah since he was a boy. I knew his father. His grandfather is still a friend, the old man up there in his log cabin in Fort Yukon. Noah West was…stable."

I sipped my wine. "You make it sound like a curse."

Hank looked over my shoulder. "In Alaska young men drift or wander and disappear. They have mercurial passions; they have pie-in-the-sky dreams. Wanderlust. Days of twenty-two hours of sunshine make them antsy. Months of winter grayness and darkness make them morose. Noah, as I say, was stable. It's a blessing."

"And yet you think he's capable of murdering your daughter."

My abrupt words stunned them. They shot looks at each other, Irina dropping her eyes into her lap. Hank downed his whiskey. Tasteless, perhaps, my tone, but so be it. Something had to be said.

"Not now, Edna, please." Irina was trembling.

"I like him."

"Everyone likes him."

Grabbing the edge of the table, Irina stood up. Sobbing, she rushed out of the room. I could hear her weeping in the kitchen. Hank watched me carefully, sadness in his eyes.

Hank poured me more wine, refilled his whiskey glass, and then stabbed at the dying fire. He seemed obsessed with the task, meticulous and steady, and watching, I said nothing, stared as he attacked the embers, added new logs, used a bellows. Bent over, face hardened, he looked mesmerized with the brilliant blaze.

For a while we sat there quietly, the two of us, lost in the fire.

There was a knock on the front door, someone was let in, and Clint Bullock's gravelly voice roared that he was late, sorry. Hank looked back at me. "I asked Clint Bullock to join us. I know you like that old prospector."

I nodded. Yes, I do.

Divested of parka but still clutching his gloves, Clint walked into the room, mumbling his apologies. "Had to help a man with a dogsled. For the carnival." He watched Hank resume his seat, and he nodded at me. "How you holding up, Hank?"

Hank smiled. "All right."

Clint's chuckle was dry. He scratched his beard. "Well, you ain't telling me the truth. I've knowed you since you was a young boy. Even then your shoulders turned in like a frightened bird when you was troubled."

Hank was nodding. "Clint, pour yourself a drink."

The sourdough went to a corner hutch and poured himself a tumbler of whiskey, downed it, refilled his glass. Hank and I watched him, and I caught Hank's eye—worry there, concern. Clint walked crookedly, as though favoring his left side. Bending, he winced, closed his eyes.

Hank looked distracted as Clint, sitting back, watched him closely, sizing him up. The crusty old pioneer settled in, scratching his beard again—I'd observed that it was a nervous habit of his—and gulping whiskey.

"Heard from Lucky Willis," Clint began. And in an explanation to me, "Old hunting buddy of ours. Crazy old coot, half Inuit, half Aleut, and hundred percent loner. He spent the winter in a tumbledown shack near the Canadian border. Weather turned real bad, and he got caught out in a snowstorm, lost four or five toes, in fact, dragged hisself to a military base. Just out of the hospital, here in Fairbanks. Funny old fool…wants to go back before someone steals his pelts." He

looked at Hank a long time. "Says to say hello to you." A
pause. "Asked me to tell you how sorry he was about…Sonia."

"Where did you see him?" Hank asked slowly.

"Drinking at the Mecca. Drunk as a skunk. Taking off his
shoes to show folks his bandages. Crazy."

Hank was nodding. "Damned good guide, I tell you. I
saw him face-off a grizzly like he was shooing a house cat."

Clint chuckled. "The man gotta be a hundred now. He was
old when I was setting traplines back on the Brooks Slope
back 'round 1910 or so. First time I seen him."

On and on they talked, the two of them, breezily so, contented, and sitting back, eyes half closed, I enjoyed the lazy
reminiscences of the two old men. I marveled at Clint, cleverly
working his quiet magic as he refocused a tense and shattered
Hank. Both men leaned in, as though over a campfire, swap-
ping anecdotes about the old days. Hank talked of being a
young, happy-go-lucky boy, hunting with his father, coming
down the Yukon River on a first boat after the spring break-up
and being stranded in Fort Yukon. Of hunting lodges, of
caribou, of long days munching on stale pilot bread and
salmonberries, gnawing on roasted porcupine. He recalled
Noah's grandfather teaching him to make a fire with birch
fungus and flint. The time Clint and Hank got stuck on the
icy tundra and had to burrow into a snowdrift and cover
themselves with spruce branches, huddled together under a
lemon-yellow sky so close you could touch it. On and on,
rambling, drifting, while I sat and listened.

Something happened to Hank. His body relaxed, his dull
eyes brightened, his hands quivered like young birds. I savored
the transformation, oddly pleased, for a moment his grief
contained. This was a man who'd tackled life head on, adven-
turesome, fierce, driven, a man happier away from cities and
newspapers and money and homes—and even, I supposed,
family. The young man, fearless, striking out, headed toward

the sun-blazed horizon. The man who once holed up in a shabby cabin deep in the Arctic tundra, buried under caribou hides, lulled by the hooting of the snowy owl and the cawing of the raven as night deepened and there was not loneliness but solitude.

On and on, the two talking, the rich man in the disheveled evening suit, his tie loosened, his speech thick with whiskey; the other, the rugged prospector who never had a dime to throw away.

I thrilled to it, really.

"Edna, I'm sorry. We're boring you." From Hank, looking away from Clint.

"On the contrary, Hank. This is why I came to Alaska."

Clint winked at me. "Hank and I know the real Alaska, Edna." He breathed in. "There's an old saying: Once you've weathered the Bush, you'll never be the same."

"Those were the days." Hank's voice got melancholic, breaking at the end. My heart went out to him. "Do you know Robert W. Service, our poet laureate? The first words a child in Alaska learns, you know." He breathed in. "'There's a whisper on the night wind, there's a star agleam to guide us; and the wind is calling, calling. Let's go.'" His hands trembled. "'Let's go.'"

Clint and I smiled, and Hank bowed.

"'The wind is calling, calling,'" Clint echoed.

Suddenly Hank closed his eyes, tears seeping out, and the whiskey glass slipped out of his hand.

"Over," he whispered. "Over."

Chapter Fourteen

While waiting for Clint, I sipped steaming coffee at the Gold Nugget. I stared out the grimy window at the dull façade of the Nordale. The ice fog had passed, replaced by a bone-marrow cold, scattered ice crystals speckling the air. I sat with a paperback—the same Herman Wouk bestseller—but I gazed idly up and down the busy Second Avenue. How could folks live like this? The endless gray of the long, long winter barely mitigated by the fleeting brilliance of a summer of almost perpetual sunlight. Bad for the system. It would wreak havoc with my regimen, my eight hours of sleep (in darkness), followed by a brisk morning walk (in daylight). The way God intended human beings to live. Of course.

I watched the street, expectant. The people striding past seemed robots, numb from the bitter cold. I wondered what these hurrying folks thought of the murder of one of its most visible citizens? Poor Sonia, who'd sailed up and down Second Avenue, hell-bent on her titillating stories for *The Gold*. A car chugged by, spewing exhaust, pulling in front of the Arcade by the Cottage Café. An Air Force lad, dressed for summer in a skimpy jacket, scurried into a doorway. He threw back his head as he ran, shivering from the cold.

A contradictory town, this Fairbanks, I considered, with decrepit log cabins juxtaposed against towering futuristic skyscrapers, with craggy sourdoughs bumping into high-heeled socialites dining on Polynesian meals at the Tradewinds. Teenagers giggled at the soda fountain counter at the Co-Op Drug Store, while Indians tethered silver-furred malamutes outside the hardware store. A town where folks lined up to see the newest Disney flick at the Lacey Street Movies, and everyone seemed to be young and bustling—vibrant, thrilled. So many pregnant women, proud, happy. A town where there were ten airline offices in a half-block stretch of street. A laundry with the ridiculous blinking neon sign: The Pantorium. Prices for everything were staggering, unbelievable. Bread for a quarter. Outlandish. Bananas a quarter a piece. An emperor's treasure, coveted. A town in which people paid for everything in shiny silver dollars.

Outside a sudden blur of ice crystals slapped against the window. As I looked up, I spotted Jeremy Nunne sitting across the room, but suddenly he approached, trying to get my attention, hovering over my table and making gulping sounds.

"Yes?" I tapped my coffee cup, Morse code clicking. I held up my hand. "Yes?" I repeated.

He rolled his tongue over his lips, smiling crookedly. "I just want to say—I need to say—I know nothing about Sonia's murder. Preston's behavior is not—mine." He went on, almost panicky. "I don't know why he confronts folks."

I watched him, this gawky young man with tuffs of cowlicky brown hair, washed-out eyes, a chubby man not attractive but somehow charming, an overfed huckleberry boy. He should be painting Tom Sawyer's picket fence somewhere in a Norman Rockwell illustration.

"Why are you telling me this, Mr. Nunne?"

Exasperated, "Because I don't want to be in the middle of…murder." He shivered.

"So I'm assuming you didn't kill Sonia?"

He yelped. "For God's sake, Miss Ferber. I met Sonia a couple times, talked to her, you know, and I don't understand how this could have happened. I'm just getting to know Alaska, new here, don't like it here, I think, but…" He looked over my shoulder.

"But what?"

"Alaska confuses me."

Suddenly I was intrigued by the young man. "How so?"

"You know, I walk out on Second Avenue"—he pointed out the window—"and I feel like I'm in a foreign country. I never expected a part of the United States so…foreign. I fly to Anchorage and I walk down gravel roads in the center of town. But what gets to me are the old Klondike ghost towns, like Dyea or Knik. Falling shacks and faded signs. The shacks with the broken windows and sagging boards. Too much death, Miss Ferber. In Alaska death is only a step away. It's like a step into darkness. So the murder of Sonia strikes me as—I don't know—part of the curse of Alaska. My aunt Tessa insisted. The cannery at Bristol Bay—a horror show. And now Fairbanks—me heading Northern Lights Airways." A thin smile. "And the dark part of Alaska's soul. Jack Mabie. And Sam Pilot. Dead. Dead. Somehow it…doesn't surprise. I…" He faltered. "I don't know what I'm talking about. I'm sorry. I don't want to be a part of this."

"Is Preston part of this?"

He blanched. "He's a good man."

"That doesn't answer my question."

"Maybe it was a mistake talking to you."

With that, he turned and walked out of the café. He crossed paths with Clint, and the two men stopped, considered each other. Jeremy made a half wave that he seemed to regret. And then he was gone.

I watched Clint walk toward me. "Morning, Clint. Join me."

"Was planning to. A woman alone at breakfast is a lonely sight."

"How about a man alone at breakfast?"

"Just pitiful, that's all."

Clint settled in, ordered flapjacks and blueberries. I chose sourdough pancakes and one scrambled egg. Lots more hot coffee.

"Does everybody in Alaska have to cover everything with blueberries?"

He nodded. "Yes—and steaming coffee, a pot of it." Which he drank black, in big, hearty gulps.

Clint grumbled, "That Jeremy is a strange bird, no? He looked like he seen a ghost."

I laughed. "He did—me. We just had a strange talk, the two of us. He's so…" I stopped, startled, pointed to the doorway. "Round two, I suppose."

Preston Strange was standing in the doorway, looking around. Impatient, he ignored the waitress who approached him. I motioned to Clint. "Look."

"Fairbanks' most annoying citizen," he sneered.

"You don't like him?"

"A coward who…" He stopped as Preston, spotting us, strode across the room, pulling off gloves and a beaver-skin cap.

"Miss Ferber." His tone was all business. "Clint. Hello." We nodded. Then, without asking, he slid into an empty seat next to Clint. Preston nodded as the waitress put a cup on the table, and he poured coffee from Clint's pot. Clint eyed him, a frown on his face, but Preston was looking at me. "The hotel told me you were here, Miss Ferber."

"Can I help you with something?" I wasn't happy. "Can I pour milk into your coffee?"

He was momentarily taken aback, glancing at the cup, but shook his head. "No, thanks, I drink my coffee black."

I looked at Clint, who rolled his eyeballs.

Preston spoke hurriedly. "Miss Ferber, I've been looking for you."

"And now you've found me."

He didn't look happy. "Yes, I have. I've been sent here by my mother. She wishes to see you, if you're free."

"Now?"

"If you're free."

"What is this about?"

He squirmed and shrugged his shoulders. "I have no idea. None whatsoever. But Sonia's murder has rattled her." He looked at Clint as he took a sip of coffee. "I just do her bidding." He made a face. "This death is beyond the pale. It... baffles." He stopped, letting his voice trail off. Then, leaning in, speaking in a soft voice, "My mother collapsed last night—just passed out. The doctor said it was stress, really. And cigarettes, of course. And too much drink. We thought we were going to lose her. Now she's lying in bed, medicated." He grinned stupidly. "Though the pills don't seem to stem her tirades."

"And she wants to see me?"

"First thing this morning, she said—'Preston, implore Miss Ferber to see me. It's urgent.'" Resentment seeped into his voice. "Everything my mother does is labeled urgent. So I warn you—expect to be disappointed."

"I'm not certain what to do." I looked at Clint.

A pleading voice. "She'll only send me back to bother you, Miss Ferber."

I fussed with my coffee, indecisive. Preston sat there, a slick man in double-breasted suit, a speck of dried shaving cream on his cheek. He started to stand, but slipped back to the seat. "I'm just the messenger boy here." He sucked in his cheeks. "Don't shoot me."

• • ● • •

I found Tessa in her bedroom, a large high-ceilinged room at the back of the house, probably once a den. Floor-to-ceiling knotty-pine paneling and empty bookcases and corner hutches. A big sleigh bed was positioned in the center of the room. Black lacquer Art Deco bureaus and mirrors and chests lined the walls. Rose-colored flocked wallpaper hung on one wall, decades old, peeling. Novels on a nightstand. A stack of Francis Parkinson Keyes paperbacks. *Peyton Place* in hardcover. Another thick tome, the spine cracked. Craning my neck, I read the title: *Not as a Stranger.* Another pot-boiler bestseller I refused to read.

I glanced out the back window: a white wasteland out there, cords of wood stacked neatly against a shed, a bank of pale green spruce that led to a frozen rivulet, shadowy under the hazy sky.

Tessa was a mound of flesh, lying prone under fluffy pink blankets, her head inclined and resting against a stack of pillows.

"My request is intrusive, Edna." She struggled for breath. "I know."

"I'm sorry to hear you've had a spell…"

"I thought I was dying." She sighed audibly, motioning to a chair. "Such a moment does wonders for clarity."

Preston, nearby, busied himself in the room. Tessa looked at her son. "Could you please leave us alone, Preston?"

"Mother, I…"

"Now."

He hesitated, but her unblinking stare made him back out. She turned to me. "My son is waiting for me to die."

"Preston?"

"Yes, I only have one son, dear Edna." She closed her eyes. "Preston…he always had a temper. Unfortunate."

I pulled up my chair, closer. Tessa hadn't bathed: an odor that suggested old rags, an unwashed body, too much flesh lying there, unmoving. I pushed my chair away. "What can I do for you?"

Tessa narrowed her eyes. "First, close the door." She waited while I got up and shut the thick oak door. "Murder is so… messy." For a second she closed her eyes, seemed to be asleep. When she opened them, she stared at me. "Hand me a cigarette, Edna."

"Is that a good idea?"

"Of course, it isn't. But do it."

I took a cigarette off the nightstand and handed it to her. I struck a match and lit it. Tessa immediately began to cough, and, assailed by the obnoxious odor, I fell back into my chair.

"Smoke bother you?" Tessa asked.

I waited a second. "Why am I here?"

A long coughing fit. "I'm an old fat lady so it doesn't matter anymore. Except to him." She nodded toward the closed door.

I was impatient. "I don't see how I…"

Tessa raised her hand. "Let me finish, for God's sake. I'm the one telling the story. Our family is a powerful Fairbanks family, as you know. Of course, you know that."

"I still don't see…"

Her look shut me up. She snubbed out the cigarette in an ashtray placed on her bed, by her pillows. I could see a half-dozen butts piled there. One had slipped out onto the bed linens.

She struggled to sit up in bed, pulling herself up so that she was almost sitting, but she started coughing. "So much going on. Sonia's murder. Last night I thought I was dying. I…"

"Tessa, does this have to do with Sonia's murder? With the other murders?"

She shivered. "She came here. I wouldn't talk to her."

Surprised, I said quickly, "Sonia? When?"

"A day before she was murdered." Again the shiver, the trembling hand. Tessa's face blanched, her lips drawn into a tight line. Anger in her eyes. "Yes, she was here, but I wouldn't let her in." Tessa looked away. "Perhaps a mistake."

"But I don't understand."

She reached out and her fingers grasped a slip of paper. "She left me this note." She handed it to me. "Read it."

A short note, scribbled on a piece of lined paper:

Tessa,

I need a name. You knew the players back when. Your missionary days. The North. You have a story to tell me. Jack Mabie. The Indian. Sam Pilot. Help me name a murderer.

Sonia

The note shook in my hand. "My God."

"Exactly."

"The players? You? When? She thought you could name the murderer of those two men?"

Her body shook. "I should have called after her." A harsh high laugh. "But I didn't trust her—didn't like the girl. What players? Jack Mabie, that dreadful man she profiled. Killed by—that Indian. Sam Pilot. I never knew them, Edna. Believe me. Reputation, yes. Dangerous men from the North. Maybe I spotted them—once. I can't remember. But never...*knew* him—them."

"Then why did she need to see you? She thought..."

Her face got pale. "I'm too old for this...these shenanigans."

My words sharp. "Tessa, c'mon. Three people have died—murdered."

She avoided looking at me. "I hate that—word."

"What do you want me to do, Tessa?"

She breathed in. "Doesn't this point to Noah? The man who carried all that past out of Fort Yukon to Fairbanks? Because of the Indian. His relative—that Sam Pilot."

My fury grew. "Quite a stretch, Tessa. Noah, a little boy back then."

"You heard me. A relative of Sam Pilot, I've been told. Family vengeance. He exacted a price."

"So?"

"Do I have to spell it out for you? The sins of the father. Age-old blood feud. Indians are very tribal, Edna. I know them. Shamans, blood lust, warriors. Noah in his lawyer's suit—nothing but an Indian in the boardroom. An old wrong must be righted."

I counted a beat. "Perhaps your fears are close to home. Your Preston."

She ignored that. "It's obvious. Indian revenge."

"No," I broke in. "You're wary of a new scandal—especially with Preston. Somehow Sonia connected somebody to—you. Or your son." I glanced at the note. "This note has to go to Chief of Police Rawlins. Now. It may help him solve this murder."

She screamed at me. "I want you to understand Noah and that dark world up there, Indians, blood feuds, angers." She threw a sidelong glance at me. "Rumors, Edna. A spy told me Sonia's note to you that night had a warning at the end—Don't tell Noah. She was meeting you with information."

I paused, alarmed. "True, but..."

"Because she knew Noah was a murderer."

"You're assuming a lot, Tessa." I counted a heartbeat. "This note from Sonia... You'd better call the chief." I paused. "Or I will tell him to make you a visit."

She fumbled. "My name must be kept out of this."

"It's too late for that."

"Edna."

"No."

I grunted to make my point, gathered my parka, and fled the room. As I strode down the hallway into the living room, I suddenly came face to face with Preston. He froze as I neared, his upturned face expectant, solemn. He'd probably listened outside Tessa's bedroom.

"Miss Ferber."

"Preston, did your mother tell you about that note from Sonia?"

He blanched, stammered, "No, I...She..."

From the back bedroom came a low, moaning sound: Tessa, listening to us in the living room. For a moment we were quiet, startled by the noise. Putting on my coat and gloves, I moved past him and headed to the door. "Preston," I demanded, "I need a lift to the hotel."

Begrudgingly, he followed me to the door.

In the car he said in a quiet voice, "My mother worries that I killed Sonia."

"Did you?"

His jaw dropped. "How dare you!"

"This is a house of secrets. Your mother, you. Tell me."

His face got pinched, drawn. "I don't have a secret."

"I don't know if I believe you."

"Well, I can't help that."

"Do you think Noah West killed Sonia?" I asked so bluntly his hands slipped off the wheel.

Mechanically, he drummed his fingers on the dashboard. He spoke through clenched teeth. "Of course not. He wouldn't swat a fly, that man."

"But..."

"None of this makes any sense to me." His voice broke. "I'm an innocent man, Miss Ferber."

"Does your mother believe that?"

He didn't answer.

A long pause as I watched his profile. "Your mother is a liar, Preston."

A slight pause, then he burst out laughing, ending with a dry chuckle. "Miss Ferber, this is not news."

Chapter Fifteen

Clint Bullock asked me to go for an early supper, and he suggested a restaurant he liked at the edge of town, out on the dirt road that led to the airport. I'd suggested pan-fried chicken at Count's Dinner House on Noble and Lacey, but Clint pooh-poohed that. Too highfalutin, he claimed. So, bundled against the bitter night cold under a clear, bright sky, I waited outside the Nordale as Clint pulled up in an old beat-up Army-surplus Jeep that spewed blue-black fumes into the still air.

"It ain't mine," he confessed.

In the front seat I felt smothered under jets of warm air. In the night sky, far overhead, wispy tracks of aurora borealis appeared, drifting ribbons of pale green and yellow and rose. To me, it looked eerie, a narcotic reverie, these Fairbanks nights, but what startled me was that most citizens seemed to take the fairy-tale splendor for granted.

At first glance the Bunker Roadhouse looked like no-man's land. Clint just chuckled when I said I was hesitant to enter a place that was a ramshackle two-story log cabin leaning precariously to one side, with one window boarded over and two rusted Standard Oil drums positioned by the entrance, with running pickups and sagging station wagons lined up in front, some hooked up to headbolt heaters.

"You got that right. If I had to lay odds for a bar fight that landed one or both parties in the hospital, odds are here's the place. Tonight." He looked at me. "But the food is damn good. I know you're an eater, Edna."

"True, though I prefer my dessert not be served to me as I lie on a gurney in some emergency room."

He punched me in the arm.

I expected booming jukebox music, some irritating and horribly nasal country-western song about lost or unrequited love or honky-tonk licentiousness. I wasn't disappointed. We walked through a packed barroom, noisy and boisterous, and Clint yelled over the hoopla. "Place was a typical roadhouse in the old days, but the city sort of growed out to reach it. Neighborhood place, locals. No tourists—the place scares them."

"It scares me."

He looked at me. "Nothing scares you, Edna."

I breathed in. "Always a first."

"You're old. Too late to start being scared."

He led me into a small dining room, away from the front bar, where folks sat quietly at the pinewood tables, and no one seemed to be talking. Too quiet. Not a waitress in sight. The smell of burnt grease in the air. I sniffed.

"Bear grease," Clint announced, and I looked to see whether he was joking.

At one point, glancing back to the bar, I saw a young girl working her way among the men. I whispered to Clint. "A call girl."

"Yeah," he answered, nonplused. "That what you call her." He was enjoying himself. "So what?"

That stunned me, this cavalier manner, but I thought, *Yes, so what?*

"Who are these people?"

"Place was abandoned some years back, just walked away

from, but Johnny Miner picked it up. Mainly-white but part-Athabascan gent from up Chalkyisik, in the North. Drifted down here, opened this here tavern, and probably is responsible for the dereliction of a good many of the Indians and shanty whites around here."

"How noble."

"Hey, I didn't say it was good. But the place attracts the locals, mostly Natives, but some whites, down-and-out guys, especially the ones married to Native girls. Lots of stuff happens here, and most of it ain't nobody's business."

"Why do you like it?"

"I already told you, Edna. Some of the best damn food in town." He grinned. "Why else would I drag you here?"

And he was right, as it turned out. I asked for a menu, was told there was none. What was served was what the cook— Johnny Miner's wife—concocted that night, take it or leave it. And what was served, I noted, was heaped upon the table, gigantic portions slipping off the edges of the chipped, stained plates. I viewed it all with righteous disdain, but Clint dug in like a hungry wolf, and I, starved, gingerly sampled something at the edge of my dish that didn't look life-threatening. It was delicious. "What is it?"

"Just a wild duck fried up in a spider's web frying pan, splattered with a thick huckleberry sauce. Nothing fancy. What you're nibbling at is a little reindeer hash, done with duck eggs." He laughed. "Duck everywhere on your dish. Johnny must have had the shotgun out this morning."

I no longer believed Clint's recitations. I simply assumed it was a roast chicken, probably bought at the local Piggly Wiggly down the street. But certainly savory—done just right, skin crispy and peppery, the meat juicy and rich. We didn't talk, and the waitress, a sullen high-school girl in a dirty smock, hovered nearby, ready to whisk the crockery away. For dessert there was a wild cranberry cobbler, light and airy, slightly tart, undercut by the wetness of the brown-crusted cake. I sighed, sat back.

"I told you you'd go for it," Clint said.

Over cups of tea I filled Clint in on Tessa's strange conversation. "She wants Noah guilty."

"But why you, Edna?"

I shrugged. "She knows I'm Noah's advocate. Maybe she was trying to convince me."

"And take the suspicion off of Preston."

Clint was lighting his pipe. He grunted.

"And she brought up Sonia's line on her note to me—'Don't tell Noah.'"

He fumed. "Yeah, that sticks in my craw, too."

"What was she up to?"

A young couple sat down at the table next to us, noisy, a little drunk. Clint turned, frowned, and I saw his face tighten. Even I started. Noah West's pretty sister, Maria, was laughing too loudly, and, throwing back her head, she spotted us. She stopped, glanced at the man she was with. For a moment she looked uncertain, but yelled out, "Clint Bullock, you old coot. And…I've met you. I met you with Noah. You're the lady from Outside."

"Edna Ferber."

"The writer," she said. I nodded. "You're writing something, Noah said."

Maria was sloppily drunk. So was the young man with her, who seemed unable to follow the threads of the meager conversation, his head sailing back and forth until, spent, he stopped, looked for a waitress.

Maria was dressed in a faded blue dress, a decade out of fashion, with shoulder pads and polka-dot collar. A canteen girl from the last war, some Arctic Andrews Sister. The dress was ill-fitting, too snug at the shoulders, and there was a tear in a sleeve. Worse, when Maria grinned at me, she showed a smear of brilliant scarlet lipstick on her front teeth. Under the stark overhead light her makeup, foolishly applied, seemed garish, a young woman's copying of a look she'd spotted, say, in a Lana Turner movie at the Lacey Street Movies or, perhaps, in the glossy pages of *Photoplay* or *Modern Screen*. Whatever the source, it suggested a bar girl, and at the moment, a tipsy one. The waitress came to her table and she ordered a couple of beers. The man she was with, bellowing after the waitress, called for food. He wanted reindeer steak, but the waitress, shaking her head, said, "Stan, come on, you know you gotta eat what Lila makes in the kitchen." She laughed and took off.

"This is Stan," Maria said to us. She reached out and poked him in the shoulder.

Surprisingly, Stan stood up, walked to our table and vigorously shook our hands. An unsteady half-bow. "Stan Stepkowski. Newark."

"New Jersey?" I asked.

"Yeah, born and bred. Raised on pirogies and a whole lot of boiled cabbage." Again, the gallant if failed half-bow. He toppled back down into his chair, stretched out his long legs.

I found myself liking him, this big buffoon of a man, not fat but broad and sturdy, a thick barrel chest, with a crew cut that still revealed an arguably very blond head. He flashed dusty pale blue eyes in a wide freckled face. A hill of a man, in flannel and denim.

"Stan is my boyfriend." Maria slurred her words.

Stan winked at her.

"You live in Fairbanks?" I asked him.

"I'm at the Ladd Air Force base outside of town. Career man, I am. I fought in Germany, final days of the war, flew over Germany with the last of the bombing. A sight you never forget, ma'am. Now I'm in exile in this here Alaska, which they keep telling me is part of the U.S. of A., but I don't believe it."

I noticed Clint had gotten quiet during the exchange,

glaring at the ebullient Stan Stepkowski, but avoiding eye contact with Maria, who was giggling and playfully tapping the young man in the chest.

Finally Clint said, loudly, "Maria, you do know Noah is in trouble?"

For a second Maria looked wild-eyed, glancing at Stan, then back at Clint. "Yeah, I know." A stark, deadened voice.

"They think he murdered Sonia."

"He didn't do it." Flat out, fierce. She glanced at Stan who looked baffled at the shift in conversation.

"How do you know?" I asked her.

She waited a long time, running her tongue over her lips. "Noah's up-and-up, always."

Stan was leaning into her, stroking her neck. She tried to brush him away.

"But…" Clint was livid.

"Look." Maria shook herself free of Stan. "Stop it, Stan." She glanced toward the bar. "I love Noah but, you know, he don't know how to play the game." She paused, glanced at Stan, lowering her voice. "With white people."

"What do you mean?" I asked.

"I mean, you don't go to the schools. Their schools. Then go after rich women, the—you know, that life. And then, you know, you don't start mouthing crap about Indian injustice and Athabascan legend and stuff. No one wants to hear that. If you're gonna be in that world, you gotta…like…smile and…" She shook her head as she looked at Stan, a fake smile on her face. "You smile." She looked back at us. A boozy hiccough escaped her throat. "Never mind. Noah is my little brother. I love him. Nobody ain't more important to me. But I can't make no sense out of him. Never could. I always looked out for him, no matter what. And he can't make no sense out of me. Never could. But he…you know…he got a problem with my life. My life."

"Sam Pilot was staying with you," I said.

"Yeah. Blood."

"Did he ever tell you anything? His thoughts…I mean, Noah thinks he was murdered. So do I."

Maria looked scared. "This is real crazy."

"Is it?" Clint asked.

"He was a drunk—damn drunk."

"What about Jack Mabie?"

"I didn't know him."

"Did Sam talk about him? After all, he was staying with you."

"Something was bothering him." She held up her hand as she watched me closely. "I don't want to think about it," she mumbled, her slurred words running together. But suddenly she looked nervous, stealing a glance at Stan. "It don't make no sense to me." She sucked in her breath. "When Noah was a small boy, we was walking around Fort Yukon, our cabin, you know, and some white guy up there had shot this white ptarmigan, like just for the hell of it, blew it to bits in front of us, leaving the carcass there to rot on the banks of the Yukon. He didn't do it for food or nothing. And Noah starts to bawl like a little baby, and he's digging a hole in the ice with a stick to cover the bird. That's Noah. I mean, he was always a nutty little kid." She shook her head. "I don't want to talk about this no more. Stan and me wanna have a good time. He has to be back in a couple hours." She turned away.

I persisted. "What was bothering Sam?"

She shrugged. "Dunno. I *told* you." A panicky look. "Come on, Stan. We ain't staying here."

She left the table, and Stan, baffled, waved dumbly at us and rushed out after her.

• ● ● ● ● •

Driving back to the Nordale, Clint confided, "She loves Noah, you know. She does, Edna. They only got each other. But she don't want too much to do with him. Him and his la-di-dah law degree and his fiery letters to the editors about the Gwich'in language, the injustice to the Dené."

"Tell me about her."

He sighed. "If you look at her, you know her, Edna. That girl wears her life on her face. She's been in and out of Fairbanks since she was a teenage girl. Had a real tough life back then. Trouble. Lots of it. A pretty girl, but she fell into the seamy life here. The Row. Back when the area was behind an eleven-foot fence with a gate, and the girls sat in their cribs and waited for men. She used to be one of the hookers at the roadhouses. That's how she lived. The only life she knew back then. Drifted into it."

"That's why Noah is crazy?"

"Yeah, mostly. She's older now, hooks up with lonely Air Force men. Like this Joe Palooka fellow. It lasts a while, they buy her nice things, make promises to her that even she don't believe, sometimes they beat her up, which she expects, and then she's running around with a new guy. Same story over and over. Gets more desperate year after year."

"This Stan…he seems decent."

"Maybe. Maybe not. All men are decent when you first meet them, Edna." Clint shook his head. "She likes blond and big and nothing that looks like he was bred on caribou steak and salmon candy. Now and then she slips back into the bar scene, you know, a working girl. Mostly she works at the drug store in Indian Village. She drinks too much. Lots of Indians do. End of story."

"It's amazing how much she and Noah look alike."

"Yeah." Clint nodded. "Two kids with great looks. She uses her looks to get silver dollars."

"And Noah?"

"I don't think he owns a mirror."

The Jeep chugged to a stop and I peered out into the night. Clint had stopped in front of Noah's cabin. He pointed. We stared at the dark cabin. I saw one light on in the front, a shade-less window, but the rest of the place was pitch-black. As we sat there, Noah—I assumed it was Noah—moved across the room, paused by the front window. Did he spot the Jeep idling there, heater blasting, headlights probing the fierce night air? But the figure disappeared, and then there was nothing but the block of solid yellow. I felt like a voyeur. Yet it was overwhelmingly compelling, sitting there. Doubtless Maria was back at the roadhouse, sloppy in the arms of that bulky military man. Here Noah, her brother, stood in his bright, square room. Suddenly the yellow light disappeared, and the house was gone, disappeared into the heavy darkness of the night.

I felt a chill pass through me. I shivered. "Take me back to the hotel," I demanded of Clint, touching his sleeve. He put the Jeep in gear, but it stalled, sputtered. He started it again, but I panicked, my voice high. "Take me back, Clint. I don't want to be here."

Chapter Sixteen

All of Fairbanks, it seemed, packed St. Matthew's Episcopalian Church for Sonia's funeral. It was a day of impenetrable ice fog, the dense air thick with fuzzy, mottled light from the car headlights. Cars inched along, a ghost train, and once inside the church, people seemed drugged. Even the aisles were filled with standing black-clad mourners.

I disliked attending the services, though I knew I had no choice. I also had no black dress, so my dark gray wool skirt and creamy white frilly blouse had to suffice. I disliked all funerals, always had. They reminded me of war, of nightmare, of dying. And these days it was my own demise that I thought of. Not that I feared death—it was perhaps preferable to lunch with some New Yorkers I knew—but I didn't like the idea that others would survive me. I fully expected a nasty obituary. My enemies would do me dirt. That fellow at the *Saturday Review*, that bilious critic who routinely skewered my novels. And, lamentably, my sister Fannie, older, but rangy and venomous. No, Fannie would have to go first.

Such were my vagrant thoughts as I sat, demurely and unobtrusively, in a back pew, my mind far away and unable to focus on the flower-draped coffin in front of the altar. The words of the minister, singsong and hypnotic, lulled the hot chapel, and an old man, two pews over, was snoring so loudly a woman on his left had a fit of giggles.

I surveyed the crowd of mourners and caught Clint's eye, giving him a slight nod. To my surprise, Clint was dressed in a suit. Used to his shabby wool shirts, denim, mukluks, and ragged parkas, I was wide-eyed at his lime-green, wide-lapelled suit, something I imagined Xavier Cugat might employ in conducting his marvelous band. Clint nodded at me, and, conscious of his incongruous attire, pinched the collar of his suit and grinned. I smiled wanly.

I looked for Noah. He wasn't in the chapel, but I suspected he wouldn't be, of course. That bothered me. He was the one who should have been there.

After the service ended, friends gathered at Hank and Irina's home, and the housekeeper Millie dutifully offered coffee and cake, though I noticed most of the men headed for the sideboard for drinks. A man I didn't know saw me watching and asked if I wanted a rye-and-ginger highball. I took nothing. When Paul passed by me, I touched his arm. "Paul, tell me, why wasn't Noah West at the service?"

He looked surprised. "He probably knew every eye would be on him. Accusing eyes, hostile. Would you want that?"

"Of course not. But he must have wanted to come, no?"

"He sent flowers."

"Which ones were they?"

Paul sucked in his cheeks and shook his head. "The ones you didn't see. My father wouldn't allow them in the chapel."

"Oh, Paul, he still believes…"

Paul leaned in, and I saw how tired he looked, how red his eyes were. "My father's always been a stubborn man, Miss Ferber. A whole part of him knows it's all foolish, that Noah West is innocent, was obviously set up, but another part locked onto that idea of Noah leaving that hotel room, blood staining his cane. It's like he can't shake himself free of an idea he knows isn't true."

"How sad." I looked around the room. "How very sad."

Hank stood among a cluster of men, one of them with a comforting hand on his shoulder.

"Not so much sad as…pathetic. Really, Miss Ferber. It's tiresome, really, this…" He made a clicking sound. "What the hell." He walked away.

Weary, I sat in an armchair in a corner, quiet, hands folded in my lap, watching people move up to Irina and Hank, mumble a few consoling words and then slide away, a curious and beautiful rhythm I marveled at, this civilized ebb and flow of regard and sympathy. But I still wondered about Noah—bothered, even annoyed. My question to Paul had been purposeful because I wanted to gauge the temper of the family. I hadn't seen Noah in two days, not since that late-night glimpse of the solitary man in the cabin window, and that abrupt shutting of his light. The dark cabin. That image stayed with me, nagged at me.

But this morning, leaving for the funeral, I'd found a brief note in my mailbox in the lobby, a few words that oddly comforted then alarmed me.

"Edna, my apology for silence. And, I suppose, moodiness. I'll buy you lunch tomorrow. My office at twelve? I've been dreaming of black ravens, but that's a good thing. Noah." In parenthesis he'd scribbled, *"Innocent, as charged."*

Tomorrow—back into the world.

On the day of Sonia's funeral, he'd be hiding out, the outlaw in his cabin.

The afternoon dragged on. As folks began straggling away, hand-shaking and hugging, I gathered my purse, adjusted my pearls, and prepared to say goodbye. I'd said nothing to anyone, other than those few words to Paul and a thank you to Millie who offered me tea, and, given my imperious demeanor as I sat in the blue velvet wing chair, no one had dared approach me. But as I sought out Irina, I watched her leave a small cluster of women and approach me, take my hand.

"Don't leave, Edna. We haven't spoken. I've been trying to get to you. Please stay for an early supper. Just the family."

"I'm not family."

Irina squinted. "I'd like you to stay. Hank needs people he likes around him now."

I tried to soften my voice. "I'm not sure Hank would want me at the supper table, Irina. I'm Noah West's advocate. Frankly."

She tightened her grip on my hand. "I'm asking you to stay."

I nodded. All right.

So I lingered in the den, my hands idly leafing through a dog-eared *Look* magazine as the guests straggled out and the house grew quiet. At one point Millie walked in and quietly, stone-faced, placed a pot of tea on a silver tray at my elbow, nodded, and started to leave. I called her back. "Millie, how long have you worked for Hank and Irina?"

The Indian woman seemed hesitant but smiled. "Twenty years, maybe. Since I was a young girl."

"Were you born in Fort Yukon?"

"No, in Eagle, nearby." She started to back away.

"You know Noah?"

"Of course."

"You like him?"

"Everybody likes him."

"Are you bothered by the accusations of murder?"

Millie fidgeted, looked back to the doorway. "You do not know the Dené," she whispered.

"I'm making you uncomfortable. I'm sorry."

Millie turned, then seemed to change her mind. "Noah took my brother's case when they said he took stuff from the store he worked at. It was a lie. And Noah tells them that."

"And what happened?"

She glanced toward the door. "And Noah, he takes no money for it. Not a penny. My brother is out of work for months, with seven kids. In a two-room cabin." Then, her voice rising, strong, "That's Noah."

"How can we help Noah, then? Help me."

Millie looked confused, but seemed to be thinking. I waited. She stared at the wall. Then, in a loud, clear voice, "Don't let him hide."

"What?"

"Don't let him disappear." She smiled. "It's easy for us sometimes. We go back to places where we understand the rules."

I said hurriedly, "Millie, please. I don't understand. Where is that?"

"Not in Fairbanks."

"But where?" Helpless.

"In the snow where you are alone."

She left the room.

I sat mulling over Millie's cryptic words, and then, my mind racing, I walked around the room, stopping in front of a bookcase. Numbly, I leafed through a book on Hank's shelf and settled back into my chair. I'd chosen one of Ernest Gruening's tomes on Alaska and saw it was heavily marked up with (I assumed) Hank's annotations, marginal comments like: *yes, emphasize this; underscore; good rebuttal; weak but possible; Eisenhower is wild card…*A flurry of black ink in the margins.

Someone tapped me on the shoulder. I woke with a start. Irina was smiling. "Edna, you dozed off."

I shook the cobwebs out of my head. "Alaskans like their rooms overheated."

"Come dine with us."

I had no idea why I was asked to be at the mournful supper, but immediately I regretted it. Sitting with Irina and Hank at the long mahogany table, candle-lit, I watched as Paul walked in, tardy, mumbling an excuse about some valedictory with an old college buddy from the University of Alaska who'd arrived late to pay his respects. No one answered him, and he slid into a seat and fumbled with the napkin. Four of us seated there, uncomfortable.

Millie served a supper of pot roast, boiled potatoes, a salad of stewed tomatoes, and lots of coffee, at least for me.

"A nice service." Irina's voice was louder than I expected.

Hank looked up. "What?"

She cleared her throat. "The day—a nice service."

For a while Irina chatted about unseasonably cold March weather, about a planned trip to Sitka to visit relatives, about a letter from a distant cousin in Nome. Telegrams from everyone, a flood of them: Ernest Gruening and Bob Bartlett in Washington. Walter Hinkle. Eleanor Roosevelt, surprisingly. James Cagney. Even Carl Lomen, an arch-statehood foe from Nome, who sent a heartfelt wire. Irina turned to me. "He's the Reindeer King"—a remark that confused me. Wildly, I thought—Isn't that Santa Claus? And I almost said that out loud, though immediately I thought better of it. It seemed almost a monologue, Irene's reverie, though I interjected appropriate vocal responses. Paul quietly picked at his food and looked ready to flee.

Finally, out of the blue, Irina concluded, "Life will never be the same for us, I'm afraid." But her voice was strong, as though she were fashioning a vow.

Hank muttered, "The heart has been cut out of this family."

An awful silence in the room.

"What?" his wife asked.

"Something died long ago."

Paul, snippy, "Why do you say that?"

Irina spoke energetically. "We are a family, Hank. We can't forget that. Because we lost Sonia…"

Hank cut in, "We didn't lose Sonia, Irina. She was taken away from us."

She snapped back, "You know what I mean."

"It doesn't matter," Hank snarled, his eyes glassy.

Paul looked at his father. "What does that mean?"

Irina was frowning. "You're not making much sense, Hank."

Hank banged his fist on the table. "Well, thank you."

I blundered into the storm. "Maybe we shouldn't…"

Hank sat back, closed his eyes. When he opened them, he reached for his glass, downed his whiskey.

Irina muttered, "We have something. We have a family, Hank. What do you think you're looking at?"

Hank sank into his chair. "I guess so." His smile was lazy, a waking man's. "I suppose so. But, you know, I woke up this morning and lay in bed and I thought: What a hole in our lives. Sonia was such a…presence." He paused. "I vacillate from that to"—a long pause, frightful—"Noah. Noah West. It's hard to say his name. One story. The other. Both. I don't know."

Paul pleaded, "God, Dad, come on."

Hank narrowed his eyes. "I think, somehow someone… you know, she pushed the wrong button, probed somewhere, asked someone the wrong question. Alienated people with money to lose. She told everyone she was on the hunt for two murderers. That scared people. At the church today I saw Preston Strange and Jeremy Nunne. At Sonia's funeral. Why were they there?"

Irina bit her lip. "For God's sake, Hank. In times like these people show respect in a town like this."

"My daughter is dead." He spat out the words, then teared up.

"For Christ's sake, Dad." Paul crumbled a piece of bread, pieces falling onto the table.

Hank shook his head. "I drive myself crazy. I can't help

it. I look at the people and I think: Who did this to my girl? Did you? Did you? Did I do something that led to it? Could I have stopped it? And then I look around for Noah West, expecting him to be in church. A part of me wanted him there, not because I wanted to hurt him, but because he's always been around us. He's always been there when we needed him. Then I think: But maybe he murdered Sonia…" Paul grunted, rolled his eyes. "Yeah, yeah, I know, but I can't get that image of him leaving Edna's room out of my head."

"Hank, you do realize that Noah was purposely set up, don't you?" I said quietly. "Someone waited to leave my room, so that there'd be a witness. That parka…"

"Yes, I do," Hank admitted. "Of course. That's obvious, but it doesn't help. But she told him goodbye. Go away. The day before."

Paul muttered, "Do we have to have this conversation now?"

Irina reached across the table and touched his arm. "Paul, enough, for God's sake."

Hank wasn't even listening to them. "You know why I can't get Noah out of my head? I'll tell you. It's not just the witness who saw Noah—or someone like Noah. And that remark on the note to Edna—'Don't tell Noah.' But I lay in bed that night and I remembered something Sonia said to me. I'd forgotten something else she said the day before. We were sitting in the Gold Nugget having coffee, our afternoon ritual. She said when she told Noah she wanted…you know, to be apart, he said, 'This time I think you're serious.' And she said a real hurt came into his eyes. She said it *scared* her—that bad. 'I'm gonna have to hurt him real bad,' she said."

Irina protested, "Scared *for* him, Hank. Not *of* him."

"I know, I know. But I can't help it."

Paul, in a hollow voice, "Did you tell this to Chief Rawlins?"

"Of course."

"Great," Paul said sarcastically. "You're trying to put a noose around his neck."

Hank spoke in a barely audible voice. "Maybe it belongs there."

Shutting his eyes, Hank seemed to tire of the meal and the conversation. His fingers gripped the whiskey glass, but then he pushed it away. Paul fidgeted, shoved his plate away and lit a cigarette, sat back with his arms folded over his chest. Irina sat stiff-backed, hands on the table, glaring at her husband. Hank, the dominant leader of the household, now appeared to have lost his energy. Whenever I'd thought about him before, I considered a robust man, hearty, backslapping, boisterous. A man who liked control, impatient with contrariness, a man who blustered his way into millions and power, a frontier titan.

Curious, this sea change in Irina. She was the obedient wife in the shadows who spoke in whispers, the quiet cheerleader behind her quarterback husband. Now, bizarrely, there seemed a switching of souls: Hank, lifeless, negative, a man whose brio had vanished, a man whose wilderness energy was no more. And Irina was like a piece of ice-cold glass, iron-rod spine, in control, as though she figured any salvation in this family had to begin with her.

Irina was talking about the cousins, then about Tessa Strange. I hadn't been listening. "What did you say about Tessa?"

Irina glanced at the sullen Hank. "Tessa sent a note in the morning. To Hank and me. It was beautiful, really, a few sentences that I thought nice, a real understanding of our loss."

Hank looked up, but said nothing.

Paul seemed irritated. "You didn't tell me she'd sent a note."

Hank glowered at his son.

I tried to change the subject. "Hank, did you finish going through Sonia's papers in her apartment?"

"Yes."

"Nothing helpful?"

"Nothing that relates to the murder."

"Did you tell Chief Rawlins?" Irina asked. "I mean, they did want to go over everything themselves…"

"Yeah, he and his men also went through them."

"And?"

"Nothing. As expected." Then a long pause. "Before they got there…I burned her journal."

"What?" From Paul.

"And some bits and pieces of her life at *The Gold*," he said. "I burned them." He drew his lips into a thin line. "I don't care. Nothing to do with the murder. I didn't want the public reading about her personal life."

"Do the police know you did this?" I asked, unhappy. "And how do you know? You could have missed something."

"Dad, do you know how wrong all this is?" Paul said.

He frowned. "No." A pause. "And you're not gonna tell them."

Paul narrowed his eyes.

"Did she talk about Noah West?"

Hank refused to answer, but there was a sidelong glance, a slight thrust of his head, that told me he was not being truthful. He'd discovered something. I was convinced of it. There had to be more to his easy condemnation of Noah West—there had to be! If so, why burn them? Why not give them to the police? That was logical…

"What bits and pieces?" I asked quietly.

He shook his head back and forth. "Nothing. Scraps of paper. Nonsense."

"Dad."

"Stop it," Hank yelled. Then softer, "I want to mourn my daughter." He closed his eyes.

No one spoke as Millie came in to clear away the dishes.

Chapter Seventeen

As I walked to Noah's cabin to meet him for lunch, I spotted Clint, also headed there, and we fell in together. "I thought I'd drop in. I'm worried about him," he told me.

When Noah opened his door, he seemed surprised to see us both together. "Good." A pause. "The three of us can have lunch."

Noah moved quickly around his small room, grabbing his parka, gloves, scarf. A lot of clutter in his cabin, I noted, but clutter I condoned—stacks of books on the floor, on a table, even on the sofa, and an uneven stack of newspapers, *The Gold*, the *Fairbanks Daily News-Miner*, even *Jessen's Weekly*. A well-read man, and I liked that. But he seemed in a hurry to leave the rooms. Antsy, he kept up a flow of chatter.

I put my hand on his sleeve as he pulled on his parka. "Slow down, Noah."

He looked at me and blinked wildly. It was as though I'd turned off a switch because the Noah who walked outside with us was a different man, taciturn and withdrawn. I didn't know what to make of it. When I called his name, he paused in his stride, turned to me, and the look on his face was of a startled schoolboy, called to task for some antic.

"Are you all right?"

He nodded. "Cabin fever." A quiet laugh. "From someone

who actually lives in a cabin." But there was no humor in his voice.

As we walked, I noticed his limp seemed more pronounced, as though he'd not stretched his limbs for days. I watched him closely. And as we settled at a table at Mimi's, we struggled for words, then finally gave up. Again Noah ordered for us and slapped down a pile of silver dollars on the table—at the beginning of the meal. What was he telling us? I wondered. Homemade bread, thick and crusty, with smoked salmon. Sweet, teeth-numbing blueberry fudge for dessert.

We ate in silence, Noah famished, chomping on the food, rushing through it. Nervously, I watched him.

"Your note surprised me," I began. "About meeting you today."

He looked sheepish. "I was feeling guilty about my silence— hiding away. I do that sometimes, you know. I hide from friends." He waved his hand across the crowded room where now I was conscious of Indian eyes on us, steely, protective. "Outside of here, you are my connection to that world."

I remembered what Hank's housekeeper said. "Why do you hide away?"

He wiped his mouth with a napkin, looked down at his empty plate. "It helps me check in with myself."

Clint was clicking his tongue, though he never took his eyes off Noah's face.

"But you don't want to…disappear."

He gave me a weak smile. "In Alaska people disappear. Right, Clint?" The old sourdough nodded. "In the dark night of winter, out on the glassy crevasses and glaciers and tundra, people head out and don't come back. Planes vanish. Hikers become ghosts. Alaskans accept that. Every family has people who've disappeared. Certainly every Indian or Eskimo family…"

"And you?"

He ignored me. "Plane crashes, wild animals, a sudden

gale, an ice storm, and you're a memory. But, you know, the Athabascans—at least the Qwich'in folk I love—are used to isolation. That's all I mean, Edna. We live alone on the trap-lines in isolated cabins in winter, enduring the long brutal cold. It's our nature. It's not a bad thing, such disappearances. When we need to deal with something serious, we pull away, hide in the spruce groves under the shadows thrown by the walls of ice. A good thing, most times, but it can be danger-ous."

"Dangerous?"

"Because sometimes it's tempting not to return."

I was confused by his words, unhappy. "Return to what?"

"This." He pointed out the window at the busy street. "I mean Fairbanks. Or Anchorage. Nome. Towns out there. The more Athabascans move away from ancient lands and into white man's cities, the more our power is taken away. We lose our spirit. You know, I've been thinking about that for the last couple days, as I hid in my cabin. The only way to survive is to keep that power." He tapped his chest. "Inside."

"I don't want you to disappear." For a second I choked up, and turned away.

"It's not a choice sometimes." He sighed. "I know the Dené need to integrate with whites to survive—this is the world we inherited—but we have to keep our past intact, our touch-stone to those herds of caribou roaming across the taiga. Or the grizzled elder of the village sitting alone for a long, long winter in a wilderness cabin. Solitary confinement makes white people go mad," he grinned, "but for Athabascans it's a way of talking intelligently to yourself."

"I don't like your use of the word 'dangerous.'"

He laughed. "I don't mean to scare you. The fact of the matter is that most souls find a balance. Don't worry about me..."

I was nosy. "Who in your family disappeared?"

Clint cleared his throat. "A long time ago, Edna."

I got the message, and was quiet.

Noah said, "Come with me now, Edna. I have to stop in at the tribal office. Some of the militants don't cater to white folks, but they know Clint, and he's one of us." Clint beamed. "And, Edna, everyone knows who you are. You have the seal of approval from Noah West, poster boy."

Noah needed to pick up some legal papers at a small hall a few streets over, a general store with a gritty bar attached, a smoky pool hall, clanging pinball machines, and in the rear a long, narrow room filled with folding tables and mismatched chairs. At first I assumed the room was empty, but from a side room I heard off-key singing, an old woman's voice, cracking and scratchy.

"Aunt Lucy," Noah called out and the singing stopped. An ancient woman, tiny and bony, appeared, wiping her hands on a towel. Dressed in a plain cotton smock bleached as white as her abundant hair, the woman rocked as she walked. When she saw Noah, she smiled broadly—she had almost no teeth—but then narrowed her eyes as she focused on Clint and me. Then, blinking, she recognized Clint and nodded at him, said something in staccato Qwich'in, and he nodded back, even said a few words. Noah introduced me.

"Oh, my boy, I know who she is. The famous Outsider."

"The story of my life." I bowed, smiling.

Noah introduced me to Lucy Children, the great-grand-mother of the Dené. The People. "Leastwise," he grinned, "the Fort Yukon branch."

For a few minutes Noah bustled around, showing me Lucy's homemade crafts sold at the tourist shops in the hotels. A ceremonial mask made of caribou fur and bone. Beaded floral barrettes, splashes of clashing color, fashioned from moose hide and seed beads. The old, gnarled fingers still moved deftly through tough hide, he said—years of tanning hides and harvesting king salmon from the fish wheels. Her fingers reaching into a cabinet, Lucy presented me with a gift: a sun-catcher made of caribou skin and beads dyed yellow from ground wolf moss. Flushed, I said I would send her one of my books.

"I can't read no English."

We sat there while Noah leafed through the papers he'd retrieved from an inner office. Clint chatted with Lucy like old friends, their fragmented talk a haphazard mix of Qwich'in and crude English.

When we were ready to leave, Lucy leaned into me. "I understands that your heart beats alongside Noah's."

"What?" Surprised.

"I understands you helps save our boy from the wolves."

Clint grinned. "The mukluk telegraph, Edna. News walks through Alaska."

Flustered, I mumbled, "Who said I have any power…?"

The old woman got too close to me, her face a mask of deep wrinkles, and I stared into her old cloudy eyes. "You don't have to tell me. Your eyes do. And the way you look at Noah."

Noah looked embarrassed. "Grandmother believes that goodness heals."

"And so you do," Lucy admonished, sharply.

"I…" I began, but Lucy shook her head. Her expression told me to be quiet.

Rocking in her chair, Lucy talked. "Back in the old days a young man was careless with himself and others of the village, no respects for nothing. He don't listens to the elders. In those days there was shamans who cast spells, talked to spirits, talked of the future, talked to the dead. The young man, foul-mouthed, one day he kills a caribou for sport. He is showing off for his buddies. He shoot the animal on the edge of town at twilight, and he, lazy, lazy, cruel, he leave it there. The wolves ravage it, the bones they clanged and knocked and the wind blew them across the land, down into the village.

No one thanked that animal for giving its life—for food, for clothing." She stopped and looked into my face. "You understands? The need to thank?"

I nodded. "I've heard..."

But her words rolled over mine. "And all winter the peoples in the village they suffers, and the wind never stops and the snow is hard. Fires go out, bears walk on the trails, wolves howl, little children die. In the spring everyone wait for thaw, breaking up, and the swimming salmon. They wait. Nothing happens. The Yukon stays frozen, buckled. March, April, May, even June." She turned to Clint. "Youse remember the ice in the summer?" She shivered.

Clint leaned in. "A bad summer. You can't forget..."

"People are skeletons. It's a village that's icebound. The elders saw the lazy young man—he wanders the tundra, crazy, skinny, hungry. And someone remembers the caribou bones strewn here and there. So the elders talk to the young man and tell him—go into the wilderness, you go alone without a parka or mukluks, without a stick, and you finds the caribou king and beg forgiveness. Crazy, he did, he got to, and he finds a caribou bone, and carves an amulet to wear around his neck. At night, sleeping on the snow, the caribou come to him and thank him for the amulet, and the boy, waking, is saved."

She winked at Noah, flashed that toothless smile. "The happy ending, yes, my boy?"

He grinned back. "Grandmother, all the endings of your stories are happy."

She waved a hand at him. "He bring justice back to the village. And the boy, shirtless in the cold, his feet bare, comes home, and as he is walking the temperature rises, red poppies bloom in the snow, and the Yukon is no longer icebound. And the caribou come back, led by a blessed raven, and the fox and the rabbit and the otter and the seal. Then everyone understood that, yes, a wrong had been righted."

She nodded at me.

"But Fairbanks is not a Qwich'in village, Grandmother," Noah said quietly.

"All Alaska is our village. There is a lazy evil boy out there. The white elders think it's you. They must be shown the truth." Turning to me, a twinkle in her eye, she whispered, "Your job, old woman."

But Noah leaned into me, whispering, "No, our job, Edna. The two of us. For Sonia. For Jack and Sam."

"The two of us," I echoed.

• • ● • •

Clint left us, headed back to his log cabin. "Got me a touch of the sniffles."

I lingered with Noah. He wanted to drive, so I climbed into his battered clunker, a decades-old Ford with ripped seats and cruel springs, with a grinding sound whenever he made a left turn. He grinned. "I'll do my best just to make right turns only."

A chilly, gray afternoon, but the air was clear, windless. The heater blasted. He drove and drove, out past the gold dredge, onto the university grounds, then to Ladd Air Force Base, and dreamy from the puffy heat, we talked. He asked about the funeral, about Hank and Irina, about Paul. "I sent flowers. I don't know why. It seemed wrong for me to do it. I don't know why."

"I know."

He looked at me. "Does Hank still hate me?"

"No, Noah, he's filled with grief."

I noticed his hands tighten on the steering wheel. "I'll never understand what happened. You know, lately I've been thinking a lot about the years I lived in the Lower Forty-eight. I mean, my years in prep school, at the University in Washington.

"Why now?"

"Well, I never really thought about difference—skin color, race. Not until I went down there. Hank's family sheltered me. Sure, prep school in Massachusetts was a safe haven. I made friends right away. I was an Alaskan and damned proud of it. Back home, the few redneck slights bounced off me. I was a kid. Some drunk oil bum spitting at me in Nome. Hank and Irina have always been courageous folks. Those were the days of heavy-duty discrimination, though it's outlawed now. Natives couldn't go into some stores, hotels, even bars. Keep out. One sign actually said: 'Indians and dogs not served.' I used to have that sign—I stole it with some friends of mine, hanging it on my bedroom door. But, you know, educated people—the Hanks and Sonias and Pauls—made no distinction."

"Your heart was in Alaska."

"I couldn't wait to get back to Alaska. This was my home. I ran back to Hank and Irina, almost out of breath. And they welcomed me."

"And they will again."

He snapped at me. "I don't know if I want to go back there."

"Don't become hard, Noah." I touched him on the sleeve.

He shrugged. "Too late."

"I don't believe that."

He pulled into a parking space alongside a landing on the Chena River. "Let's walk a bit, Edna." Outside he said, "Cover your face."

The air felt good after the warmth of the car. Twilight now, the early setting of the sun. A blue-gray light in the air, the wispy pastel strands of aurora borealis hazy in the distance. Walls of packed snow, turquoise-blue. We strolled along the banks of the dead winter river.

"In your note you mentioned dreaming of ravens."

Noah laughed. "A good omen, Edna. The black raven,

chulyin, created the world, dug rivers with his feet, survived, tricky, but with a spiritual power. I value that dream."

"Tell that to Edgar Allan Poe."

Noah got serious. "The police stopped in to see me again. Rawlins and his deputy. Some commissioner. A bigwig I didn't know who reminded me that Hank and his family are powerful—that this murder has to be solved. More questions. Even less friendly than before. It was like they were ready for a confession from me. The man kept saying that lots of folks saw me on the street outside the Nordale that night, looking suspicious, waiting, in my famous parka…"

"But we've been through this."

"What else do they have? I fully expect to be arrested for murder."

"Why haven't they arrested you?"

"I asked them."

"And?"

"Well, the witness didn't see my face—just the red parka and cane." Noah smiled. "The chief said they're gathering evidence."

Startled, I looked into his face. "Like what?"

He shook his head. "I guess I'll find that out when they come for me."

"What will you do?"

"What do you mean?" He stopped walking and stared off at rosy-tipped Denali, disappearing into the darkness.

"I don't know what I mean."

"Edna, I'm a lawyer. An American lawyer. I've been trained in American jurisprudence. I value the law. To me it's not white man's law—but law. Law is imperfect, but the concept of law is sacred to me. I have to trust…"

"Well, I have less faith in our system than you do, obviously."

He was staring at the darkening hills to the north. "I spend my life defending Indians. I tell them to trust the law."

"Who killed Sonia?" I blurted out. "You must have thought a lot about it."

"That's all I think about."

"This is scary. Three murders."

"And the killer probably feels safe now."

"These murders are connected."

"I agree. Someone killed Jack..."

I interrupted. "Then Sam—to cover up. Because Sam knew the killer."

"And then Sonia—because she learned who killed the men."

"But who?"

He checked off reasons with his fingers. "My conclusions are obvious. Someone from the old days. It was someone who wouldn't be out of place in the Nordale Hotel. Someone who knew I stopped in most nights, lingered in the lounge. Someone who knows the hotel, especially the little-used back entrance, the dark parking lot in back, stairwells, the hallways, even the shifts of the housekeepers. The easy-to-open locks. How else to pull off such a murder...and to implicate me?"

"Why you, Noah?"

"Because of Sonia?"

"Maybe."

"Your connection to Sam?"

"Few knew that."

"Someone who had to get rid of Jack first."

"Jack knew something."

"But what? An old drunk."

"And Sam knew it, too."

"Sonia's death was necessity. She learned something. She had to be stopped—and quickly."

"The first two were—vengeful."

"Yes," I agreed. "The men were easy targets. Outside a bar. Late. Drunk. But Sonia's was carefully planned." He was nodding at me. "Someone intended to implicate you. The parka was chosen because everyone recognizes you in it. Someone slapped on that trim. Maybe not even Athabascan. The red color was what was important. And that cane. The killer wanted to be seen by that tourist."

"Not hard to locate a red parka in Fairbanks."

"But someone who also knew *my* plans. Someone who knew I was at the high school till around nine. My obligation."

"And someone who knew what Sonia's plans were that day—her flying alone to Tanacross, gone for the day. Someone who must have talked to her and knew she planned on meeting you that night, knew how to orchestrate a change at reception. Someone she felt comfortable talking to."

"A spy at *The Gold*, maybe. Tessa mentioned her spies."

"Someone phoning Preston? News for Tessa?"

I shivered from the cold. "And, most importantly, someone who knew what she wanted to tell me that night. Obviously, someone who knew her secret."

"True. If only we knew who'd she'd talked to that last morning, we'd know who did it. Who was in *The Gold* offices early that morning? Anyone? Or the night before? Did she stop there first? Who did she talk to?"

"That's the problem. Sonia talked too much—but never enough. Maybe she blabbed to someone at breakfast, at the airport, anywhere, hinting at solving the two murders, mentioning meeting me that night, and someone overheard her."

Noah nodded. "Everyone in Fairbanks listens in on others' lives. That's what we do here."

"Your winters are too long and dark."

"Edna, I want to fly up to Fort Yukon in a few days. I need to see my grandfather. If they let me leave Fairbanks. Away from here. I need to breathe again. Come with me." He reached out to touch my wrist.

That surprised me. "God, no. It's winter. I was in Kotzebue

two years ago, Eskimo land, and it was forty below. I still feel numb when I think of it."

He tapped my wrist. "Come with me."

I shook my head. "God, no."

He smiled and faced me. "You're…you're cold, Edna, I can see. Back to the car. C'mon. I need to get you back to the hotel and a pot of hot tea."

At the entrance of the Nordale I asked him, "Are you all right?"

"At first I couldn't sleep at night, rolling and tossing, agitated as hell. But last night I slept like a baby."

That surprised me. "How?"

He grinned. "I finally remembered something. Surefire medicine. I rummaged in an old bureau and found a tattered blanket my grandfather gave me when I was home in Fort Yukon one winter and caught sick. He wrapped me in the smelly old blanket. It's moldy and musty and smells of rotten apples and seal oil. But last night I covered myself with it, and I slept."

"It has magical powers," I said, smiling.

"Of course it does."

"It's a blanket, Noah."

"No, Edna, you don't understand. It's my grandfather's breath."

Chapter Eighteen

Late afternoon, an empty hour, I sat by myself at a window table in the Gold Nugget. I'd ordered a powdered doughnut and hot coffee but touched neither. With lazy, half-closed eyes, I gazed out the grimy plate-glass window across Second Avenue at the frozen cars and the occasional scurrying pedestrian, and considered the Nordale Hotel with its drab beige exterior, built on a block overwhelmed by airline offices, their clunky signs cluttering the façades: Wien, Alaskan, Pan Am, Pacific. Northern Lights Airways. Tessa Strange's company. Jeremy Nunne strolling in, a newspaper tucked under his arm. One after the other. What a strange land, this Alaska. Folks spent their time trying to get off the ground.

Hank Petrievich, hatless, walked by, gazed at something in the window of the Co-Op Drug Store, looked at his watch, and headed to *The Gold* offices. When I left the café, I decided to drop in to talk to him.

He seemed surprised to see me. I pointed to his clothing. "A new look?"

A checkered wool shirt, open at the neck. I couldn't remember him in anything but a pressed dress shirt and bolo tie, the kind a sensible western businessman might wear, with cuff links made of whalebone, the man of affairs in the rough-and-tumble town. Now Hank looked like a man who no longer knew how to wear clothes. His shirt was wrinkled, too resolutely casual, and too—I winced—dude ranch.

I slipped into a chair across from him. For a moment he gazed out the window. "Nobody's in town." The title of one of my books, I realized, but I doubted he knew that. "I'm expecting Paul." Another glance out the window. "He avoids me. He spends so little time at home now that I gotta make an appointment to see him." His words clipped, low.

"You seem angry, Hank."

His tone was biting. "You're our guest in Fairbanks, Edna. Our friend."

"I am that." I watched him. The corners of his mouth crinkled, tightened, and he sucked in his breath.

"I wonder about that."

"What's going on, Hank? I can't believe you're mad at me. Are you?"

A long silence. "I sure am."

"Tell me."

"Noah West." Two words, weighty, explosive, an epitaph. I nodded knowingly. "I spent all of yesterday with him."

"I know."

"So that's it. The mukluk telegraph. I'm not allowed to do so?" I bit my lower lip. "There was a time when you spent days with him."

"That was before he murdered my daughter."

"For God's sake, Hank, a little over the top, no? What has happened to innocent until proven guilty? You, of all people. A newsman, First Amendment rights, all that Constitution language…"

His eyes closed a second, then popped open. "I know, I know, I'm being unfair. I don't know what I mean anymore."

"Yes, you are."

"I don't care."

"What does that mean?" I asked.

"I know I'm being irrational. I *know* Noah was set up. A whole part of me believes that. Well, a good part of the time. But then, waking up from a nightmare, sweating, frightened, I think—maybe not." A deep sigh. "How do I know? I keep playing that scene at the hotel in my head—him striking her over the head over and over. In a fit of passion, jealousy. Old lovers—a quarrel that got out of hand. I don't know."

"This was no spat between lovers that got suddenly nasty. You know that."

He nodded furiously. "I know, I know." He looked me in the eye. He scratched his face, and I noted his nails were bitten to the quick: a thin line of dried blood. "Then I've horribly wronged someone I love, and I can't go back."

"Hank, you're better than this."

He looked at me and his eyes got watery. "Am I? I used to think I was, lofty and smug and liberal and tolerant…"

"You're still that man."

"I never was that man, maybe."

"Noah has done everything you've ever wanted or expected from him."

"True," he admitted. "Except…"

"Except what?"

"Marry my daughter. I wanted that."

"And now he's a leper."

He shook his head. "I'm discovering whole parts of myself that are ugly." Abruptly, he shifted the subject. "What did the two of you talk about yesterday? And Clint, my old buddy. Another one. You were at Mimi's, you went to the Brotherhood Hall, you and Noah walked along the Chena at twilight…"

I smiled. "Spies?"

"You don't build a great newspaper in Fairbanks without a network."

"It's not important what we talked about, Hank. And it's private."

A flash of anger. "Yes, it is. Did you talk about Sonia?"

"Of course." A pause. "Noah mentioned sending flowers."

I actually saw his face flush. "That was childish of me, throwing out those flowers."

"Yes, it was."

"What else?"

"Hank, please. I can't do this."

He slammed his fist down on the table. "It's important."

"I will tell you one thing. Noah and I believe the murderer is someone who knew Sonia's plans intimately, someone who had already killed Jack Mabie and Sam Pilot."

He got quiet. "I've thought the same thing."

"Any word from the police? Anything?"

He glanced over his shoulder, back to the small cubicle that had been Sonia's office. "The police spent another morning in Sonia's office, going through her papers, examining all her files, something I protested—to no avail."

"But why would you have a problem with that?" I was surprised.

"First Amendment issues," he said. He rolled his eyes. "Paul fought me. He said there's a larger issue than the Constitution here."

I smiled at that. "You probably didn't like that."

"No, I didn't. I'm a stubborn man. I'm an old newspaper guy—that kind of thing. But maybe I want the answer before the police find it."

"Did you find the anonymous letter some crackpot sent to Sonia? A threat on her life."

He seemed surprised. "Sonia showed you that? You know, she received all sorts of nasty letters. She…enflamed passions."

"But a death threat."

"The cops took it—thought it untraceable. Empty threat." He sucked in his breath. "I went through Sonia's papers before the police got to them."

"I know, Hank. That seems questionable." I looked around the office.

"I suppose that's true, Edna. I've been thrown off by this."

The door opened, and Paul came in. He seemed surprised to see me sitting with his father. "Ah, Miss Ferber."

Paul looked hesitant, standing back until I pointed to a chair. "Paul, please."

Finally, Paul asked, "What are we talking about?"

Hank sucked in his cheeks. "I was just berating Edna for spending all of yesterday with Noah West."

Paul stared at him. "Dad, please, for God's sake."

"We're just talking, Edna and I."

"Obviously, you're not," Paul countered. "Miss Ferber can do what she wants." He turned to me. "How is Noah?"

"As well as you'd expect. He feels betrayed by your family." Blunt, to the point.

Paul made a *tsk*ing sound. "Not by our family. Not all of our family."

Hank was following the exchange. "Edna wants to convince me that Noah West is innocent."

"I don't think I need to," I said, flatly. "Common sense…"

"She's just told me that Noah believes the murderer is someone close to our family. Someone—an acquaintance maybe. A spy in the bowels of Fairbanks."

An edge to my voice. "I said—someone who knew Sonia's plans, her business."

Paul frowned. "Well, of course." He nodded at me. "It stands to reason, no?"

Hank seemed surprised by that. "Who else knew Sonia's plans that night…her appointment with Edna?" Hank's voice got thick with sarcasm. "Only probably everyone in *The Gold* office. And, ironically, possibly Noah himself."

Paul whispered, "Not here, Dad. Not here."

"Then where?" He looked around the empty office. "At home, where we pass by each other in the hallways like ghosts?"

"Christ!" Paul thundered.

Hank rubbed his temples. "I'm really tired."

"Then maybe we should not be doing this now."

"No one is here," Hank said.

"I'm here," I said, sitting forward and interlocking my fingers.

"But you already know all our dirty laundry."

A heartbeat. "Not all of it."

Hank looked at me. "What does that mean?"

"Somebody is not telling me something."

"What?" asked Paul.

"I don't know," I went on. "If I did…"

Hank smiled. "Now you're being mysterious, Edna."

"Look," I declared, exasperated, "I'm involved with this, whether I like it or not. The lobby of the Nordale is noisy, and everyone stares at me like I'm some dark nemesis come to haunt Fairbanks." I stared into Hank's face. "Answer me something, Hank. You told me you burned some of Sonia's papers, including her journal. I wonder why."

Surprise in his voice. "I told you. It was nothing."

"Then why burn them?"

"I wanted no one else to be hurt." The line exploded in the air.

"What does that mean?"

Hank frowned. "I didn't want the police going through her letters. Yes, I know it was wrong. A whole part of me kept saying—stop, stop. But there was nothing in those pages that pointed to a murderer, or I wouldn't have burned them. Believe me. I'm not a fool. But you know how Sonia was—she said some nasty things about the anti-statehood people, about others, about Preston and Tessa in particular, well-known folks, even about our family. A private journal, so she talked to herself. It would be all over Fairbanks." His eyes got moist. "I didn't want people to remember her by her secret words."

"I don't know if I believe you," I told him.

That surprised him. "What else could it be? I was protecting our family. It had nothing to do with the murder, I swear."

"How do you know?" Fire in my voice. "You set yourself up as the one and only judge. Unfair to her, no?"

"I know. I wasn't thinking, really. I was filled with…" He sighed. "She said stuff like: 'Tessa raised Preston to be a dishonest coward.' Okay? I remember that line. So I burned her journal." A hesitation. "And she wrote some pretty graphic stuff about guys she knew—a little too lurid." He shivered. "Her writing about Noah, in particular—too candid."

"And you think that he murdered her?"

He looked away from us. "Her rambling about sex with him was, well, too colorful…and embarrassing. I wouldn't want people reading that. Chief Rawlins." He locked eyes with mine. "My daughter, Edna."

"A grown woman who made her choices."

Hank's fist slammed the table. "I don't care."

"Does Chief Rawlins know you burned the papers? I'm assuming he does. He's not stupid."

He shrugged. "I don't care."

"You're a journalist," I offered.

Hank sat back as his face tightened. "I'm a father first." A pause. "Anyway, enough." He threw his hands up in the air. "Paul"—he glanced at his son—"I want to say something. Something I just told your mother this morning. She's sitting home now. Unhappy with me. But I can't help that." He took a deep breath. "I'm leaving the paper, Paul. I'm retiring. Over. I'm walking away from it."

"What's this all about?" Paul turned pale.

His voice was scratchy. "It no longer matters to me, I've decided. You and your mother both know I've been losing steam these past years, and Sonia's death was the final straw. The paper, the corporation, my investments—none of it matters now. Statehood will happen within the year, I suppose, but that doesn't matter. I mean, I want it, of course I do, but

I don't care. I'm happy it will happen. But do you know what I want to do?" He actually grinned. "Head back to the Yukon, go fishing, trapping, hunting. Me—maybe Clint. Not have to face another edition of newsprint."

"This is nonsense," Paul said.

"It's time. It's not a big deal." He drew in his breath. "You can take over."

"Me?" Paul scoffed. "What?"

"This was Sonia's empire," Hank answered. "What she wanted someday. She wanted to be publisher. Everything she did moved her in that direction. The paper was her baby—she breathed journalism. You know that." He nodded at his son. "So Paul, now it's yours. It passes on to you."

Paul half-rose from his chair, his face red. "Do you hear yourself?"

"I'm tired," Hank was speaking over Paul's words. "There's a fishing pole that…"

"That's not what I mean," Paul yelled.

"I got all the money in the world. What it got me is a murdered daughter."

Paul roared, "The money didn't kill her."

"It's time. I—"

Paul interrupted. "Stop it, dammit. You're not listening to me." He looked at me. "God, I am the cipher in this family."

I stared into my lap. A family, I thought suddenly, is nothing but a wound that you can't heal.

I started to gather my things. This was nowhere I should be now. But Paul, watching me, put his hand on my sleeve. "Stay."

"I don't…"

Paul laughed as he turned to his father. "Dad, I don't want your empire."

"Of course, you do. I've groomed…"

Paul's hand flew up, palm out. "No, I think you got that

all wrong. You groomed Sonia to take over. My sister. She's the one who wanted it."

"But what difference…?"

Paul spoke through clenched teeth. "I'll tell you what the difference is. Sonia wanted to be in control of things. To be in the center of things. Sonia as epicenter of a solar system she created, her in the middle. 'Look at me. Look at me.' The beautiful Sonia Petrievich, belle of the Fairbanks ball. I was the little boy in the backyard catching one more winter cold and praying for sunshine."

Hank twisted his head to the side. "What does that mean?"

"I'll tell you what it means. How many decisions at *The Gold* were made in your office with Sonia…and I'm not even there?"

"But now you have a chance." Hank looked baffled.

"Christ, you don't get it, Dad. You just don't. I'm not second best. If Sonia wasn't dead, we'd never be having this conversation. You know, all my life I played by the rules, the good boy. Even at *The Gold*. Do this, do that. The twin born about a minute after Sonia. And I'm ignored."

"It's because we trusted you. Never worried about you, Paul." His father's voice was mournful.

Paul looked to the door, seemed ready to leave. "And this last nonsense with Noah. I like Noah, always have. We go out to dinner, we laugh over coffee, we travel together, he calls me up, and he asks me what I think of things. He's my friend, Dad. And what do you do? You accuse him of murder. Probably the only man who ever really loved Sonia. Wanted to *care* for her."

"People kill out of love…"

"Yeah, yeah, I heard that come out of your mouth before. Just stop it— it sounds pathetic. But not Noah. Not the way he's built. Shit, Dad, you know him."

"I don't want to discuss Noah today." Hank closed up.

"Yeah, let's wait until they hang him. Front page in *The Gold*. Well, I won't be publishing that edition, let me tell you."

"Your sister…"

Paul held up his hand. "My sister was a frail, faulty woman who could be funny and charming and loveable. But she stuck her nose into everyone's life. We had our good times, the two of us. She was bright, clever. She got a little crazy, maybe a lot crazy, power mad, and she liked to hurt people. She obviously hurt someone to the point that they murdered her."

"Enough." Hank looked around the room.

"No, not enough." He leaned forward in his seat, then stood up, faced his father. "This is my last oration on the subject. Chapter and verse. You closed your eyes to Sonia's weakness. Even her affairs. Lord, I remember how you condemned Maria West, years back, when she was selling her body on The Row to drunken Indians and horny miners in from the Bush. I remember how you told Noah to his face—'Can't you do anything about your slutty sister?' Poor Noah! How embarrassed he was, sitting there, unable to talk back to you, his master and benefactor. So I guess he repaid you, right, by killing the one thing you loved?"

Hank stood now, eye to eye with his son. His slapped Paul on the side of the face. Then, madly, he bulldozed into Paul's chest. The man expelled air, gagged, and toppled into the doorframe. Hank grabbed his neck, throttling him, and Paul slipped to the floor, thrashing about but not fighting back, his hands covering his face, his head turned away. Hank, on top, pummeled him, short jabs to the neck. Blood squirted from the corner of Paul's mouth.

Dizzy, I tried to find the word "Stop!" but was surprised that I had lost my voice.

Suddenly Hank stopped, that spurt of anger dissipated. He toppled back into his chair. I noticed a smear of blood on his skinned right knuckle, and glancing at Paul, then pulling himself up into a sitting position, his arms cradling his knees,

I saw a thin line of blood on his cheek. He rubbed it, looked at the trace of blood on his fingers, whimpered, and looked ready to cry.

Paul sputtered, "Say nothing. Do you hear me?"

I stared at the sheets of papers knocked off Hank's desk onto the floor. Sitting up, my foot shuffled some papers, and, leaning down, I picked up a snapshot of Noah West, Noah as a young man, standing in the Arctic wilderness, his arms cradling a huge king salmon. What was the photo doing on Hank's desk? I wondered. Noah, the handsome young man, virile, rough, beautiful. That shock of black hair. The sun-burned neck and chest. A man in his early twenties, perhaps. I held it in my hand. I tucked it into my dress pocket. A thief. I'd become a common thief.

I didn't care, because I wanted that picture.

I needed to end this. "Paul, it's best you leave."

He turned to go. I noticed blood on his sleeve. His parting shot: "I have an announcement, too. I'm leaving Alaska. My health is one reason, to be sure—I'll die if I'm here one more winter—but not the main one. I've been planning to tell you for some time, but Sonia's death stopped me." He looked at me. "But maybe this is a good time. I've got myself a job on *The Oregonian*. You know why I went to the Lower Forty-eight a month back for a long weekend—and you *wink wink wink* thought that I hung out at a whorehouse—I was interviewing for a job. Which is now mine. So that's that."

"Leave." From Hank, furious.

Paul walked out, slamming the door.

Silence. Hank and I sat there quietly. Hank was staring over my shoulder at nothing, I stood up, put on my coat, and said goodbye. He didn't answer me, nor did he look up.

As I opened the door, I looked back. Hank hadn't moved, a big heap of a man reduced to hunched shoulders and ashen face. Just before I closed the door behind me, I glanced back again. Hank sat there, frozen.

Chapter Nineteen

I had second thoughts about flying to Fort Yukon with Noah in his Super Piper Cub. He'd called me the night before, charmed me—"an adventure, and only mildly dangerous"—and I'd reluctantly said yes. Changed my mind—"No, really"—but finally said yes. "It's only thirty below there now." Yes, I noted, I'd been above the Arctic Circle in even lower temperatures. "Then, you're an old pro."

"We'll see," I grumbled.

"Chief Rawlins cleared my leaving Fairbanks, though reluctantly. So long as I'm not flying into exile to the Lower Forty-eight."

Sitting in the lounge with Clint, he scrunched up his face. "Mighty cold up there, Edna." He mock-shivered.

Setting a cup of tea at my elbow, Teddy mimicked Clint's shiver. "Ain't Fairbanks cold enough for you, Miss Ferber?" Laughing, he dangled a foot in the air. "Frostbite can take a foot. Or maybe a little toe." In an annoying singsong, he said, "This little piggy lost a toe on the way to an ice-box church."

"Or a life," Clint added. "Icebound."

"You two aren't helping me."

But the next morning, around ten, the air clear though frigid, windless, with just an occasional ice crystal slapping my face, I stared at the flying crate he'd talked of, parked in a busy hanger at Weeks Field in a line of similar battered Cessnas and Piper Cubs, all looking like gerrymandered junk heaps. He'd bought the plane, he told me, from a bush flyer who'd gone south—that is, to the Banana Belt, around Kodiak. Flaky red paint, strips of what looked like gleaming silver duct tape— worse, bits of faded canvas flapping in the slight breeze. To me, it looked a frivolous play toy, some little boy's abandoned model plane left in the family garage until, years later, it was ready to be hauled to the trash bin. Noah watched me eyeing the relic. He'd been talking about its value as a bush plane, its low-cost maintenance, its durable tail, its...

I closed my eyes. "Noah..."

"It's not how they look on the outside," he promised, "but what's inside. It's like the people you write about, right? Insides more important than outsides?"

"I have been known to make that comment."

"I know. I read that in a biography of you in the library."

I stared into his face—he was grinning. "You surprise me."

"Well, they did teach me how to read."

The inside of the plane, though cramped, looked obsessively neat, indeed sleek, despite the piles of boxes and packages filling every available corner, including my unwitting lap. Noah was bringing some medicines and foodstuffs to his grandfather and others in Fort Yukon. But, as well, there was a part for a generator for a neighbor, a bolt of fabric for a woman, boxes of candy for some children, some ammo, and a stack of *Reader's Digest*s for an old woman who craved them. "In Alaska bush pilots are cabbies."

"You're like an old-fashioned drummer from my childhood, piling his wares in a beat-up jalopy and heading out into the boondocks."

"You can't get to Fort Yukon by road. And in winter, before the break-up, no boat comes down the frozen Yukon. It's dog-sled or plane. Ten years back, they built an airstrip. We used to land on ice or snow, dangerous because of hidden ridges in the ice, ripples, or sometimes even mushy springtime ice. Now, even with skis on my plane, it's effortless."

I squirmed. "What about bad weather? The hotel said not to fly in winter. March, young man, is still winter. You do use the same calendar, right? God, up here, June feels like winter sometimes."

"You gotta trust me." His eyes had a faraway look. "Given my bush pilot experience working for a small bush feeder airline, I joined the Air Force, was shot down in the Pacific, came back with a bum leg and a purple heart, a proclamation from the mayor, my photograph on the front page of *The Gold* and *The Fairbanks Daily News-Miner*, and the back-slapping gratitude of the First World War veterans of town." A hint of sarcasm. "Look at me—now."

I started to say something but he repeated, "You gotta trust me."

And immediately I did. Noah had a slick, deft sense of flying, and a cautious regard. He'd inventoried a compass, an ax, signaling devices, matches, sleeping bags—a methodical emergency checklist. A two-way radio. Little comfort, there. The plane slid, bumped, and rose into the air. I said something about the weather because I thought the sky, at breakfast so pale and blue, now was fast becoming a grayish-white, deadened. But Noah simply nodded and pointed out the window. All I saw were white-topped mountains, with a sweep of descending jagged ice, naked valleys, oases of dark trees speckled with the glint of the sun.

Over the clanging, chugging motor and the whistling wind that seeped into the cockpit, Noah spoke into my ear. "Hard to talk up here. All the noise. Relax. Enjoy."

Relax. Enjoy.

I pulled at the wool blanket he'd tucked around my legs, tucking it in securely. And so, for more than an hour, I found myself staring down at a barren landscape, humped ridges, vast, endless stretches of white and gray, and even black, frozen rivers and streams. No people, no cabins with comforting wisps of smoke from chimneys, no winding trails, not even a harum-scarum rabbit or muskrat venturing out of its warren. I looked to see herds of caribou and even a few menacing grizzlies. I saw nothing but a deep yawning crevasse where, I imagined, planes plummeted and disappeared—for good. Noah had explained, *People disappear in Alaska*. Well, Doubleday would love this. *Edna Ferber disappears in Arctic crevasse in winter blizzard.*

One way to sell my novel…

"There," he said finally, and I found myself staring at the Yukon River, a wiggle and spiral of frozen brownish water. He pointed to the narrow Porcupine River with its crystal-clear ice, where it met the Yukon. Noah tracked the plane along its curves for a few minutes, dropping too low for my comfort, and he pointed in the distance until I thought he said it was Yukon Flats. He was grinning. And then, making a whooping sound, reminding me of the Navajos who were his blood brothers, he indicated a settlement of scattered cabins and caches and trails, and yelled, "Fort Yuk."

I saw a small village spread out along meandering trails with no signs of life. The squat cabins, even the rambling two-story log buildings, seemed a ghost town. Circling, he pointed. I saw an American flag fluttering over a squat log cabin. And suddenly, as effortlessly as sliding into a warm, sudsy bath, the plane banked from the north, dipped, taxied on a snow-covered airfield, its skis bumping gently, and came to a stop. I turned to look at Noah. He was jumping up and down, back home.

He apologized. "I'm here…I always feel a…a rush…"

I grinned but lectured him, "You know, young man, the proper element of man is land. Not air, not water, especially not fire." I looked toward the bleak, winter-shrouded village. "Though right now I'd relish a fire burning in one of these cabins."

He helped me down from the Piper Cub, and I found myself up against two waiting dog-teams, with yelping, frisky huskies, bucking, straining. Two red-faced teenaged boys, their round faces barely seen in huge parkas with massive fur-lined hoods, stood at the head of each team. Noah nodded to the boys. "They were expecting us. Edna, my cousins Henry and Jonah, twin troublemakers." The boys, hearing Noah's joke, giggled and one actually stuck out his tongue.

But, without delay, they fell into a practiced rhythm. The boys unloaded the cargo onto one sled, except for some packages for Noah's grandfather, while Noah tucked me into a seat and smothered me with blankets and caribou skins. He talked to a man who'd come out of a building, discussing what needed to be done to keep the plane warm and ice-free while we visited. Noah himself assumed the lead of one team of dogs, and feeling very much the pampered medieval maiden—or a doomed character in a gloomy Russian novel by Tolstoy—I found myself gliding over snow, a biting wind in my face. But in seconds the sled stopped at the doorway of a tiny cabin with one small window facing front, a sagging Arctic porch, and a snake of gray smoke rising from the roof, a line of color etched against the bleak white sky.

● ● ● ● ●

I had no idea what to expect from Noah's grandfather, but, romantic that I was, I thought he'd be like Clint Bullock, a leathery man dressed in patched buckskin and moose-hide Indian moccasin, with a gnarled face—though handsome like his grandson. I was wrong. Yes, the man who greeted me was ancient, probably in his late eighties, maybe older, but tall and slender, with a clean-shaven and unblemished face, with long white hair worn straight down his shoulders. I looked to see Noah in the man, but little, save the height and deep coloration, suggested kinship. With his high cheekbones, fierce black eyes, and bushy white eyebrows under a high forehead, he had an intense, albeit bemused, look about him—a cracker-barrel intellect in a country store. Oddly, greeting me with a half-bow and an extended hand, speaking in clipped but labored English, he reminded me of an ancient professor, decades-long emeritus, because he wore a tattered cardigan sweater on which I read: W-A-S-H-I-N-G-T-O-N, in blue letters, the "W" nearly disappeared. He wore creased brown gabardine slacks. He looked ready to deliver a lecture.

I settled in, sitting by the hot rumbling Yukon oil-drum stove, a pulsating machine whose makeshift opening was fed log after log. The cabin was steamy, and, glancing out the small window, I saw sudden wisps of light snow flash up against the cabin. A howl of wind. A dog barked. I shivered.

Comfortable, I watched the curious and touching dynamic of Noah and the old man, who'd introduced himself formally as Nathan Elijah West. Noah gave his grandfather a hug and clung to his forearm, a warm and necessary gesture. For a moment they chatted in Gwich'in, and I was fascinated with the shift in Noah's voice: melodic, yet startlingly abrupt and staccato, high-pitched, a wonderful counterpoint against the old man's raspy, guttural voice. The old man raised his hand. "We are rude to Miss Ferber, who is the author of *Show Boat*."

The line struck me as comical, and, glancing at my quizzical face, he said, "I lived in Seattle for ten years, off and on, working in the timber forests. One summer I saw *Show Boat* at a little theater…in Tacoma, I think." He smiled, and I saw missing teeth. "I can still hum some of the music."

"So can I," I laughed. "Noah, can you hum a few bars?"

Sheepishly, he answered: "I have to confess, Edna, I've never read one of your books." A sloppy grin. "Yet."

"That's probably why we're still friends."

I looked around the cabin. There was a tall gas lamp switched on, though now and then it fizzled, a small wind-up gramophone with a stack of 78-rpm records nearby (I remembered Noah telling me that his grandfather listened to Paul Whiteman and big band music), a short-wave radio, an oil-cloth-covered wooden table, one recliner, and a wool-braided rug on the pole-wood floor. A fifty-gallon water barrel rested up against a kitchen area. A kerosene lantern was hanging from the ceiling. A rack of caribou anthers hung by the door. The smell of old grease, burnt wood, oil. Pungent brewed tea, not unpleasant. Rustic, yet warm. A colorful red-and-white checkered gingham curtain on the window, a little lopsided, but neat; one of Noah's "Go Native" posters; a series of unframed photographs tacked to the wall, black-and-white snapshots of a man in front of a fish wheel, a man standing over a fallen grizzly, a man holding a huge salmon—I thought guiltily of the photo of Noah I'd stolen from Hank's office—one of white men, rifles slung over shoulders, one foot triumphantly placed on a big-antlered caribou.

The old man saw me looking. "Pictures from when I was a young man."

He served tea that calmed me, brewed from the needles of the Hudson Bay plant, a faint hint of turpentine, and I munched on some soda biscuits laced with cranberries. Chewy as hardtack.

The old man looked at Noah and sighed. "And we have to talk of your troubles, Noah. Bring me up to date on this dreadful mistake." He looked at me. "There is a phone at the post office I use, we all use." He nodded at me. "When my Noah calls, he tells me that you are helping him." He nodded, approvingly.

I said quickly, "I'm not really helping, I'm afraid, but I know Noah will be vindicated. It's a stupid matter."

The old man closed his eyes for a second, snapped them open. "It's not a stupid matter from somebody's point of view. Someone planned this evil."

Noah recounted his visit to the police, the support of the local Athabascan Tribal Council, even Paul—I learned that Paul had phoned the night before, quietly—but I waited to see if Noah had told his grandfather of Hank's betrayal. Hank, I knew, the old visitor to Fort Yukon, had long been the hunter-friend of Nathan Elijah West.

"And Hank Petrievich," the old man said finally. "Is his heart still hard?"

Noah nodded.

"Sonia's death has twisted a good man into nonsense. Grief can push folks into madness." He smiled at Noah. "Trust me. Hank will someday apologize to you."

Noah said sharply, "And maybe I won't want to accept Hank's apology." His eyes flashed, angry.

"Of course you will. You're not built for holding grudges."

Noah looked ready to say something, but his grandfather stood up. "We can talk of this later, you and I. Edna Ferber is here for a short afternoon. I'm making food for us. You take her around the village and show her the beauty of Fort Yukon." He looked at me. "Fort Yukon was settled in 1847 by the Hudson's Bay Trading Post, and it has a long history. Back then we Indians were nomadic, and we just came here with our fur pelts. Now, with five hundred souls, it's home to the Dené—Qwich'in Athabascans—and white traders and missionaries and teachers. Noah, show Edna Ferber your boyhood home."

It was, of course, too frigid for a long walk, but I savored the meandering on the old trails, with Noah carrying a stick to fend off pesky dogs. The cabins with the faded chalky logs, some nearly covered in snowdrifts, were desolate, but every one had a trail of dark smoke escaping roofs, some of which,

I noticed, were made from flattened oil drums. We strolled by high-pole caches, storage for smoked salmon, the caribou meat—safe from the menacing wolf packs. The grizzlies.

The main road, he said, was called First Avenue. I smiled. It seemed just an ice-packed, gravel-imbedded dirt road. Noah pointed out the Alaskan Native Service School—"where I went as a boy," he said. The BIA school. "Two schools," Noah said snidely. "One for Indians, and the Territorial for the whites. They taught us moccasin-sewing and how to build a birdhouse. The white kids read Dickens. Some of my teachers refused to drink from the same cup as the Indian kids. If I spoke Qwich'in, I got my knuckles rapped with a switch."

We strolled past the Show House, where he'd watched John Wayne and Tom Mix westerns, whites killing Indians.

"Summers, when I returned home from boarding school, I learned to smoke Lucky Strikes between features." He sighed. "Nowadays, the young kids just chew tobacco and spit."

After barely an hour, I was getting chilled. I was too old for this. Noah noticed, tucked his arm under mine, pulled my scarf tighter around my neck, and led me back.

The cabin smelled of roasted meat. We sat at the small table, and the old man served more tea, a wild celery and carrot soup, and a crispy rabbit. It was leisurely, an abundant meal, which surprised me. I expected some pale string beans from cans, powdered potatoes, a slab of prickly meat. Instead, a feast. I savored it all. At the end, sitting with coffee that tasted like the hearty chicory blend I recalled from my days scooting around Oklahoma, I ate a creamy confection of crushed blueberries and low-bush cranberries on cream-slathered pilot crackers. Incredibly sweet, almost cloying, the berries melted in my mouth, the frozen berries thawing out in the warm milk, releasing their fragrance. I licked my fingers.

"I like this restaurant," I said.

I noticed Noah glancing out the window, and I could

hear a growing roar, a rumbling. A sudden banging against the eaves, a swirl of snow covered the window, and I jumped.

"A snow squall," Noah told me. He went to the window. "Maybe a white day"—sky and ground and air all white, a landscape of no shadow. "A bottle of milk, we say."

"What does that mean?"

"It means we can't fly out this afternoon. We have to sleep in." He shook his head. "Sorry, Edna. I didn't expect this…"

But the old man grunted. "The ancient shamans are smiling on me, a blessing, truly. I have my grandson and Edna Ferber into the night."

I was not so joyous. I thought of my cozy Nordale room, the sizzling aroma of bacon and sourdough pancakes in the morning. Wind slapped the boards, and I jumped again. Strangely, looking out the window, standing next to Noah, I thought of the old Athabascan woman's legend of the lazy boy and dead caribou: an icebound village. I'm trapped here, I told myself. Snowbound. Icebound. Bound.

As night fell and the wind roared, we sat before the fire. I was surprised that I could relax. After all, for once I had no choice but to sit there. I liked to will my moments, to make the world conform to my demands. I liked my schedule followed, exact and rigid. Now, helpless in this Arctic room, a millions miles from Earth—God, if Kitty Carlyle Hart could see me now!—I closed my eyes and drifted.

The men talked animatedly, then softly, and at times seemingly aggressively, other times with a mellowness that lulled, like a child's song. I listened to the rhapsodic words.

"In the old days we had shamans," the old man said to me. "They told us how to live. They told us what was wrong." He smiled. "I was told and believed that they could bring the dead back to life. The American military were afraid of our priests, and of superstitions, and they cut their hair off, shaved them, covered them with red paint to humiliate them. Missionaries told us they were Satan."

"Have you passed down your stories to Noah?"

He nodded.

"I remember, Grandfather." Noah sounded like a little boy.

I looked around the tight, heat-flushed room, Noah leaning into his grandfather, the old man's elbow grazing the side of his grandson.

"It's the way you view the world," the old man went on. "Everything is a cycle, Edna Ferber. A goose feather tossed into the Yukon becomes a new bird. A crow's feather in a boy's hair makes him have swift feet."

At one point, sipping a last cup of tea, I asked about his family. The old man talked about marrying young. "I was sixteen, she was thirteen." When his young wife died, his sister helped raise the children, including Noah's father. The grandmother, Noah added, of the two twin boys who'd met our plane. "Silly boys," the old man grumbled, "though they work like packhorses." He mentioned Noah's father and mother, and Noah stiffened.

"Was Noah's father as handsome as his son?" A stupid remark. Noah frowned.

The old man nodded. "The girls followed him around the village, even out to the traplines on the Flats. Sitting in the mission church on Sundays, they giggled behind his back. He married the daughter of the chief, in fact, a beauty, who sadly died in childbirth. Little Maria was left with her younger brother, Noah."

"And Noah's father, a sad story, this one." His eye still on Noah. "Noah's father was a good hunting guide for white folks, but they taught him how to drink. One icy afternoon, drunk, he hitched up his dogs, wouldn't listen to reason, headed to the traplines, and he took out the dogs. He never returned."

"Oh, my God." I was stunned. I looked at Noah. He had his head down.

Noah got up and tended to the fire, his back to us.

A long silence in the room.

The old man watched Noah's back, then cleared his throat. "The end of one chapter of our lives."

I decided to bring up Hank Petrievich. "Your family is tied in closely with the Petrievich clan."

"Going decades back, generations. To the turn of the century. The end of last century, in fact. Hank's father and cousins came here, had a hunting lodge, hunted caribou and seal and moose. Good people. Clint Bullock—you know Clint. Wonderful Clint. A heart of gold, that man. After his gold-seeking days ended, he was a guide. I spent winters with them out on the Flats. Mostly we didn't stay in Fort Yukon. Only summers. They ate at this table. You know, it was Hank who got Noah to go to school in Massachusetts. The white boys' school."

"I know."

Noah, his voice edgy, said, "I've already told her that story."

The old man kept talking. "Our families were close. Not white man and Indian. But real friends." He looked at Noah. "The ties not of blood but of goodness."

"So you know Tessa Strange?"

He laughed out loud. "Ah, fat Tessa. A pistol, that girl. She was a young girl, not so fat then, but maybe plump. But with a Bible in her hand. She was a missionary at the Episcopal Mission over to Venetie, forty-five miles away from here. On the Chandalar River, the Gquchyaa Gwich'in. But she'd come here, first with the Featherwells, an old Episcopalian Mission teacher and his wife. With other missionaries. Tessa, Tessa. Lord, a crazy woman she was."

"A crazy missionary?"

"Is there any other kind?" He laughed. "I resisted all efforts to become a Christian, though other Gwich'in did. She was a zealot, but she liked to sing and dance and carry on. A drinker, though it was forbidden. They ran the mission there, and we used to laugh at her husband, Lionel Strange."

"Why?"

"He was a small man, the size of a small boy, runt of the litter, maybe, with a big round head, who talked in memorized lines from the Bible, and he followed her around like a puppy dog, though he had a roving eye for the ladies. That drove Tessa nuts. Everyone made fun of him. He had this strange accent—he was born, I believe, in Kansas. I guess Tessa had been sent there by her parents—to calm her down—and she fell in with him. He came to Alaska with Tessa, his bride, up to Venetie."

"So Preston was born in Alaska?"

He nodded. "But Lionel died when his boy was small, falling into a river, freezing to death. And Tessa went to Fairbanks, where she married some rich man."

"What about Hank?"

"Oh, Hank comes up for hunting now and then. But he has other guides now. I'm too old now. I just serve dinner."

I was in a hurry to ask a question. "Sonia wrote Tessa a note. She mentioned that Tessa knew the players. From the North. Jack Mabie. Sam Pilot."

Nathan looked puzzled. "I don't understand."

"What can you tell me about Jack Mabie and Sam Pilot?"

Nathan shook his head. "Not good men. Sam is my blood, as you know. But the dark shadow of Jack, a vicious man."

"You knew them?"

"Slightly. Sam from a nearby village, yes, of course. Once they stopped here. The two of them needed a place to sleep for the night, but the next morning silver dollars disappeared— and the two men. After that, I wouldn't let Sam cross my doorway."

"Was Jack really the meanest man in Alaska?"

He narrowed his eyes, and smiled. "I am always amazed that a man can label himself one way—and the world believes it." A pause. "But he was evil."

"A killer?"

He nodded. "In his younger days folks really feared him—walked the other way. He shot a trapper out in Venetie, a squabble over furs. A posse caged him, but Sam said he saw the whole thing. Self-defense. A lie. Nothing happened." He clicked his tongue. "The pattern, you see. Jack robbed and cheated and—killed. A prospector in Dawson, we heard. An ambush in Eagle. Like the others who plundered the Arctic. Soapy Smith and his gang. Fred Hardy, who killed the Sullivan brothers at Unimak. Thieves who lay in wait for the gold-rushers on the White Pass Trail."

"Did you ever witness a murder?"

A long silence. "Not witness firsthand—but here. Sadly."

"Grandfather, maybe you shouldn't…"

He held up his hand. "So far in the past, it's—it's like a story I was told." His eyes focused. "But I didn't see it. Jack lusted after a beautiful woman, a married woman who was frightened of him, a mother, a missionary wife, and Jack accused the husband of robbing his cache of pelts. This was 1925, maybe earlier—around then. Trumped up accusations, of course. But Jack accused—a lie—and the poor husband, a missionary who didn't even trap, confronted Jack. I didn't see what happened, but Jack Mabie shot the man in the heart. In front of his children." He closed his eyes for a second, shook his head. "When we got there, the man was dead, a hunting knife lying near his hand. The wife screamed that Jack dropped it there, set him up, and Sam Pilot said no—the missionary lunged at Jack. A lie."

"So Jack walked away."

He nodded. "A miner's court. You know, a bunch of local men got together, they listened to Sam, refused to hear the wife, and Jack and Sam rode off…"

"Into the midnight sun," I said.

"Evil, evil."

Noah interrupted. "It's late. Time for bed."

It was midnight. Looking out the window, Noah said the sky was clear now, the snow ended, and the heavens were brilliant with color. So Noah and I bundled up and stepped outside the cabin. What struck me first was the silence, except for a faint distant hum, which Noah said was the generator that gave power to the village. But it was the sky that held me: a wash of violet and blue and green and rose at the far north horizon, moving, dipping, swirling. Noah said, "If you whistle, they say the stream will come down to you." The air glistened, wrapped around me. But it was too cold to whistle, and I rushed inside. There, Noah glibly quoted, "'They danced a cotillion in the sky; they were rose and silver shod; it was not good for the eyes of man—'twas a sight for the eyes of God.'"

"Let me guess. Robert W. Service."

"Who else?" Noah laughed.

The old man watched us. "The aurora lights lead you to heaven. They are nothing more than the spirit of our dead who stay with us, quietly advising us. Our dead return in our dreams, and talk to us. My father often visits me."

Noah kept repeating. "Bedtime. Bedtime. You two will talk forever."

The old man insisted I have his room, though I protested not very much. His bed—layers of caribou and fox hides piled high, soft and cushy, near a cherry-red-hot stove—dominated a quiet room, Spartan almost, with a rack for clothing, one pineboard bureau, some makeshift shelves. No windows.

Noah and his grandfather slept in the front room, both wrapped in blankets and pelts, close to the oil-drum stove. Lights off, one kerosene lantern flickered in a corner, the room peaceful. Outside the wind roared and shrieked and moaned. I heard the sled dogs howl—or, I thought, is that the sound of wolves? I shivered. From the front room came the soft whispered voices of Noah and the old man, talking softly, back and forth. I couldn't hear what they were saying, but now and then I heard chuckling, suppressed laughter. I smiled, lulled by the warmth of their whispering. Then, suddenly, the buzzing stopped, as though by signal, and I heard faint snoring. I slept.

Now and then in the long night I'd awaken and forget where I was, but the smell of burnt wood, acrid and rich, and the sighing from the men feet away, soothed me. At one point I woke and caught the last fragment of a dream: my father Jacob, a young handsome man with a moustache and a Prince Albert coat, was talking to me, whispering. In the darkness I cried out. I drifted back to sleep. In my dreams I was alone on a vast tundra, snow fierce, wind deafening, and the sky above was heavy with stars and wisps of undulating light. I buried myself in a snow cave, mole-like, so that I was encased in a velvety cocoon, and the snow was not cold but warm to the touch, invitingly so. I could almost taste it. As I folded my arms around my body and pulled up my legs, I heard a raven, hovering nearby, not really cawing but talking. I woke from my dream, and it rushed upon me, and I wanted it back because it was so beautiful and it belonged to me.

Chapter Twenty

I woke refreshed, the hum of soft voices drifting in from the front room. When they realized I was awake, the men bustled about, and the aroma of toasted bread and strong coffee came to me.

"*Vun gwinzee*," Noah said, grinning. "Good morning."

He said the weather was fine, and we'd be leaving in a couple of hours. He'd sent one of the twins to see about the plane, warming it up, readying it, checking for splintered propellers, a broken strut, anything that might have happened during yesterday's flight. I didn't care, really. I thought I could linger in Fort Yukon for days. But, of course, I couldn't, nor could Noah.

But I'd woken up with a few questions, and I didn't know how to ask the old man. After eating breakfast and too many cups of hair-raising coffee, I asked about the old hospital, even the Episcopalian mission, and the Indian school.

"Tell me about the schooling," I probed.

"Two schools, as I told you," Noah said. "One for Qwich'in kids, and one for the children of the whites. I remember reading a tattered Dick and Jane primer with some of the pages missing. To me, it was like reading science fiction. Who were these people? Once, telling a story in class, I faltered, called a bear a *ggagga*, our word, and I was sent home."

"Horrible."

"Well, the laws have changed," Noah acknowledged. "One school for all now, even though it's been ignored in some places."

The grandfather added, "Having two schools was always a real problem, though."

"Why was that?"

"The children of mixed marriages. So many white men, trappers, hunters, end up with Dené women, often marrying them, and the children are half-breeds. Some of the white men wanted their children in the white school, so that's where they went. One foot in one world, one in another. Most half-breeds went to the mission school."

"Such intermarriage isn't a problem?"

"Not really, but two different cultures. Well, there's bound to be trouble. And there are always some souls—Indian and white—who blame the others for their sad lives."

Noah left to check on the plane, and so I sat with the grandfather, and the old man suddenly looked worried.

"What is it?" I asked.

"Noah is precious to me."

I nodded.

He presented me with a gift, a carved walrus-ivory figure, smooth and elongated, and staring at it I realized it was a boy, an abstract rendering perhaps, but a simple piece. "I made this decades ago. When Noah was leaving for prep school in Massachusetts. It reminded me of him somehow."

I held it in my hand. "I can't take such a gift."

"I no longer need it," he insisted. "Noah is always with me now."

I closed my fingers around the statue, so light in my hand, so delicate. "Thank you. I'll cherish it."

"That's why I'm giving it to you."

I relaxed in my seat and stared at the old man.

"You want to ask me something?" he said, smiling.

"As a matter of fact, I do. I didn't want to bring it up with Noah here. But yesterday you were talking of Hank and Tessa, the old days up here, and I started to think of something…"

"I know. I saw your curiosity. So I ended up giving you so much of the story…"

"But not enough, I'm afraid."

"You have a question?"

"Questions," I emphasized. "I keep coming back to Sonia's note to Tessa. Jack Mabie. Sam Pilot."

"I don't think Tessa ever knew Jack Mabie."

"Maybe, maybe not. She can't be trusted. But in her missionary days she had to have heard of him." I thought of something. "The missionary who was murdered by Jack. Tessa must have known him?"

Nathan sat up. "Of course." A look of panic in his face. "Yes, they did know each other, but when he died she was long gone to Fairbanks."

"But maybe Sonia knew that…that connection."

He was shaking his head. "I don't know…"

"I have the feeling the answer to Sonia's murder is up here."

"In Fort Yukon?"

"Maybe. Somehow up here."

"I can't see how." I saw him thinking. "Let me show you photographs of those years."

Nathan walked to a bookshelf and pulled out an oversized scrapbook. A wisp of dust flew into the air. "Good housekeeping," he joked, his fingers brushing away the thin layer of dust. "Appropriate for an old relic—our young lives."

He sat down next to me and placed the scrapbook on the table. Black pages with Kodak photographs inserted into corner wedges. He started to leaf through the pages. "Let me find a photograph of Tessa and her husband."

I touched his wrist. "Let me see the others," I told him.

He smiled, indulged. "Words most people never hear when threatened with an evening of family or vacation photographs."

For the next half hour, slowly, quietly, enjoying the exercise himself, Nathan shared different snippets of the Fort Yukon of fifty years back. "Noah's father," he pointed.

"Looks like him."

"Noah as a little boy."

"Looks like him now—looks mischievous."

"Too smart for his own britches." But there was pride in his voice.

Self-consciously, he pointed to a snapshot of himself—a regal-looking young man at a salmon skein, brawny, thick-chested, a shock of long black hair. He joked, "That man reminds me of myself as a young man."

A picture of Maria and Noah, both fifteen or sixteen—tall, striking, smiling at each other, a backdrop of the Episcopalian chapel.

Nathan sighed. "Happy days. Noah ready to go off to boarding school. Maria to Fairbanks to work in someone's kitchen." He *tsk*ed. "A life that went off the rails."

"I've met Maria."

"She avoids me, Edna, though I beg her to visit me here. She is my granddaughter."

He thumbed through some pages. "Here, look. The visiting missionaries."

A grainy snapshot of a small cluster of people congregated before the Episcopalian chapel. "Tessa," he pointed.

Unrecognizable. Yes, slightly chubby, but the bright-eyed attractive young woman holding onto the arm of a smaller, wiry man bore little resemblance to the mammoth Tessa.

At the corner of the photograph a small child gazed at the camera, his arms circling a small ball. A head of curly hair, a frail face.

I nodded at Nathan. "Preston?"

"When he was innocent." He squinted at the photograph. "He's maybe two or three then. A toddler."

I laughed. "When we were all innocent at that age."

But Nathan's face suddenly twisted, and his fingers twitched. "I'd forgotten…"

"What?" I peered at the crowd in the photograph.

His fingers touched a man's head. "Ned Thomas, the Episcopalian missionary. His…his beautiful wife."

For, indeed, the woman standing next to him was beautiful. Lithe, willowy, her fingers touching the large wooden cross she had hanging around her neck.

"What?" I repeated, impatient.

"I'd forgotten. Tessa was close to them." He turned to look in my eyes. "The man shot to death by Jack Mabie. And got away with it because of Sam Pilot. An innocent man of God, slaughtered."

I felt a chill go up my spine as I stared at the man who'd shortly be one of Jack's victims. A pleasant face, long, almost bony, a strand of blondish hair drifting down over his forehead.

"I'd forgotten," Nathan mumbled. "So sad to see this. A man taken away from his wife, his children." He drew his face near. "This photo is—maybe a couple years before. Preston born in 1921. I remember that."

"And then Tessa's husband died."

His eyes flashed.

"What?" I asked.

"I'm gossiping, Edna. Tessa, the missionary with the party gown in her closet, flirted with this Ned—much to the horror of his wife. For years. Rumors of an affair, nasty, talked of. A long-standing secret affair, supposedly." He winced. "Horrible rumors that little Preston was Ned's child."

"Possible?"

"Who knows? Tessa retreated into her marriage. Her

church. But the rumors persisted. Ned and Tessa. And Lionel in the dark. So devoted to his God that he had no eyes for the real world." A smile. "Although he liked the Indian women." He chuckled. "My, my, I am a worse gossip than Noah."

"Then he died?"

"Rumors that he killed himself in the icy river. Someone whispered to him about Ned and Tessa. I never believed that."

"But then she left Fairbanks—and Ned was murdered."

"Yes," he said, "two or three years later, maybe more. Tessa was in Fairbanks."

"A new page of her life began there. She forgot about God." I paused. "Sonia's note, Nathan. Somehow she connected Tessa to Jack's murder of Ned Thomas."

"Both missionaries."

"Preston's real father?"

He hesitated. "A rumor." He stared into my face. "And decades now in the past." He sighed. "Tessa demanded no one tell Preston—even to this day."

"But perhaps he found out. Maybe…"

"But Jack still lived."

He frowned. "And someone still wanted him dead."

"And Sonia was convinced…" Another pause. "But what?"

There was whooping and yelling outside. Noah had returned, but he was romping with some frisky children, including the twin boys, his cousins. They were rough-housing, tumbling into one another, rolling onto the ice-packed ground, the air filled with their infectious laughter, and they were sputtering in Qwich'in. I stood by the window, watching, enjoying the scene. At one point Noah looked up, spotted me, and started to wave, just as one of the boys barreled into him, pulling him onto the ground. I heard his throaty, high-pitched laugh.

Hurriedly, I said to the grandfather, "Tessa's husband died young—?"

He smiled. "Not murder, Edna Ferber. Lionel drowned in icy water."

"You liked Preston?"

"I knew him as a little boy. As a man, I hear he presents problems."

I smiled back at him. "So I gather." I looked at him. "From this isolated village, you seemed to have learned a lot."

"In the early years, Hank visited, talked a lot. Even Tessa sent letters. An interesting lady, that Tessa, one who has drifted from child of God to Satan's daughter. She seems to have passed some of that legacy to Preston, the wastrel."

I grinned. "I love that word. How did you hear that?"

He grinned. "Noah is a gossip, too."

"Nathan, the roots—maybe here. Jack and Sam had murderous lives here. The three murders in Fairbanks. It's just that I can't find the connection. Sonia was on to something. Tessa is afraid of something."

The old man spoke rapidly. "You're making me question a lot of things, Edna."

He stopped abruptly. Noah came tumbling in, snow-covered, black hair slick with ice pellets, cheeks reddened, eyes flashing.

"My cousins get all their manners from the huskies they sled with."

His grandfather stood and moved to brew hot tea. "You overgrown boy," he said to Noah, who beamed.

But, as he sipped his tea and watched his grandfather pack a bag of food for us—"Grandfather, you know we do have food in Fairbanks"—his mood shifted. He grew quiet, holding the cup with two hands, blowing on the hot liquid. Then it was time to say goodbye, and I saw him stiffen. Yes, back to Fairbanks and all that nonsense. Yet, I told myself, he probably underwent a similar metamorphosis whenever he left the idyllic village of his boyhood. A bone-marrow-deep melancholy.

The old man suddenly embraced his grandson, his eyes watery, and I noticed Noah's shoulders shook.

"Edna Ferber," the old man said, "you must come back in summer, our short but lovely season. The wildflowers are brilliant colors, the forget-me-nots and purple fireweed and blue larkspur and wild pink roses and mountain azalea. Fields blazing in the hot sun. Fort Yukon is not just frozen wasteland—it can be paradise." The old man nodded. "Life is a short season."

"Grandfather." Noah hugged him again.

"Edna, you must come back."

"I'd love to." But I knew I never would.

The dogsledders appeared, almost on cue, and the giggly, energetic twins tucked Noah and me in, poking fun at both of us, to my delight.

In the air, in the rattletrap matchbox of a plane with the hiccoughing motor, Noah sailed out over the Yukon and Porcupine rivers. It was a calm day, brassy and flinty with sharp sunlight, and Noah, though subdued, swooped and dipped and showed off. The plane sailed north, I thought, toward the pole, and Noah directed my gaze to herds of caribou. Then, turning south, he pointed. "The Yukon Flats." I nodded, gazing at frozen ponds and foothills. Ice-locked ridges toward the west. "Look." An animal—a fox? A lynx? A mink?—scurried into a copse of spruce. For a while the plane followed the river, then dipped away, farther out, over the flat, mundane tundra, with banks of squat, stunted spruce, a speckling of pale green and black against unrelenting pale white.

In the middle of nowhere the plane banked, seemed to hover, a hummingbird, though I knew it didn't, and Noah pointed downward. "My trapline cabin," he yelled.

I stared at the tiny log cabin sheltered in a grove of old black spruce and naked birch trees. Nothing around for miles and miles. A dot on the landscape. "There. My cabin."

"I don't understand."

"Where I learned to be a man. Where I go to be alone."

I could barely make out his words, but the tenor of his speech alarmed me. Images of disappearance, of wandering, of extinction flooded me. The plane turned again and seemed to be headed now in one direction.

Then the plane swooped over a bleak stretch of bitter rolling ice, a ripple of buckled blue-glass mound and crevasse. "My father died there." He looked at me. "Somewhere his body rests in the ice. Deep now in the permafrost."

His jaw set, his eyes avoided mine. For the rest of the short trip to Fairbanks, Noah was silent, and I knew I'd best be quiet. I could see his neck muscles jutting out, thick cords of sinew and blood. I could see his hands gripping the controls—white-knuckled, frozen.

When we landed at Weeks Field, he taxied to a stop, but just sat there. I started to fidget, but I watched his impassive profile. He stared straight ahead, then cleared his throat. "I didn't mean to be rude."

"You can never be rude, Noah."

He turned, looked into my face. "Whenever I fly over that part of the tundra, I think of my father."

"But you seemed to head in that direction."

He smiled thinly. "Nearly thirty years and I'm still looking to see him out there. Bush pilots talk of seeing visions there. Spirits come to them as they fly over that world. I wait and I wait." He bit his lip. "But I shouldn't have made you a part of it."

"Don't apologize. No."

"I suppose, it's the not knowing. He—never returned. So it's like he's still out there."

His fingers trembling, he sat back, his face turned away from mine.

Chapter Twenty-one

I sat up in bed.

I had an idea.

An hour later, after coffee and some harried note-taking on a sheet of creamy Nordale Hotel stationery, I knocked on Hank's office door. He was sitting at his desk, rifling through some copy, though he looked listless. A lit cigarette, unsmoked, lay in an ashtray, a snake's coil of ash. There he sat, busy, and I wondered about his decision to give up *The Gold*. I also wondered about Paul. Was he in his office across the hall? The editorial rooms of the newspaper were eerily silent, even the receptionist missing from the front desk.

"Can you spare me a minute, Hank?"

"Of course, Edna. Come in. Please." He motioned toward a chair.

Sitting opposite him, a little nervous, I began, "I spent the last two days in Fort Yukon with Noah and his grandfather…"

"I know."

"I figured you did."

"How is old Nathan?"

"A man easy to like."

For a moment his eyes got cloudy. "A great soul."

"He says good things about you."

A pause. "Even now?"

"Especially now."

He looked down at the stack of papers. "I don't know what to say." He blinked fast and managed a sliver of a smile

I locked eyes with him. "Nathan West told me a lot about the old days, the early hunting days, the interwoven lives of you, Tessa, the Athabascans there. Noah's early days. The missionaries. Quite an education for me. Quite wonderful, in fact. And it got me to thinking about Sonia's note to Tessa—as though Tessa holds answers."

Hank wet his lips, running his tongue over them. "Answers? Tessa? My Sonia?"

"I'll tell you what I think. Sonia started looking into the early days, especially all that interplay up at Fort Yukon and Venetie. She was obsessed with her 'White Silence' columns—the old pioneers. After Jack was murdered, and then Sam, she started to investigate—mainly in response to Noah's pushing her. She learned something—probably because of Sam Pilot's behavior. It troubled her. His cryptic remarks in the lounge. Jack's remarks to him. And somehow she thought Tessa had an answer. Jack Mabie."

Hank whispered, "Sonia asked me about him, Edna. I told her about Jack killing that missionary, Tessa's old friend."

"And rumors of Tessa's affair with him? Rumors about Preston?"

He nodded. "Gossip."

"But Sonia started to connect some dots. *Some* dots. There was no reason someone would murder Jack *these* days. An old drunk man. But maybe his ugly past from the North demanded someone here—now, in Fairbanks—take revenge."

"But Tessa?"

"Sonia didn't know. She wanted a name. She wanted Tessa to tell her something."

"What?"

I shrugged. "I don't know yet. But Tessa was only concerned with Preston—her fear that he was a murderer."

"So she tried to blame Noah?"

"She never talked to Sonia, but Sonia knew she was on to a story. The real murderer. Jack was dead. But Sam still alive. Though not for long. Does this make sense, Hank?"

He shook his head. "You know, Edna, I don't know what makes sense anymore."

I caught a yellow taxi to Tessa's home. Raina let me in, but said that Tessa was in bed. I persisted: "Please, just a minute of her time." Quietly, the girl left me in the vestibule, and when she returned, she simply nodded to the back of the house.

Tessa lay in her rumpled bed and looked as though she'd been there for days. A musky odor, almost of dried autumn flowers or decaying fruit, sweet but oddly noxious, filled the space, and Tessa, propped up against a bank of mismatched pillows, looked sloe-eyed, drugged.

"You intrude again," she mumbled.

"I'm trying to save a life."

"And diminish the lives of others?" Tessa spat out, bitingly.

"Only if necessary."

"What do you want now?" Nervous, she looked to the nightstand. For cigarettes? But Tessa left the pack of cigarettes untouched.

"I spent the last two days in Fort Yukon."

"I know."

I smiled. "Was it in the papers? Banner headlines? My lovely photograph in the rotogravure?"

Tessa snapped at me. "We are a powerful family, Edna. Rats and sycophants and low-lifes cannot wait to deliver news to us, to curry crumbs of favor."

"What favor can you still provide these days?" I knew it was a cruel line. I noticed Tessa avoided eye contact.

Tessa smiled. "I can provide silence."

"Even if it's destructive?"

Her head swiveled as she spoke to the wall. "Well, that's your judgment call."

"I'm still asking about Sonia's last failed visit with you— that note that frightened you so."

"I've had heart attacks—I'm easily cowed."

I neared the bed. "I doubt that."

Silence, then a shaking of the head. "Nothing lies buried under Arctic snow for very long. The crevasses eventually spit up their secrets."

"I want to ask you about the murdered missionary up North."

That startled her. "Why?"

"Jack Mabie and the cruel murder of your friend."

For a moment she dipped her head to her chest, trembled. "I still think of that…that poor, innocent man, a man of God, butchered…"

"Did you know his killer, Jack Mabie?"

She shook her head. "I already *told* you—no. Yes, I heard of him. Maybe saw him. I don't know. Who hadn't?"

"But he killed your friend."

"Because he wanted his wife."

"But Sam Pilot lied for him."

"Him I knew, though faintly."

"Tell me why Sonia thought you had an answer. Was it because of Jack murdering that missionary?" I sucked in my breath. "A man you supposedly had an affair with. Rumors of little Preston…"

She shrieked. "Enough." She rubbed her temples. "All these years later. The lies. Again. It never happened. Never. Never."

"I'm only repeating…"

"Lies." Tessa looked scared. "But why now? All these years later. Really, Edna. Preposterous, no?" She started to laugh, a gurgling sound that made the rolls of hideous fat weave and buckle. She ended up choking and reached for a cigarette. When she lit it, her hands trembled.

"The reason for the three murders points back to Fort Yukon. The Arctic. Your life there."

"I was a child of God."

"Whose friend Ned was shot to death. An innocent man." I breathed in. "Nathan remembered, gossiped"—I smiled as I remembered his hesitant use of the word—"you and this man, this Ned Thomas became…involved."

"He was a married man. His wife my friend."

"Nevertheless, the gossip suggested…an affair."

"How dare you!"

"When Sonia said 'Jack Mabie' and 'Sam Pilot' in her note, you knew she connected you to the murdered missionary. Yet you kept quiet."

"So long ago." Her eyes narrowed. "That part of the story was years later. I was already in Fairbanks. I'd met my new husband. A letter told me that Ned was shot to death. I was stunned. But I hadn't seen him—his family—in years. It was just a horrible story I read about then. I cried for him—for them. The name Jack Mabie, yes, was mentioned, but I…I was far away then. It was like reading a newspaper article."

"Yes, but one that included the mention of a man you'd loved."

She shivered. "*Did* love. As a friend, really. And his wife."

"But when Jack Mabie was murdered here in Fairbanks, didn't you think that it had something to do with the past? Maybe your past?"

"No, of course not. I'd"—she looked away—"forgotten about Jack Mabie. He supposedly killed so many others—his shameful reputation. Sonia's story in *The Gold*. Ned was but *one*. Yes, I knew him—so what? But Sonia somehow wanted to tie me into the story. Or, worse, my Preston. I'm a powerful woman. Why would I want that scurrilous note circulating around Fairbanks?"

"As you say, long ago. Maybe three decades."

"No matter," she snarled. "The horrible killer."

"Whom someone now killed. And then his sidekick, Sam Pilot. Maybe someone wanted both men dead—keep them quiet."

"How naïve, Edna, you are. Killing would make people talk of the past—bring up rumors." She laughed. "Crazily, I'd want to keep them alive, no?"

"I don't know. But perhaps righting a wrong? Revenge?"

She gasped. "You don't think I would...stupid revenge? Really! You think I...employed my Preston to do murder? A balance sheet, to even out the edges of what happened years and years ago?"

"I didn't say that."

Tessa looked frightened. "Are you saying I... Are you saying the murder of that man...Ned...that I wanted revenge?"

"Preston's real father?"

She closed her eyes. "Stop this. Stop this. Lies. Lies."

I interrupted. "You knew a man whom Jack murdered."

She stammered, "Decades ago. Preston knows nothing of those years—of Ned Thomas."

"But you did."

"So what?" She roared, "Look at Noah West. Sonia was warned about him. You will do anything to take the light off Noah West."

Her words stunned. "This is not what I'm talking about."

But she was through with me. Her hand shot out, in my face. She sucked in some cigarette smoke.

She pointed to the door. "Out."

"I..."

"I'm tired of being pleasant to you, Edna Ferber." A drag on her cigarette. "Out."

Bundled up at mid-afternoon, I walked to Indian Village. I wasn't looking for Noah—he'd told me he was flying to Tok that day to settle some legal matters for some Athabascans at war with each other over the loan of a few dollars. But I found what I was looking for—a small drugstore called Mussey's. Clint had told me where to go, offered to come with me, but I'd said no, not this time. I sat at the narrow lunch counter and ordered coffee. The other diners, perched on stools, gaped at me. Indianland, I thought, and I'm the intruder, an old lady with a black patent leather purse and cumbersome mukluks. The waitress stood in front of me, chewing gum and frowning.

Finally, I said, "Is Maria West here today?"

"She's in back. Why?"

"A friend."

"I doubt that."

But at that moment Maria walked out of a back room, in her hands a tray of glasses, and she stopped short. Her sudden frozen face told me she did not want Edna Ferber approaching her there.

Breezily, I called to her. "I need your help. To save your brother."

Maria peered at me, wary. "Noah?"

"You have more than one brother?"

Maria put down the tray, glared at the waitress, and walked around to the front of the counter. She slid onto the stool next to me.

"What do you want?"

I stared at her. Too much lipstick. Too much rouge. Too much of everything, this naturally pretty woman. A stunner, she was, but a web of wrinkles at the eye corners, along the lips. The ravages of a life of…what? Poverty? What did I really know about her?

I spoke in a soft voice. "Sam Pilot stayed with you his last days. I've asked you before, and I'm asking you again—he must have talked."

She was shaking her head vigorously, then a broad smile. "You didn't know the old man, Miss Ferber. A rock, granite, sitting in a chair and staring at the wall. I come back from the drugstore, greet him, fry an egg or a chop, something to eat, and he barely moves."

"But once he learned Jack Mabie was in town?"

She nodded. "True, that made him—well, maybe lively." She laughed. "For a split second." Her eyes darkened. "Happy, then angry, then...blank. His look used to scare me."

"He liked you?"

"Blood—and I left him alone."

"When Jack was murdered, did he talk?"

She thought for a bit. "Yeah, actually he did. He got this... like talking jag one night, rambling, then when he met with Noah—I guess they talked at the Nordale—he clammed up. But I could see something was bothering him."

"Okay, you told me that before. Why?" I looked into her face.

"I don't know."

"And then he was murdered."

She started. "I thought he just, you know, got drunk and fell against a wall. Froze himself."

"Murdered," I said, emphasizing the word. "That's what Noah and I believe."

She shivered. "Oh, Christ, Miss Ferber." She sucked in her cheeks. "You know, Sonia Petrievich visited him at my apartment."

I sat up. "What?"

"Right before he died. She rushes in, bombarding him with questions. I'm in the kitchen so I don't hear most of it, but he don't answer her. He stares at her, puts his hand over his heart, and stares her down."

"Sonia thought he knew why—not by whom—Jack was murdered."

"When I walked in, he's there, hand on his heart, and he said, 'Get this woman outa here.'"

"What did she do?"

"She left."

"What did he say afterwards?"

Maria bit her lip and gazed over my shoulder. She spoke in a hollow voice, so low I had to lean in. "He said, 'I have lived long enough to see the dead come back to life.'"

Someone called to her from the back room, and she jumped. "I gotta work. Sorry."

"Maria…"

But she was moving away. Over her shoulder she said, "Tell Noah I said hello."

Chapter Twenty-two

Noah and I sat in the Gold Nugget waiting for Ty Gilley. Mid-afternoon, the place empty, the waitress poured us coffee and then disappeared into the back kitchen. Noah, restless, kept looking toward the doorway. I reached out and touched his wrist. "Calm down."

"I can't." Then he laughed. "I'm always calm, Edna."

"So I noticed." I followed his gaze to the doorway. "He's late, but I know he'll arrive."

Noah fidgeted. "You know, I think I scared him. I knocked on his door, stared him in the face, and said, 'Three people have been murdered, Ty Gilley. And Edna Ferber and I suspect you know something about it.'"

I laughed out loud. "As good an opening line as I can imagine, but perhaps not even true. He didn't cower in fear?"

"He turned white, stepped backward, grabbed the door-jamb for support. I couldn't believe what he said back to me. 'We want to talk to you,' I added, and he simply nodded. 'I know. I suppose it's time. I don't want people suspecting me.'"

"I knew we were on to something." My palm slapped the table, and Noah flinched.

He went on. "'Is there a reason they might suspect you?' I asked him. 'Yes.' That was it. And he agreed to meet us here"—he checked his wristwatch—"a half hour ago."

"Be patient." But I checked the doorway. "I've felt that Ty Gilley, mystery man, creeping around the Nordale, holds one answer. I'm not certain what—but a step we need."

"But a murderer?" Noah asked, wide-eyed.

"I think we'll know that this afternoon—if he shows."

Again the quick, nervous glance toward the doorway. "I'll hunt him down."

"Like a sun-dizzy caribou on the taiga."

He laughed a long time. "You've started talking like an Alaskan."

I sipped my coffee and watched him over the rim, my words now dark. "Who gains by murdering these three souls, Noah?"

"Jack was killed for a reason, and then Sam Pilot, who'd probably suspected who killed Jack."

I held his eye. "And then Sonia, investigating, probing, interviewing, a shadow on the wall, suddenly suspected who did the murders." I qualified that. "Though she first assumed Sam had killed Jack."

He blew out his cheeks. "Which meant she had to die. She got too close to the answer."

"Who gained?" I asked again. "Sonia learned—and rightly so, I now believe—that the roots of the first murders could be traced to the far North. Maybe even Fort Yukon."

"Something to do with Tessa and the murder of her missionary friend?"

"Or lover."

"Preston's father?"

I thought about that. "I don't think so, but who knows?"

"Jack and Sam—so many murders they committed, real or imagined. Legendary."

"Probably the one that mattered here and now—Ned Thomas. The only one with a connection to Tessa. Hence Sonia's note."

"Tessa's scandalous past coming back to haunt her? Her

vast power now. She knew but kept her mouth shut when you questioned her. She played games."

"Preston," I said. "Preston had problems with Jack, despised him, hated how he hurt his business, fought in the street. Jack threatened him. But I don't know if he knew about his mother's connection to Ned Thomas. Tessa may have feared something would come out—tarnish her name in Fairbanks. The old rumors might resurface."

Noah sighed and checked the doorway. "I can't see Tessa commanding Preston to kill Jack. And then Sam." His voice trembled. "Then Sonia."

"Unless there's a deeper story we don't know about. A darker motive."

He made a face. "Always possible. But what about Jeremy Nunne, the one who started the rumble with Jack down at the Bristol Bay cannery?"

I considered that for a moment but shook my head. "Jeremy strikes me as an overblown frat boy with some sentimental urges—remember how he went to see Jack in the Frontier Home?—a man floundering, probably unhappy in Alaska, unhappy with his imperious Aunt Tessa."

Noah broke in, "And probably disliking his gruff but slick-as-polished-leather relative Preston Strange."

"Preston intrigues me. All that money and so little control of his temper."

"Another mystery man. I keep thinking of Sam's line—'He was there.' And Jack's—'Maybe it ain't him.'"

"Those lines tell us something. Told Sonia something."

"They talked, Jack and Sam. They both were face to face with…" I stopped.

Ty Gilley walked in the door. He stood in the doorway, bundled up, his face almost hidden behind a dark purple scarf, though his gloved hands clutched a manila folder. For some reason he waited there, watching us, until, impatient,

I waved him over. He shuffled, stopped, then moved. May I take two steps? Children at recess.

He stood by the table. "Please sit down," I stared up into his face, but he still didn't move. "Is there something the matter?"

A harsh, guttural voice. "Of course, there is. I didn't come to Alaska for this."

"What you came to Alaska for is the subject of our invitation to you, Mr. Gilley." My voice louder. "Sit, please."

Unburdened of his layers, dropping a glove on the floor, bending over to retrieve it and banging into Noah's side, he finally settled into a seat opposite me. His shoulder brushed against Noah's, and he breathed deeply. He placed the manila folder on the table, and the three of us stared at its worn, crumpled edges, scribbled pencil markings, a food stain perhaps, a coffee ring. He smiled at it. "My life." He touched the folder tenderly.

A small, round man, he shifted on the chair, adjusting himself, uncomfortable, tugging at the sleeves of his bulky green and red sweater. Santa's elf, I thought grimly, though gone to seed. A haggard, freckled balloon face. When he smiled, he revealed a prominent overbite. A pug nose, unlovely on the flushed face. Strands of whitish hair floated above his head, loosened by the static of his hat removal. Self-consciously, he drew his hand over his scalp, an attempt to flatten the vagrant hair, though his quick gesture did nothing but send his electrified hair in different directions. His small brown eyes darted from Noah to me, back and forth, waiting.

I began slowly, softening my words. "Coffee?" He nodded, and the waitress, who'd been hovering nearby, rushed over and filled a cup for him. He gulped it down, black, hot, his lips twitching from the heat.

"Mr. Gilley."

"Ty," he said. "Please."

"Ty, you approached Sonia, then Jack, then Sam, all with

your story about searching for information about your father. All three of these folks were murdered."

He shuddered. "But not by me."

"Then help us. Your story…"

"Is true. Every word. My father came to Alaska and disappeared."

Noah watched him closely. "But that's not the whole story, is it? Something else is going on?"

He smiled thinly at Noah. "Yeah."

"Tell us." I spoke so sharply Noah glanced at me, a hint of a smile on his face.

Ty relaxed. "I never knew my father, but Mom told us stories about him—heroic, wonderful stories." He laughed out loud. "A wonderful hero, bigger than life, though a wanderer. A man who craved adventure but, real poor, wanted more for us. He headed to the Army but wandered to Alaska to make his fortune…and never returned." He breathed in, bit his lip. "He was hanged. For a crime he didn't commit."

I sat up. "Hanged?" The word caught in my throat.

"Somewhere. Who knows where? We thought Dawson over to Canada. Then Skagway. Then Circle City. We never found out. We found an old magazine he left behind—he circled a small village called Old Crow. Far, far up north."

"What happened?"

Slowly, he opened the tattered folder and pulled out a folded sheet of typescript, opening it carefully, the edges of the yellowed paper crackling. "As a young man I spent hours in libraries, old bound newspapers that talked of the North. Nothing, no records. Like it never happened. Until by chance in a Seattle paper, an article on Alaska, a territorial marshal's notebook, found on his frozen body and published—I found and copied this."

He slid it across the table. I read: "Clay Fowler, 40 or thereabouts, drifter, hanged for common thievery outside an Indian village."

"Your father?"

He nodded. "1915. The only thing I ever found. And by chance, really."

"So it set you on a lifetime mission?" Noah asked sympathetically.

"Yeah, though life got in the way. A bad marriage, this and that, sickness."

"But not much to go on." I hesitated. "You said an innocent man, Ty."

He reached back into the folder. "After my mother died, I went through her stuff. She never mentioned a letter she got around that time. It's a letter that got me nuts—like a sense of injustice, everything wrong, horrible. It's what finally got me to take a job here in Alaska."

His fingers gripped a yellowed envelope, jagged tears at the edges, and a childlike block address on the front. Gingerly, he withdrew a small slip of lined paper, so chalky now, gray at the edges. When I reached for it, he held it back, but held it out so I could read it, though he read the words out loud—and from memory:

"Dear Mrs. Fowler, you don't know me a friend of your husband Clay. A good man he was, and tricked. Somebody stole a cache of miner tools, not him but blamed him said he done it. A crooked man done it blamed your husband, testified like before the posse of men and swift justice hung Clay a good man. The notorious scoundrel runs off with the stuff. I liked your husband Clay and found this address inside his wallet and said to myself send a letter with the bad news. A good man I'm sorry ma'am. He talked of you and his children. His friend Lonny."

Sad silence at the table, the awful deed covering us. The smell of old paper, so intense, like old winter apples in a farm bin. His fingers shaking, Ty carefully folded the letter and tucked it carefully into the envelope, and then back into the folder. For a moment he closed his eyes, moist at the corners.

"No return address," Ty said. "No nothing."

"Mr. Gilley...Ty," Noah began, "how horrible for you."

He nodded up and down furiously, his eyes still closed. "It haunts me. Still."

"So you thought Sonia could...?"

"When I read her 'White Silence' interviews, all those old times, the old-timers from the Bush, I thought, hey, someone will know where it happened. Remember him. Someone still alive to this day. How do you forget a hanging?"

Noah added, "And you thought Jack Mabie, a man who boasted of killing, might be the man?"

Again the furious nodding. "Yes." His voice rose. "I thought—God is giving him to me. Here in Fairbanks."

"But you got no answers?" I went on.

"Nothing. Not from Sonia, from Jack."

"Sam Pilot? You approached him in the Nordale." Noah waited.

"Yeah, another one who dismissed me." His tongue rolled over his lower lip. "He made me feel foolish."

"The inscrutable Indian," Noah said.

With a note of desperation in his voice, Ty said, "I even tried to see Tessa Strange."

"Why her?"

"I had a talk with Sonia in the lounge, the night before she died. She mentioned Tessa Strange. 'She was there.' Strange words. Sonia told me she was up in the North in those early years. A missionary. Fort Yukon. Venetie. I figured she might remember the awful story."

I sucked in my cheeks. "But she wouldn't see you, right?"

He gulped. "I couldn't get past her son, Preston. He got real belligerent, said I was crazy—even said his mother was never up in the North. A bold-faced lie that made no sense. Everybody I talked to knew that. I figured what is he—or even she—hiding?"

I caught Noah's eye. "Good question. Tessa seems always to be hiding a lot of things. I wonder how much she's told Preston."

Noah grumbled, "Preston, the hatchet man of her empire."

"And then there's Jeremy."

Noah drummed his fingers against his lips. "The court jester, maybe. The fool who may be privy to the inner workings of the empire."

"But it seems to me Tessa is more concerned with her reputation now—she believes the events of long ago mean nothing."

Ty was following our exchange, anxious to say something. "I sometimes wonder if Jack Mabie was involved with my father. Farfetched, yeah, but…an evil man."

That stopped me. "True."

"I even told that to Sonia."

"In which case," Noah went on, though his voice softened, "the police might still consider you a suspect, no?"

Ty's jaw got slack and he fumbled with the folder, seemed ready to bolt. Suddenly he became nervous, twisting in the seat, one hand gripping his parka. "But I'm not."

Noah looked into his face and summed up, "Jack Mabie was legendary in inflicting his wide-ranging misery across the Arctic for decades, and real proud of it. Sam Pilot often was there to lie and scheme and rush the evil man out of town."

Ty's voice broke, ragged. "Do you believe me a killer, Miss Ferber?"

I didn't answer him. Instead, thinking aloud, I said, "The first time Sam Pilot sat in the Nordale lounge, up against the back wall, facing out, he seemed to watch you when you stepped into the room. I remember thinking—what in the world? That glassy stare, that frozen face that stayed focused on yours. Almost a trance. Do you remember that?"

He swallowed noisily. "Yeah, I do. It wasn't pretty, that moment. I walk in and there's this frightening-looking Indian, that old leathery face and that long white hair, like someone from a goddamn nightmare, and he catches your eye."

"And held it, right?"

He shook his head. "No." He reconsidered. "I mean, I turned away, uncomfortable. But I thought maybe he got an answer. But he scared me that first time."

"But something happened," I went on. "Within seconds, flummoxed, he stood and fled the lounge. Perhaps trailing you." I turned to Noah. "You heard him say something in Athabascan."

Noah nodded. "Gwich'in. 'He was there.'"

Ty pursed his brow, confused. "What the hell does that mean? Really. I wasn't anyplace, for God's sake."

"But he seemed to recognize you," Noah insisted.

"No, I don't think so. How? Maybe because I was staring at him so hard, so crazily."

"You never met him before?" I asked.

He thought a second. "'He was there.' Those words can't mean me. No way. Christ, I don't remember my father. You know, I was maybe two when he took off. A toddler. Not even one memory of him. Some faded picture of him, yes, but that's it. In a few years my mother remarried, a fool named Gilley." He grinned sloppily. "He adopted us, and I got this goofy last name. In school—'Silly Gilley, will he?' Nice gift for a bumbling kid, right?" His voice trembled. "I was just a son trying to get some feeble justice for a wronged father."

"Justice for a wronged father." I echoed his words.

My mind roiled—yes. A father-son bond that stretched out

across a half-century, tenuous, mysterious but always there. Suddenly I got dizzy as an idea percolated in my brain— a fierce image that settled in the corner of my mind and intruded, like a pebble in an old shoe.

Noah and Ty were staring at me, Noah's eyes wide with alarm. "What, Edna?"

"Ty, I think you should share your story with Hank Petrievich. He was part of that world. He knew folks. And maybe Clint, another old-timer. In fact, Preston and Jeremy."

Puzzled, Noah said, "Edna, what are you up to?"

I smiled. "What makes you say that?"

"I don't know," Ty began. "I don't like talking about the… the hanging."

I cut him off. "I know the ending of this story now."

Chapter Twenty-three

Hank Petrievich paused in the doorway of the Nordale lounge, stopping so abruptly that Irina, close behind him, crashed into his back and whimpered. Clint Bullock, shuffling alongside him, frowned as Hank announced, "Christ, I haven't been in this lounge in so long." His eyes scanned the room and held mine. "Nothing's changed. Everything still cherry red and old and worn." But there was a nervous timbre to his voice as he threw a small wave at me.

I sat with Noah in a corner of the lounge. Eight o'clock at night, the lounge largely deserted, though a foursome of businessmen bunched near the reception desk, a cloud of cigarette smoke over their heads, sheaves of papers in their laps. They glanced up as Hank passed, one of them nodding at him familiarly, but Hank was focused on Noah. The two men watched each other warily. When Hank sat down, at angles to Noah, he nodded slightly, a tacit acknowledgment of the man he believed murdered his daughter—or believed it in vagrant moments. Irina, leaning forward, suddenly grasped Noah's hand and squeezed it. Clint looked at me, a look that suggested he'd brokered the inevitable reunion.

Ty Gilley strolled in, his head spinning around as if on ball bearings, and took a seat to my right. He mumbled at Hank, "Sir, Miss Ferber wants me to tell you my story."

Gruff, coldly, Hank replied, "I know. I still don't understand why."

At that moment Preston Strange and Jeremy Nunne walked in together, Preston loudly announcing to a gaping Teddy at the reception desk that he did not like to be summoned places. Jeremy, his face grim, tried to shush him. Teddy purposely looked down at some papers on his desk, though from where I sat I could see his eyes followed Preston as the officious businessman shuffled past. An amused look on his face, Teddy was a man used to dealing with self-important guests at the hotel.

Though Jeremy said nothing, his eyes wide with consternation, Preston began chatting with Hank about some business venture long on the drawing boards for Fairbanks, a purposeful avoidance of Noah and me—and a cavalier dismissal of the unknown Ty Gilley. Hank replied in monosyllables, unhappy with Preston's nervous bluster.

As I cleared my throat, I noticed Paul Petrievich slip quietly into the room, something his mother spotted as she raised a welcoming finger at him, though he settled into a chair a few feet from our group, a chair turned halfway toward the doorway, so that I observed his profile—tense, his jaw rigid.

"Paul," I said, "welcome. Join us."

"I have." Then he laughed. "I think I'll be able to hear what's going on."

Preston grumbled, "I have no idea why we were asked to come here for this…this carnival show." He threw back his head and smirked.

"Quiet," Jeremy whispered. "Let's get this over with. This is not going to be good."

Preston glowered at me. "Entertainment for a cold Fairbanks night? Usually it's getting royally lit at the Pastime Cocktail Lounge."

"You'll still have time for that when you leave here," I told him.

He spoke through clenched teeth. "Oh, I'm allowed an escape plan?"

"You may need it," Hank suddenly said, surprising himself, and Irina reached over to place her hand on his wrist. A look that communicated *Not now, Hank.*

I cleared my throat again. "The reason Noah and I asked you all here is simple." I looked at a fidgeting Ty. "Mr. Gilley, as some of you may know, or maybe not, has come to Alaska to find out, if possible, what happened to his long-missing father. A common enough story in these parts, the old prospectors and wanderers disappearing. But I learned there's more to the story. I figured at first Hank, long a traveler to the North, especially decades ago, might offer him a clue—might recall a story told over a campfire. But then I thought—why not all of you? Because all of you have roots in the North."

"I was a child," Preston protested. "I remember ice and snow."

Jeremy grumbled, "I am new to Alaska."

I cut them off. "Preston, your mother lived there for years. She knew the players." Purposely I employed Sonia's prophetic words in her note to Tessa. "Your mother cannot come here, of course, but perhaps you can remember stories." I stopped, not convinced by my own words. Not my real intent, this ruse, but the cloudy look in Preston's eye told me he was buying none of it.

"Then let's get this over." Preston rolled his eyes.

"Ty," I motioned to him, "tell your story."

And he did, his voice halting, at times a whisper, other times firm and confident. A folk tale, fireside Homeric, yes, flat and colorless, but very effective. The hanging of his father somewhere in the Yukon, trickery, thievery, false accusation, lies, an honest man betrayed, a family's destruction. Talking, he gathered steam, his words rising in squeaky crescendo, and he stopped suddenly, his final word—"Murdered!"—hurled into the quiet space with such force that Irina yelped.

Interesting, I thought, watching the faces of the listeners. Hank at first seemed indifferent, his head dipped, a man still covered in grief for his dead daughter. But as Ty went on, Hank looked up, paid attention, focused, at one point nodding. Irina began crying. Although it was difficult to gauge Paul's face because I saw only a profile, it was clear he was fascinated. When Ty finished, Paul turned his chair, stared directly into Ty's face, and actually saluted him. A whispered, "Good for you. The good son."

But Preston and Jeremy fascinated me, both men sitting so close their shoulders brushed against each other. Jeremy had an eager look, the frisky puppy in the store window, head bobbing up and down, but a stranger's indifference. You're telling me a story, a good one at that. Got any more chilling Arctic tales to waste this cold, cold night? Occasionally he'd glance at the roaring fireplace, rub his hands together as though he were chilled, then start to bob his head again.

Preston never took his eyes off Ty. A steely, unblinking look, almost fierce, his body rigid and unmoving, his hands folded decorously in his lap. Only once did his gaze shift—to me, in fact—a look that said: *All right now, what's the game here? What's afoot? What horror are you planning to drop at my footstep, Miss Ferber? This is about me—yes? I'm no fool, sister.*

Ty's heartfelt talk over, a babble of voices erupted. Irina left her chair and hugged him, which made him uncomfortable. Hank and Preston spoke at once. Hank said he couldn't help— he never saw the incident, nor had he heard of it. Not this one. Others on the Yukon trails. Other shootings, hangings, ambushes. Shell games that ended in violence. But most were legend, maybe mythic, campfire stories. He ended, "I never heard of Clay Fowler. Sorry."

"Preston," I began, "your mother was a missionary in Venetie. Minto. She spent days at Fort Yukon. Years in the territory. Did she ever mention—?"

He sliced into my words, almost angrily. "No. Of course not. My mother looked back on those years with—I was going to say a spiritual journey she left behind—but no, she would have no reason to fill her little boy's ears with tales of treachery and hanging and wrongdoing. The topic was taboo."

"She knew the murdered missionary, Ned Thomas," I broke in.

I could see the name resonated because he flinched, a bead of sweat on his brow. "I don't have a clue what you're babbling about, Miss Ferber." He glanced at his watch and reached for his coat. "Well, this has been delightful."

"Wait a second," Noah insisted. "There's more to all these stories."

"What does that even mean?" Preston remarked.

"It means that there have been three murders in Fairbanks."

Irina cried out while Hank flinched. Preston half-rose from his seat.

"Jesus Christ," Preston bellowed, "a little decency, no?"

"Murder isn't decent." Noah said.

"But," sputtered Jeremy, looking at his uncle, "there's a time and a place."

I sucked in my cheeks. "This time's good as any." I smiled. "And I like this place. The Nordale lounge is where stories of the far North end up."

Silence as everyone checked out the others, conspiratorial, accusing. I realized that everyone here had thought—maybe had uttered outright—the name of someone sitting in the room that person suspected was a killer. An awful moment, tense, as everyone looked around, then turned away.

"All I'm saying," I began slowly, "is that Ty's sad story got me thinking about the bond between father and son. About the invisible cord that stretched from the far North down to Fairbanks. Indeed, even to the Lower Forty-eight. A cord that stretched for decades."

"Your point, Miss Ferber?" Preston, again checking his watch.

"My point, Preston, is that the idea of a son in search of a father set me on a path to consider the why of three murders. Jack Mabie, Sam Pilot, Sonia Petrievich."

A faraway voice from Paul, now facing us. "Sam murdered? I thought he froze to death drunk."

Noah looked at him. "Sam was murdered because he knew who killed Jack Mabie."

Explosive words that brought about a rush of confused voices.

I waited.

Then, I breathed in. "'I and the Father are one.'"

"What?" From Hank, baffled.

"Am I misquoting the Bible?" I said, wide-eyed. I smiled. "Does anyone have a Bible? I thought all hotels had Gideon Bibles. I'm making a point here."

Paul laughed out loud and called to Teddy who was hanging over the reception desk. "A Bible?"

Teddy squinted. "A prayer service here?"

"A Bible?" Paul repeated.

Teddy disappeared and walked over with an old Bible. "My personal Bible," he said. "Not the hotel's. Treasured. My morning scripture to begin the day."

Preston was rolling his eyes. "This is all ridiculous."

I reached for the Bible but Teddy cautioned, "Fragile, Miss Ferber."

"Then could you please turn to Matthew 3.17?"

A quizzical look on his face, but he slowly opened the old pages. The crackle of old pulp. In a scratchy voice he read: "'And lo a voice from Heaven, saying, this is my beloved son, in whom I am well pleased.'" He added editorially, "A lovely passage."

"Thank you, Teddy." I took the Bible from his hands, ran my fingers over the weathered old leather, smiled at him, and placed the Bible in my lap. "I won't harm it. Teddy. Trust me, I promise. I value old books. If you don't mind, I will need it for one other quote."

Hesitant, he shrugged and walked to the reception desk.

Irina spoke up. "Edna, are we going somewhere with this?"

"The Biblical quotations came to mind last night as I thought about things. Fathers and sons. The Lord God and Jesus. Mortal men. A father and his son. Ty and his father. Others."

Noah looked at me. "Folks, this is the story of a father and a son." His eyes drifted across the faces staring at him. "Sonia investigated the murders with her usual dogged determination to get a story."

"And look where it got her," Paul mumbled.

His father shot him a look, but Paul wasn't looking at him.

Noah continued. "Sonia obviously was intrigued by Sam Pilot. What did he know? She also probably realized that the murder of Jack Mabie, admittedly an annoying and crusty old man, probably dated back to his outlaw days. These days he was a garrulous old drunk."

I went on. "Somehow she connected an old murder—that of a missionary in Fort Yukon—with Jack."

Hank interrupted. "God, yes. In fact, we talked about it. No, wait. After her interview with Jack, the meanest man in Alaska, I told her—'You know he was the man who killed a missionary in Fort Yukon.' Later on she asked and I told her—he was an old friend of Tessa Strange. That surprised her."

Paul spoke up. "Yeah, we know about that murder. We heard about it as kids. The guy shot in front of his kids. But I never connected a name—Jack Mabie—to it. All we knew was that a harmless missionary guy had been murdered."

Hank looked at his son, nodded. "When I told Sonia that the man she'd interviewed was the man who killed him, she got excited."

I added, "Hence her note to Tessa. She mentioned Jack

Mabie and Sam Pilot. Suddenly she had the beginning of a new story."

Irina looked perplexed. "You're saying the murder of that man so long ago led to this tragedy?"

"Yes, I am." I looked at Noah. "We are. Our thinking."

Noah went on. "When Sonia sent that note, Tessa refused to see her. And when Tessa showed the note to Edna, it was too late. Tessa claimed she was afraid to show it to the police because it would implicate Preston. She hoped it would implicate *me*."

A loud shout. "Are you people insane?" Preston stood up, waved his fist in the air. "This is all nonsense."

At his side Jeremy reached out and tugged at his elbow. "Sit down," he murmured.

Preston stammered, "As my mother told Miss Ferber, the note implicated—Noah." His finger pointed at Noah, trembled in the air.

Noah started. "But she feared it would point to you."

"Why would I kill Jack Mabie?"

"Why, indeed?" I said. "I agree it's preposterous. Preston didn't like Jack, acted around him like a foolish hothead, but did he kill him? And then Sam? And then Sonia?"

Again Preston stood up, face flushed.

"Could you sit down and shut up?" Jeremy whispered.

I counted a beat. "All Noah and I are saying, frankly, is that Sonia made a connection with the killing of Ned Thomas in Fort Yukon with the present. The question is—why *now*? What would make someone exact vengeance all these years later? A desire to kill that spanned decades."

Silence. Everyone's eyes on me, waiting. Preston was breathing heavily.

"My blood is Sam Pilot." Noah's words broke the silence.

"What?" From Hank, agitated.

"Sam understood what was going on, though at first he

rejected the idea, confused that he was. Sam sat in this very lounge, a frozen figure, then bolted out. Then, again, later on, a long stretch of hours as he sat impassive against the back wall. A vigil that obviously got Sonia's attention."

"So what?" asked Irina. "An odd man."

"Not odd," Noah insisted. "Prescient. We have to consider some of the things we heard him say."

I began, "He saw it." I smiled. "Admittedly in Gwich'in."

"Jack's response," Noah added. "'Maybe it ain't him.'"

"'I have seen the face of God.'"

"And," Noah concluded, "to my sister Maria, he said, 'Is it possible to return from the dead?'"

"Shaman talk," Hank said hurriedly, "the mystical rattling of the old shamans. The ancient superstitions."

I shook my head. "No, Hank. Nothing mystical about it."

Noah spoke over my words. "Father and son."

Jeremy spoke up. "You keep saying that."

"Edna and I first thought Sam was talking about Ty Gilley because Sam seemed to be startled by Ty's appearance in the lounge. He fled the lounge right afterwards."

"But we were both wrong," I said. "There was no way Sam could have recognized Ty. Ty was a toddler when his father disappeared. A stranger to Alaska."

"What are you saying?" Hank was impatient.

"It suddenly dawned on me, Hank, that Sam, indeed, did see a ghost. The dead did rise again. A dead man—murdered—came back to life. He saw something that drove him to tell Jack about it. Someone else." I breathed in. "When I was visiting Noah's grandfather in Fort Yukon, he talked to me of early life there. The missionaries. Of Tessa Strange and of Ned Thomas. How Jack lusted after Ned's wife, trumped up a charge, then shot him in the heart. Sam lied to cover it."

"So?" From Preston, nervous.

"So Nathan West shared with me old photos and, by

chance, there was an old grainy snapshot of Ned Thomas with his family. With Tessa and Lionel Strange. I've been thinking a lot about that photo. I thought the image looked familiar."

I stopped, collected my thoughts. At my right Noah encouraged me, his fingers tapping my elbow, a thin smile on his face.

Teddy maneuvered his way through the others and placed a cup of hot tea on the table. I smiled up at him. "Thank you, Teddy."

He grinned at me. "You're doing a lot of talking, Miss Ferber."

Preston grumbled, "The only true words said here tonight."

I grasped Teddy's sleeve. "A moment more, please. I need you for something." I tapped his Bible in my lap.

That bothered him, his eyes shifting back to his empty reception desk, and he shifted from one foot to the other.

Noah spoke loudly. "Sam Pilot saw Ned Thomas."

My finger in the air, I corrected him. "No, Noah, he saw Ned Thomas' son."

A rumble throughout the room, Irina making a chirping sound, Hank clearing his throat. Even Clint, who'd been watching me closely, made a rattling sound.

"Revenge," Noah added, "served frozen."

I sucked in my breath. "May I introduce you all to Ned Thomas' son?" I raised the teacup and saluted Teddy.

Teddy jumped, spun around, and didn't know where to look. His voice garbled, "What are you talking about?"

I pointed at the identification tag on his shirt, a small clipped-on metal strip that said: Ted Thomson.

"I finally realized why he had that name."

"Really?" Teddy exclaimed. "How foolish. Thomas' son? Tom's son? A stretch?"

I ignored that. "Talking with Noah, I realized that Sam Pilot was not startled that day by Ty's appearance. I thought back—Teddy had just served me a cup of tea. Sam, looking up, stared into the face of the man Jack murdered. I finally remembered why I thought the image in Fort Yukon so familiar. In the back room here, where Teddy naps, a family photo. His father. The same man."

"Preposterous." Teddy's voice trembled. "I've never been north of Fairbanks."

"So you tell everyone. Over and over. But I wondered when you joked that my going to Fort Yukon was dangerous. Frostbite making me lose a foot. Or, you said, a toe of someone walking to an icebox church. I remember—this little piggy went to…an icebox church. An odd remark, not 'to the market,' as any child recites, but a missionary son's remark, no?"

Suddenly Ty Gilley spoke up. "Christ, yeah." His voice rose. "Teddy talked to me about it. I didn't pay it any mind then."

"Sonia, investigating, pursued Sam Pilot. She questioned folks in the lounge, doubtless even Teddy. Definitely Teddy. Being a good investigative reporter, she came to believe that Teddy murdered Jack. 'He was there.' 'Maybe it ain't him.' Sam's flight out the door. Who else? Lord knows what else she uncovered."

Teddy was wetting his lips, his arms swinging at his side.

Noah was watching Teddy closely. "'He saw it.' Sam's words. Ned's son was there—saw his father wrongly murdered."

"And," I concluded, touching the Bible in my lap, "a good missionary's son somehow forgot Proverbs: 'Do not say, "I will repay evil." Wait for the Lord because he will deliver you.'"

I lifted the Bible and opened it. "As I suspected, a family treasure. Here, look." My fingertip touched the faded-ink signature on the first blank page. I read out loud: "Edmund Thomas, Butte, Montana."

Teddy grabbed the book from my hands. He arched his back, and his voice thundered, "I waited long enough for God to deliver me. I had to repay evil myself."

As I watched, Clint withdrew his pipe, fumbled with the tobacco pouch, but quietly walked out of the lounge, disappearing from sight. I watched his retreating back, but said nothing.

"Why, Teddy?" Hank asked. His voice broke. "My daughter?"

Teddy's laugh was eerie. "I had no choice."

Noah whispered, "Of course you did."

"What do you know, damn it? You slick yourself in here, an Indian in a suit, acting high and mighty."

"Sonia..." Hank's voice, breaking.

"I don't give a damn." Teddy threw back his head, and his eyes locked with mine. "I waited decades for this. You don't think I've hungered for this? The name Jack Mabie stayed with me like a curse. I was a young boy, but I saw my father shot down in front of me. He ruined my family. My mother—we drifted back to the Lower Forty-eight and she died of grief. Poverty, struggle. I struggled to make a life for me and my sister. And I vowed—someday... At night, burning, I wept. One night, finally, I said—go to Alaska."

"To track Jack Mabie?" From Noah.

"I didn't know if he was still alive. I spent years chasing rumors of the man. Once, I heard of an outlaw named Jack in Kodiak. A summer there, searching. Not the man. I never forgot that evil face, the maniacal laugh. Everything about him. And Sam Pilot, backing him up. The Indian without a soul. Vacations from this dump—I wandered. Juneau. Nome. I almost gave up, but then suddenly there it was in *The Gold*." He laughed a long time. "There it was. The man was in town. Loud, drunk. Cocky."

"And so you killed him?" Hank asked.

"No challenge."

"But Sam realized..."

"The way the Indian sat here that night. He just stared

across the lounge. It gave me the willies. His eyes on me—feverish, hot—eerie. Like he seen a ghost. I knew that he knew then. Another drunk. Staggering in the night. Easy."

"Sonia." Again Hank's plaintive word, stretched out. Noah caught his eye.

"Sonia was a damn snoop. She questioned me over and over. Annoying. Why was Sam Pilot sitting in the lounge? What did he say to me? Then I came into work early, when May was on duty, and there was Sonia, sitting in back with her, chatting. She picked up my family picture, peering at it, then at me. A day later she asked if I heard of a murder in Fort Yukon. No, I said. I never went north of Fairbanks. But the lie sounded stupid, and after that she watched me. I caught her talking to the manager, asking to look over guest lists, even employee applications. I think he said no, but who knows? Foolishly, I'd written that I was born in Eagle. Years back—no matter then. Then she was nervous around me, and I knew she suspected. But she had no way of knowing for sure. One night, headed out from my rooms down the street, I saw her in the shadows, watching, watching. I knew."

"And you had to kill her, too."

Exasperated. "What choice did I have? Christ! Decades of waiting, hoping, praying, all to end with exposure?" A fake laugh. "I don't think so."

"But how?" Noah asked.

"Her note to Miss Ferber. I was off taking a towel to a guest and when I got back Silas Taylor said Sonia'd stopped in, left a note for Miss Ferber. He joked that she added something. He said she was happy to see *him*. Him, she stressed. Not me, I guess. In the middle of the night I opened the note and saw the line—'I can connect the dots.' I knew. She added that polite 'please' at the end." He tilted his head and snarled. "I added the bit about not telling Noah. Blame *him*. Because I already knew what I had to do."

"Blame an innocent soul." Paul's words were fiery.

"A morning run to the trading post by the airport. A red parka, some cheap tourist emblems. An old cane I owned for years. A call to *The Gold* changing the time to meet Miss Ferber. I knew she'd be at the school till nine. I hear everything."

"Convenient," I said. "I wondered why you chose my room."

A sickly grin. "So close to home, as they say. Convenient, indeed. When she arrived, I lied—said you'd called from your room. Go up now. She was hesitant, uncomfortable with me, but as she rifled through some papers in her purse, I scooted out the back door of the back room, hustled up the rear staircase, let myself into the room. In seconds she knocked."

"But she must have been surprised?"

"To put it mildly." A harsh laugh. "It gave me time to pull her in, smash her in the head, then beat her with the cane."

Irina screamed, grabbed Hank's hand.

Teddy ignored her. "Then I washed off traces of blood in a hurry, stuffed her papers into my vest—she'd outlined her case against me, in fact—cracked open the door. I waited until a guest came out of a room and I put on the parka—I'd actually hidden the parka and cane in Miss Ferber's room an hour before—and then, hood up, limped down the back stairwell. Back into my little space."

"My God." Irina started sobbing.

"And then waited for the hoopla to begin." He spun around, then back, glaring at me. "In the middle of the night I dropped the cane in an alley. I burned her papers in my fireplace." He grinned. "Evidence." He pointed at Noah. "I almost got him, too."

At that moment Clint returned, Chief of Police Rawlins next to him. Both men stood quietly in the doorway, the lawman with his hands folded over his chest. Clint caught my eye and cocked his head. He mouthed the words: *You're welcome, Edna.*

Teddy spotted the lawman, but turned back to us. "I don't care, you see. I got what I wanted. I dedicated my life to one pursuit. One only. A life driven by revenge." He shook his fist at the ceiling and laughed out loud. "I did what I wanted. I *got* what I wanted. No other purpose. Accomplished. Done. The final page of my book. Do with me as you will. My father sleeps easily in his grave."

Chief of Police Rawlins moved forward.

Teddy saluted him, his voice awful and fierce and echoey. "And tonight I will have the most peaceful sleep I've had since I was a little boy in Fort Yukon. I may even dream." His eyes moistened and he bowed at me, then at Noah. "Perchance to dream."

Chapter Twenty-four

"A sad story," Noah muttered as he sat having coffee with Clint and me. "Sonia, Jack, and Sam. The power of obsession."

I sighed. "Deep-seated vengeance." I looked at my watch. In two hours I'd be on a Pan Am flight to Seattle, then on to New York.

Noah was drumming his fingers on the table. He'd hardly touched his coffee. "I keep waiting for Sonia to tap me on the shoulder. To ask me to go to a movie."

"You have to make a decision," I told him.

"What do you mean?"

"I mean…Hank, Irina. After Teddy was arrested, Hank reached out to you in the lounge. He was trying to say he'd made a mistake."

"Yes, I know."

"And?"

A heartbeat. "I have lot of thinking to do."

"But you gotta give him a break," Clint said, reaching across the table and taking Noah's hand. "He made a mistake."

Noah rolled his tongue into the corner of his cheek. "Yes, he did."

"But you're not ready yet. Right?"

"I don't know what I'm ready for. You know, lying in bed last night I realized that I'm not mad at Hank anymore. His grief made him…irrational. And, I suppose, in time we'll talk again. But something has shifted in me. It had to. A lifetime of trust and love and…and believing. I learned something about him…"

"He ain't that man," Clint said hotly. "He's the father grieving for a dead girl."

Noah, sharply, "And what about me, Clint? I was like a son to him. What about me?"

Clint didn't answer.

"You say you're not angry, but you sound it." I stared into his face.

A long pause, then he smiled. "I suppose I am, still. But I talked to my grandfather last night, and I admit his words got to me…made me back off my anger." He sighed. "At least a little bit."

"What did he say?"

He looked at me. "It's not what he said. It's his silences that talk to me."

Clint grinned. "Something I'd expect you to say."

"Indians are inscrutable." Noah grinned. "Hollywood has taught us that."

"And mostly a pain in the ass," Clint said. "You forget that I was married to an Athabascan many years ago."

Clint excused himself, headed to the bathroom, and I saw him wince as he stood, and for a second he lost his breath, stumbled. Noah and I watched him walk away. I stared after him, shaking my head.

"Clint's dying," I said slowly. "You know that, don't you, Noah?"

He nodded. "I know. We all know. But he doesn't want to talk about it."

"What's gonna happen?"

Noah glanced toward the bathroom. "Clint's like most Alaskans, the old pioneers—as independent as can be, fiercely so. He once told me he won't be put into the Frontier Home, all those craggy old men sitting all day, playing cards, complaining about the food, the fact that no one comes to visit, wandering off at night to Omar's to get plastered. He wants to stay in his cabin. Or hang out in the Nordale. That's the way he wants to die…on his own terms, puttering around. Probably while chopping firewood."

"When he dies, an era ends."

"It ends a little every day, as the old sourdoughs die. Clint's one of the last."

Clint tottered back, sat down. "Talking about me?"

"Yes," Noah admitted. "We were saying you're one of the old pioneers."

Clint's voice rose. "Ain't gonna put me in the Frontier Death Camp, is you?"

"Wouldn't think of it," Noah said.

I changed the subject. "I heard that Tessa is near death. Another stroke." I sipped coffee. "And Paul has left Fairbanks," I said quietly.

Noah nodded. "Yeah, packed his bags and headed to the Lower Forty-eight."

"I think Hank and Irina hope he'll come to his senses and come back home."

"Paul called his mother from Seattle, she told me," I added. "He said he crossed paths with Jeremy Nunne on the streets, who told him Preston won't talk to him now. Jeremy's headed back to Ohio, to the family home—to forge his own life. He's sworn off Alaska—and Preston's empire."

I looked at my watch and said to Noah, "And what about you, Noah West?"

Noah stared back at me, a lopsided boyish grin on his face, almost mischievous, a boy caught in the cookie jar.

"I'm going home," he said. "I'm leaving Fairbanks."

"To stay with your grandfather?"

"For the summer." He breathed in. "Edna, I'm leaving this all behind. For now. I'm not going forever, but for a while. I got some catching up to do with myself." He grinned. "I'm a Qwich'in Thoreau, although, I admit, a pale, less reflective sort. I got to spend some time alone. This is not a place I recognize anymore. I walk the streets here and feel like a stranger."

"Well, you've been betrayed." My voice cracked. "So you will live with your grandfather?"

"No." Noah tilted his head, smiled. "No. Well, this summer, yes, as I said. In the old days we didn't live in cabins like now. We were nomadic, following seasons and the caribou. Winters on the traplines. So I want to live in that small cabin I have out on the Yukon Flats. By myself. This coming winter."

My heart sank. "The place you showed me in the plane?"

He nodded. "Yes."

"But there's nothing around it but tundra, vast and vacant and…"

"That's the idea."

"So small," I said, nervous.

"You build small cabins because they're easier to heat. Half of it is underground for insulation. One window so I can see the wolves and grizzlies coming to call. I want to trap animals. In the winter their pelts are thick and luxurious, you know. Clint knows that." Clint nodded. "I don't want to be around people."

"But I'm going to worry about you," I told him. "Out there. In the cold. People disappear in Alaska. You told me that. I can't get the idea out of my head."

He was smiling at me. "They do. I know. But one of the things I got to deal with…finally…is my father disappearing. My father and me. Even Maria and me. My lovely sister. All those years I refused to think about her life. I need to work on my life with her. I need to make her a part of our grandfather's life again."

I wagged a finger at him. "Become a real brother to her, Noah."

"Yes." He nodded.

"But if you go away…" I paused. "I'll worry."

"I promise you'll hear from me."

I started to say something but stopped.

"I won't forget you," he said.

"How will I know you're safe? Especially if you're hidden in a cabin?"

His eyes brightened. "I'll surprise you someday. You'll pick up your phone and…"

"I'll wait for that call, Noah. Then I'll know you're okay."

"Promise."

"I just did."

Epilogue

The morning doorman at my apartment house seems ready to say something, so I hurry by. Despite the starch-pressed gray uniform with the gaudy Prussian epaulets on his wide shoulders, there is always something rough-hewn about James. His face looks bronzed, enormously wrinkled, a man more at home on a Wyoming cattle range than in the subdued but still ostentatious entrance of a posh East Side doorman building. As I stroll by him, this first day of July, very early, a scorching day, he tips his hat dutifully and says a ritualistic, "Good morning, Miss Ferber."

My fingertips gingerly smoothing the lace trim of my collar, I walk past. But hearing him clear his throat, I hasten my admittedly ancient step away from the building. My morning walk, up Park Avenue, over to Fifth or, sometimes, living wildly, down Lexington, a mile and a half, sometimes more, rain or sun or ice or war or Manhattan pestilence, and then back to Molly Hennessey's sumptuous breakfast, the morning mail.

But today I'm exhilarated and feel giddily triumphant, though I've said nothing to Molly this morning. And I know why. At a news kiosk on Lexington, just before I turn back toward Park Avenue, I glance at *The New York Times*, pinned on the rack:

ALASKA ADMITTED AS 49th STATE.

July 1, 1958.

I had nothing to do with this, truly, but I find myself chuckling: well, maybe just a little. After all, I wrote *Ice Palace*, my fervent novel about Alaska and the pro-statehood movement there, published four months ago, in March. Fairbanks read it, and Anchorage and Juneau. And the impassioned Alaskan women—mainly women, I know—fired off letters to Congress, to newspapers, promoting statehood.

Without my planning it, I'd written a front-page novel, newsworthy and talked of.

Back at my apartment building I pause on the sidewalk, spotting James rushing to open the door for me.

"Miss Ferber," James says, the sleepy eyes in the grizzly face.

"James." I stroll past him.

He clears his throat, unsure. "Miss Ferber," he says again, louder. I turn back. "I just learned that you wrote that book on Alaska. The super just mentioned it—gave me his copy. I didn't know…"

"What didn't you know?"

"Miss Ferber, I was in Alaska for four years."

That stops me. "Really?"

"The war years. Afterwards. Went up there late in '42. Soon I was working for the U.S. Army, building the Alcan Highway, you know, from Dawson to just outside Fairbanks. I drove up in an old pickup, looking for work. When it was over I was in Fairbanks, a rough-and-tumble town, let me tell you."

"I know Fairbanks."

"I know it, too," he says emphatically. "Alaska got to me." He slips off a glove and holds up a hand, and I notice two of his fingers missing. "Frostbite. Fifty below in the winter." He pauses, makes eye contact. "Alaska got into my soul."

"Then why are you here?" I stare back into the rough sandpaper face.

"My wife was here. And I got real lonely." He chuckles. "But she wasn't so lonely, I guess. When I got back here, she left me for someone else."

"But you could have gone back to Alaska." I take a step away.

He stares at me a long time. "No, I was afraid to."

That gives me pause. "What?"

He runs his tongue over his lips. "Lonely in New York is one thing. Lonely there is dangerous. I lived in a cabin five miles outside Fairbanks, through a long winter." He whispers. "In Alaska people fall in love with loneliness. They disappear into the snow and ice."

That startles me. *People fall in love with loneliness.* A horrible line, that, but not new to me. Those vacant-eyed men who hid from the world among grizzly bears, wild blueberries, caribou on the taiga, the crushing ice of the Yukon, under the surrealistic Northern Lights.

As the elevator rises to my floor, I think of Noah. In my apartment I sit in the kitchen and say nothing while Molly puts coffee in front of me, and then buttery and crispy waffles, with tangy blueberry syrup sent from Alaska by Irina Petrievich. A gift. I push the plate away. *People fall in love with loneliness.*

Since I left Alaska, I've had two notes from Noah, only two brief notes, spirited, lovely. But then silence.

Now, the rumble of excitement about statehood, I feel the Earth move beneath my feet. Noah, the mukluk grapevine. Call me.

So it colors my afternoon on a day that should be a celebration. All afternoon the phone rings, the telegrams delivered. Edna Ferber, as front-page news. Katharine Hepburn, in Hollywood, sends a telegram: ALASKA AND EDNA. LOVE AT FIRST FROSTBITE. I smile. Dick and Dorothy Rodgers, out of town: EDNA DEAR YOU'RE FORCING

US TO BUY A NEW FLAG. WE'VE HAD THE OTHER SINCE ARIZONA WAS ADMITTED IN 1912. And Kitty Carlyle Hart, touring in the Midwest: DEAR EDNA YOU DO KNOW HOW TO MAKE A STATE (MENT). Clever, witty punsters, nutty, these friends of mine.

All afternoon I mumble, Thank you thank you thank you. I mean none of it.

I can't get my mind away from some tiny rickety cabin out on the desolate Yukon Flats, miles and miles and miles from anything…from anybody. And a young man, maybe…

I accept a call from Ernest Gruening, Alaska's Territorial senator, and now, most likely, Alaska's first state senator. He reaches me late afternoon, after a day of no work at my typewriter. He implores me to fly to Washington. I say no. He wants me to fly back to Alaska. I say no. He rattles on and on about my *Ice Palace* being instrumental in priming the pump—his quaint term, though I grimace—in getting Americans on Alaska's side, on letting the world beyond Alaska—the Outside—understand the pernicious workings of the Seattle-based salmon industry, the mining and transportation monopolies. "You did it, Miss Ferber," he says, formal, as always, with me. He even gloats that some are calling *Ice Palace* the "Uncle Tom's Cabin of Alaska statehood," something that makes little sense to me. When he finally hangs up, I sit there, phone still cradled to my ear, the dial tone humming. I stare at the clock.

In Alaska it is…what? Eight p.m. in Juneau, maybe later in Fairbanks. And on the churning, muddy Yukon, it is—what? There is no time there anyway. All longitudes start to converge toward the Pole, become one, cancel one another out. Above the Arctic Circle there is no time. Just loneliness…or aloneness…

I can't focus. I go to a drawer in my workroom, rummaging through my notes on Alaska, opening boxes of Alaska gifts—a walrus-bone carving, a caribou mask—and finally extract the small, frayed snapshot, three-by-five, the color fading. I put it close to my eyes. There he is, when he was a young man, maybe twenty or so. Noah. You can see the mighty Yukon, you can see a crude Indian fishing wheel, but standing in front, prominent, is the young man, tall and lanky, skin the color of mahogany, really, a chiseled jaw, a wide high-bridged nose, prominent cheekbones, a wash of thick black hair, the fierce black eyes staring at the photographer with a bemused look. He's dressed in a blue wool shirt, rolled up to his elbows, wrinkled brown canvas pants, and his muscular arms cradle a magnificent king salmon, maybe two feet long, glimmering, a ruddy prize.

No one knew I stole the snapshot.

I will call you.

I wait. I have no choice. I read of bonfires in Nome on the beaches that face the Soviet Union across the Bering Strait, the forty-nine-gun salute from the 207th Infantry Battalion of the Alaska National Guard, dancing in the streets, sirens blaring, even an attempt to dye the Chena River in Fairbanks a murky gold. Eskimos hurl one another into the air, celebratory blanket tosses, while tourists applaud.

Two days, three—waiting.

Then one night, actually two in the morning, I hear the phone ring and sit up in bed, and a panicky Molly Hennesey rushes from her small room off the kitchen, switching on lights as she moves. But she is surprised to see me, fluttering in my pink nightgown, my robe half-on, one sleeve dangling, already on the phone. "Molly, go back to bed."

I hear static, muttering, silence. "Hello."

"Edna."

My heart leaps, and I get dizzy. "It's you."

A chuckle. "I'm alive."

"I knew that."

"I was living with my grandfather. He's taken ill. But better now. I'm in my cabin." Static, hissing, beeping sounds." The voice starts to fade. "I promised you…"

"Where are you?" *Loneliness…people fall in love with…*

"It doesn't matter."

"Are you all right?"

A moment of silence. "I can't talk long. I'm using a military phone."

"What? Who?"

Then I remember his stories of those frozen communication centers deep in the wild—the sixty-foot radar towers of the DEW Line, the almost-open White Alice Communication system then being built near Fort Yukon, the two hundred U.S. airmen protecting America from the Soviets. The Alaskan Air Command at the top of the world. I'd watched, as our plane hovered, seeing the flashing red lights of the distant towers, somewhere out there, stark against the ice and snow, out on the gray-and-mauve tundra, punctuating the sweep of land, flashing on the pinched spruce and grubby grass where the caribou migrated.

"How did you manage…?"

He's laughing. "I'm charming."

"Tell me. I want to know."

"I can't talk long. They told me one minute."

Now I grin. "Well, I guess you're not *that* charming."

He laughs. "Somehow I knew you'd say that."

"Tell me."

"This call is telling you something."

"But I…"

Static. Beeping, silence. The line suddenly goes dead.

But though I stand there in the shadowy hallway with the dead line in my hand, I am not bothered by the abrupt end. I'm smiling. And then, helpless, I'm grinning.

To see more Poisoned Pen Press titles:

Visit our website:
poisonedpenpress.com
Request a digital catalog:
info@poisonedpenpress.com

31901064171749